JCB M

THE BUTTON HORSE

Center Point
Large Print

Also by Giles Tippette and available from Center Point Large Print:

The Horse Thieves
Slick Money

This Large Print Book carries the Seal of Approval of N.A.V.H.

THE
BUTTON HORSE

A Warner Grayson Novel

GILES TIPPETTE

CENTER POINT LARGE PRINT
THORNDIKE, MAINE

This Center Point Large Print edition
is published in the year 2018 by arrangement with
Betsyanne Tippette.

The text of this Large Print edition is unabridged.
In other aspects, this book may vary
from the original edition.
Printed in the United States of America
on permanent paper.
Set in 16-point Times New Roman type.

ISBN: 978-1-68324-792-0

Library of Congress Cataloging-in-Publication Data

Names: Tippette, Giles, author.
Title: The button horse / Giles Tippette.
Description: Center Point Large Print edition. | Thorndike, Maine :
    Center Point Large Print, 2018.
Identifiers: LCCN 2018006446 | ISBN 9781683247920
    (hardcover : alk. paper)
Subjects: LCSH: Large type books. | GSAFD: Western stories.
Classification: LCC PS3570.I6 B88 2018 | DDC 813/.54—dc23
LC record available at https://lccn.loc.gov/2018006446

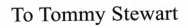

To Tommy Stewart

1

Warner Grayson was eating breakfast when Charlie Stanton came in to tell him he had a visitor. Warner said, "Set him down in the front room, and I'll be there quick as I finish. See if he wants some coffee, but ain't no need to mention I'm still at the table at this time of the morning."

It was after eight o'clock, an unusual hour for Warner to just be having breakfast, but he'd been up all night delicately working a high-priced colt out of a high-priced mare. The colt had not only managed to wrap himself in the umbilical cord, he'd somehow managed to get turned around in the womb sac and was nearly breeched. It had only been an hour ago that Warner had finally finished the job with both dam and colt on their feet, the colt sucking and the mare eating hay. It had taken him most of the hour to clean up and change clothes and have a drink of whiskey to steady his exhausted hands before he'd been able to sit down to the ham and eggs and biscuits and gravy that the Mexican woman who kept his house and cooked for him had set on the table.

Warner had no idea who his visitor might be. Likely it was about horse business, either a buyer or someone wanting a mare bred or some such. He doubted it was very important

7

or an appointment would have been made. The kind of horse business he was engaged in didn't lend itself to walk-in trade. But whoever it was, Warner wasn't going to rush. He'd been looking forward to this breakfast and a good wash and clean clothes and a smoke and a drink of whiskey since somewhere around four in the morning. It never ceased to amaze him that the higher bred the mare, the more trouble she had dropping a colt. It seemed that some old range mare could lie down, roll over, and by the time she'd got to her feet, the colt was dropped, cleaned up, the cord bit in two, and the colt was suckling and about half weaned.

But the colt he'd labored with for the previous twelve hours was nearly as high-blooded as anything that came off Warner's ranch. The sire was one of the six Andalusian stallions he'd acquired along with the widow Pico as owner and extra baggage, and the mare was of his own purebred Morgan–quarter horse crosses. The colt would be about as fine a traveling horse as a man with a good deal of money could acquire. The Andalusian stallions were a little-known breed that the widow Pico and her late husband had acquired from a part of Spain just across the strait from Morocco. The nearest thing to them that Warner had ever seen was the Arabian. But these horses were tougher than the Arabian, with more endurance and about the same speed. They weren't, however, fast enough to run against either the Kentucky Thoroughbred racehorses or the southwestern-bred quarter horses, which were about as fast as anything walking, for a distance up to a half a mile or a little less. And the Andalusians had absolutely no cow sense, so they were worthless as cattle horses even if a man was so foolish as to use a five hundred to one thousand dollar horse around half-crazy longhorn cattle.

Warner was eating in the sunny kitchen of his ranch house. It was October of the year 1886, and even though it was full fall, the weather was still seasonably warm in that part of south Texas. His ranch was sixteen miles west of the Gulf of Mexico and the Texas city of Corpus Christi and part of his 2,000 acres touched the Nueces River to the north. It was a small ranch, but then, Warner was in the selective horse-breeding business and he didn't need much land. Most of his stock was held close to the ranch headquarters either in 100-acre fenced traps or in small corrals or, as in the case of the mare who'd been about to foal, in one of the several big barns around the place.

He had been in the horse business ever since he was twelve years old. Now he was past his twenty-ninth birthday and he'd never done anything except train and handle and break and sell and breed horses. It was considered, by those who knew him and knew of him, that there wasn't much he didn't know about horses. It could even be said, if word of mouth was enough, that he was famous as a horseman. Certainly he wasn't short of orders or work. He sometimes thought that if there were two of him he would still be about two weeks behind.

He sat there, finishing his breakfast, the sun shining in through a side window on his face. His hair was bleached a little lighter by the sun than its usual sandy color, and his skin stayed the same weathered tan the year around. Most times his face looked his twenty-nine years, though sometimes, when he was relaxed and there was humor in his eyes, he looked almost boyish. But there was nothing boyish in his big shoulders and arms and hands. He was a little over six feet tall, and looking at him one way, you thought of him as slim. But then you saw that a great deal of his weight of 170 pounds was in his shoulders and his upper body and you realized he was a very powerfully built man indeed.

Sitting at his kitchen table, Warner was a fairly contented man. The only factor in his life that was either a constant irritant or a constant joy was the widow Pico. Laura Pico was his partner because she owned five of the six Andalusian horses and because she had advanced certain amounts of money to get the breeding business off to a bigger start than he had been progressing toward on his own. She lived part of the time in a big house in Corpus Christi and part of the time with him at the ranch. She was a woman of about thirty, strikingly attractive, with a body that made his throat get thick and muddled his thinking, but she had a way about her—a bossy, pushy way—that set his teeth on edge and caused him to dig in his heels whenever she opened her mouth to take a hand in the business. She knew just enough about horses to be dangerous and enough about being a woman to keep him constantly on the defensive. But other than Laura he had no complaints with the hand he'd been dealt. His debts were not cumbersome, and for a young man, he was doing exceedingly well at work he loved. He estimated, conservatively, that over the last five years he'd averaged around $5,000 a year, and that when a good cowboy was barely making $600 for the entire work part of a year. He kept four hands full-time, even though they were not needed year-round. But he figured it was better to continue to pay men who would be loyal to him and who knew what he wanted, even when there was very little work for them, than to hire men as he needed them and then have to waste valuable time breaking them in. As a consequence his ranch could nearly run itself, especially with Charlie Stanton in charge, leaving Warner free to move around the country, making himself known, looking for good buys on selected stock, and maybe taking orders for a few animals himself.

His specialty was breeding traveling horses like the colt he'd just pulled. But he also developed cow horses out of the Morgan–quarter horse cross, and racehorses from a Kentucky Thoroughbred stallion he'd had for several years. He had a few Thoroughbred mares, but they were not the quality he was looking for to produce racing stock over the longer distances. But then, even though Texas, especially the southern part, was a hotbed of match racing, the distances seldom went beyond a half a mile.

He was thinking about his Thoroughbred stock and finishing his last cup of coffee when the door separating the kitchen from the front room suddenly opened and a man stood there looking at Warner.

The man was medium-sized with a day or two's growth of beard. He was in that age area where he could have been twenty-five or thirty-five, depending on how hard he'd been used by life. He was wearing an ordinary pair of jeans with a blue flannel shirt and dusty boots. He had on what appeared to be a good quality black hat and a soft leather vest that looked to be new. He was chewing on a matchstick. He stood there with one hand on the doorknob, staring at Warner, and said, "Reckon you are ever gonna finish that meal of lunch?"

Warner's first thought was that maybe Laura was right. She would seldom stay very long at the ranch because she claimed his house was too small. It *was* small, but he'd never thought of it as being *too* small. It was four rooms—the kitchen, the front room, and two bedrooms, one of which was mostly used as a storeroom. But it was Laura's argument that, considering the quality of their clientele, their headquarters ought to be something more impressive than a four-room shack. Of course it wasn't a shack. It was a well-built little hacienda with white-washed walls of concrete brick and red Mexican tiles. It was all the room he needed, but Laura claimed it gave her a shut-in feeling. But most places would, considering she owned a ten-room house in Corpus on the bluff overlooking the bay. She said his place had no privacy and damn little room to turn around in.

Well, she'd been right about the privacy, because here was this man Warner didn't know interrupting his breakfast and not acting particularly polite by making it sound as if Warner was so late getting started that he was having lunch before going to work.

Warner took note that the man had his gun belt set up like a gunfighter's rig. The holster was a cutaway, and the butt of the revolver was slung about an inch higher than where the man's hand hung by his side. Warner was not armed. His gun belt was lying on the bed where he'd left it when he changed clothes, and any other guns he might have wanted were nowhere close. All he had for defense was a butter knife and a fork and maybe an empty plate and cup. He was not wearing his hat, and he put his hands back behind his head and yawned and stretched. He said, "Now, who might you be?"

The man said, around the matchstick, "I *might* be anybody. But I'll tell you who I ain't. I ain't some yahoo's gonna set around coolin' his heels whilst you decide it's daylight and time to get up and goin'."

Behind him Warner could see Charlie Stanton making motions and gestures to make it clear he'd had nothing to do with the man's precipitate action. Warner said, "Well, seeing as how I didn't invite you to come out here to cool your heels or to comment on my eating habits and work schedule, why don't you just state your business and then get on out of here?" He wondered if Charlie was armed. There was a clear air of menace about the stranger that made him uneasy. During seventeen years in the horse business he reckoned he'd made an enemy or two along the way; you couldn't be a horse trader and not step on some toes. But this man was in no way familiar. Of course, he thought, he could have been sent by someone else.

The man took a step into the room. Now Warner

could see Charlie clearly in the front room. He had his hand on the butt of his revolver and was watching the stranger carefully. The man said, "I got a message fer you from Jack Fisher. I reckon you know who Jack Fisher is."

Warner had never met Fisher, but he knew of him by reputation, and most of what he knew wasn't good. Fisher owned a good spread of land west of Cotulla about a hundred miles from Warner's ranch. Fisher was said to be a tough and a bully and a man you did not want for an enemy because he would stick at nothing. He was said to have killed anywhere from five to fifteen men, depending on who you were listening to, and he was supposed to be either pure death with a handgun or a backshooter with a shotgun, again depending on who was doing the telling. But he was also rich and powerful and as set on having his way as a spoiled woman; of that there was no question. Warner knew a little more about him than he should have because Fisher was a horse breeder and a man who was said to raise some of the best racing horses around. But the way Warner heard it, Fisher didn't know which end of a horse the hay went in. He'd hired some very knowledgeable people who did the actual breeding and raising of his horses.

Warner said, "I've heard the name. What about it?"

"Wa'l, Mr. Fisher is gettin' damn tahrd of you bad-mouthin' his horses, an' he intends on seein' it stopped. I've come to tell you thet as quick's it can be arranged you an' him is gonna have several horse races an' then you are gonna shut yore mouth. You savvy?"

Warner looked at him. There was nothing in his eyes or his face to show how he felt. He said slowly, "Where does this Mr. Jack Fisher come of the idea that I've been bad-mouthing either him or his horses?"

The man looked at Warner sort of pitifully. He said, "He heared it around, you damn fool. Whar you reckon he come of the idee? Reckon it was in the newspaper?"

Warner made a small smile with no humor in it. He said, "Well, you go on back and tell Jack Fisher that I have not been bad-mouthing his horses. As a matter of fact, I can't say for sure that I've ever even seen one. And not being in the horse racing business, I ain't got any interest in running him a race or a set of races." In his mind was the fact that the man had called him a damn fool and that Charlie Stanton had heard it. He had not reacted because he thought more would be coming, more that would be enough to give him justification to treat this insolent man the way he deserved to be treated.

The man took the matchstick out of his mouth and laughed dryly. He said, "Mr. Fisher reckoned

16

you'd be inclined to say no, so he give me some other messages fer you."

"And what would they be?"

"Said he'd set in on yore horses and work his way up to you. He figgers somewhere 'long the line you'll come 'round to his way of thankin'."

Warner pushed his chair back slowly and stood up. He said, "Exactly what does Mr. Fisher mean by saying he'll start in on my horses?"

The man shrugged. "Now thet, I wouldn't be knowin'. But I'd reckon a man with a rifle on a dark night might cut yore herd down a little. Reckon that's the thankin'?"

Warner kept his voice even. He said, "I still don't get it why Jack Fisher has decided to do me the honor of picking me for an enemy. I don't know the man, and I'm not sure I know anyone who does know him."

The man started to put the matchstick back in his mouth and then stopped. He said, "Sheet. Don't come that line o' talk on me. Ever'body 'n this part of the country knows Jack Fisher. I didn't ride no damn hunnert miles to listen to bullshit."

Warner still kept his distance from the man, thinking. He'd once ridden near Jack Fisher's headquarters on the east side of Cotulla. The road he'd been traveling had forked, one branch going off to the left, the other to the right. There had been a sign in the middle of the fork. It had an

17

arrow pointing toward the road leading to the left. It had said: This Is Jack Fisher's Road. You Take the Other One.

Warner was carefully not letting himself feel anything. It was the only way he knew to keep sudden anger from rising up in him. He'd learned early on that anger was your enemy and your enemy's friend if you used it the wrong way. He said carefully, "Do I understand that you are threatening my horses?"

The man shrugged, looking insolently at Warner. He said, "*I* ain't threatenin' nothin'. I'm jest sayin' what might happen case you didn't want to run some horse races against Mr. Jack Fisher's stock so we'd find out right quick who was breedin' the best stock. But barns ketch on fahr all the time. Ain't nothin' could be said agin Mr. Fisher if yore barns was to take fahr. You savvy?"

"Yeah," Warner said, "I guess I savvy." He put heavy emphasis on the word as he started around his kitchen table and across the floor to the man. He said, "I think I'm also beginning to savvy that Mr. Fisher would just as soon not have me in the horse business. I don't think he likes the competition. And I reckon he sent you up here to talk about shooting horses and burning barns to test my nerve. Reckon that's right? You savvy what I'm talking about?"

Warner had come right up to the man, who was

standing in the doorway about a foot or two into the kitchen. The man took the matchstick out of his mouth. He said, "I don't reckon you'll be talkin' so smart some of this starts to happen. Now what about these here horse races?"

Warner lifted his left arm and pointed to the left side of the kitchen. He said, "Your answer is right over there."

The man almost involuntarily swung his head around to follow Warner's pointing finger. As the man's head turned, Warner lifted his right shoulder and ducked his left, pushing off from his back right foot as he drove his big fist in a short hooking right-hand punch that took the man full on the jaw he'd exposed. Though Warner's concentration was totally on his target, he caught, in his peripheral vision, a glimpse of Charlie's horrified young face.

And then his blow crashed home, and he felt the faint crunch of something. If it was a broken bone he hoped it was in the man's face and not in his hand. The man's head snapped back like he'd been struck with a heavy-caliber bullet. His body followed, slamming into the door frame and then bouncing off. He bounced toward Warner, but Warner had let the blow carry him past the man, and he simply twisted sideways, making no move to catch the man, and let him fall face forward on the kitchen floor.

"Lordy!" It was Charlie Stanton, standing

there with his eyes big in his head. He said, "Mr. Grayson, you shore done knocked the jam out of him! What a lick. Reckon he's dead? He just be layin' there."

Warner shook his head. He said, "Naw, he's just out cold. Let him lay there for a minute, and then we'll drag him out the kitchen door and throw some water on him if he don't come around in a minute. We get water all over Rosa's kitchen we won't see no good vittles for a week."

They stood there watching the man. Charlie said, "What you reckon this is all about, Mr. Grayson?"

Warner shook his head. "I don't know, Charlie. I've heard that Jack Fisher is mean as a snake. I don't know, myself. But anytime a man goes to talking about shooting horses and burning barns I tend to get mighty nervous."

"But you ain't been bad-mouthin' the man like this feller said."

Charlie was barely twenty-one. He was Warner's top hand because, like Warner, he'd started out with horses, doing a man's work, when he was very young. But being an outstanding hand with horses did not make him wise in the ways of the world. Warner gave him a look and said, "Charlie, how many times have you known me to bad-mouth anyone? Especially somebody I don't even know."

"I didn't mean the same kind of bad-mouthin'

20

this here feller was accusin' you of, 'bout Jack Fisher's horses," Charlie said. "Truth be told, I never even heard that Fisher was in the horse bidness like us. I thought his main trade was either runnin' folks off they land or else buryin' 'em on it so as he could have the use of it. I thought maybe he was a-talkin' about that."

Warner took a slow deep breath. He'd let his anger out of its cage when he threw the punch, and it was still out, walking around and hard-eyed. But his was a quiet anger, not given to growling or bluster. Very little, if any, ever showed on his face or sounded in his voice. Now he looked down at the back of the man he'd hit and said, "I ain't real sure what he was talking about, Charlie. I'm waiting to talk to him some more soon as he comes around."

"Wa'l, what'd you hit him for, Mr. Grayson, if you wanted to talk?"

"Wanted to get his attention, Charlie. Got tired of listening to what he was going to do to my horses."

Charlie knelt down by the man's side. He said, "He shore is still, Mr. Grayson. That was one hell of a lick you give him. You reckon his neck is broke?" He didn't wait for an answer, but said, "I seen an old boy get his neck broke, an' it wasn't from nowhere near as hard a lick as you hit this feller. 'Course, that old boy snapped his neck over the edge of a saloon bar. Still, you did poleaxe him pretty good."

Warner walked across the kitchen and opened the door that led to the outside. The house was built low to the ground so there were only two steps from the door to the backyard, which held a vegetable garden and some chicken coops that Rosa tended. Warner propped the door open with a board and then walked back to where the man lay on the floor. The floor was made of heavy wooden planks and covered with Mexican throw rugs. Warner said, "You get him under one shoulder and I'll get him under the other and we'll drag him outside and bring him to."

Even though they were both strong men, it was a hard pull dragging the deadweight of the man across the floor. They tugged him out the door, his boots bumping down the steps and then, with difficulty, laid him down on his back in the yard. Warner said, "Charlie, go pump up a bucket of water."

Charlie ran for a pump that was near one of the three big barns that stood back and off to the west of the house. One was mostly used for supplies while the other two stalled hurt or sick horses and mares near to foal. Some of Warner's stock dropped their foals on the prairie grass, but most were too valuable to leave to the vagaries of nature. Surrounding the barns was a succession of wooden corrals, some fairly big, some small, depending on their use. Off the corrals were traps of a hundred acres down to a couple of only ten or fifteen. They were fenced with smooth wire. Barbed wire was already making an impact on the range, but Warner wouldn't have it on his place. Once a horse got cut or snagged by it, the animal would go loco and fight the wire until he'd cut himself to ribbons. Warner had heard that the huge King range some eighty miles south of him was in the midst of fencing itself in with barbed wire strung on cedar posts, but he hoped it wasn't true. Of course the Kings had a cattle operation, and cattle wouldn't hurt themselves with the fanged wire, but Warner hated the idea of the range, the prairie, being chopped up into little self-held lots and thus not free for the use of all. He had only 2,000 deeded acres, but he could have grazed his herd, if he'd wanted to, over an area twice that size. Most cattlemen did that, because of the number of cattle they had and because they couldn't feed their herds on just the land they held but had to depend on the use of public acreage. Barbed-wire fencing would seriously interfere with that common method of running cattle, and Warner had already heard words of trouble about the fencing that was starting up.

But he had trouble enough, he figured, right here. While Charlie was getting the bucket of water he leaned down and picked up the man's hat and dusted it off against his leg and then laid it on the steps. The man had a little string of silver

Conchos for a hatband. The hat was definitely not that of a working cowhand. And neither was the man's revolver. Warner leaned down and pulled it out of the holster. The hammer was on safety, on half cock, but Warner could tell that the double action mechanism had been filed away and the gun set up to be cocked and fired. His own revolver was altered the same way. No man who was fighting for his life pulled the trigger to pull back the hammer that then released and fired the gun. The effort of pulling the trigger hard enough to cock the hammer caused barrel deviation and could throw your shot off two or more feet even at a distance of ten yards. A man cocked the hammer with his thumb and aimed and fired at the same time. And if his trigger pull was adjusted right, it would take a very light touch to make the gun fire.

He stared down at the man. A little blood was trickling out of the man's mouth on the side where Warner had hit him. He clenched and unclenched his right fist. It hurt a little, but he didn't think anything was broken. He reckoned he'd broken something in the man's face, maybe his jaw, maybe his cheekbone. The face he thought was mean-looking, even with the man unconscious. But that didn't mean anything. His good friend Wilson Young had one of the meanest-looking men Warner had ever seen working for him, a black Mexican named Chulo.

Chulo wasn't mean, but he was dangerous if you got on the wrong side of him or Wilson Young.

Charlie came running up, looking as young and excited as he'd been five years before when he first went to work for Warner part-time. He was tall and thin and looked gawky and awkward until he got on a horse. After that, it was hard to tell where the horse left off and Charlie began. Warner reckoned that Charlie had almost as light and as good a seat as he did.

Now Charlie stood there, bucket in hand, looking a question at Warner. Warner said, "Douse him down, Charlie. Hell, the water ain't gonna do him any good you keep it in the bucket."

It was a five-gallon bucket. Charlie had spilled some on the way over, but there was still plenty left to make a deluge when he poured the water square into the man's face.

For a second nothing happened, and they stood there staring down at the man, waiting for some reaction. Finally his lips parted and his mouth began to work. They heard him gasp for breath, and then his eyes suddenly came open. He stared straight up for a second, unseeing, and then, slowly, consciousness began to return. He blinked and focused his eyes on Warner. He opened his mouth, started to speak, and then stopped and put his hand up to his jaw and worked it back and forth. He said something that sounded like "Shiiis."

25

Warner knelt down by the man's side. He said, his voice even, "You awake? Can you hear me?"

The man glared at him and worked his jaw some more. Finally he said, the word not coming out whole, "Sunbish."

Warner said, "Yeah, I hit you. You come in here talking about killing my stock and burning my barns. What'd you expect, an invitation to supper?"

Now that the man was fully conscious, Warner could see the venom burning in his eyes. He made an effort to raise his shoulders off the ground to sit up, but Warner put out a hand and pushed him back.

"Just wait a minute. Me and you are gonna have a little conversation and I like it like this. Now, what the hell is your name?"

The man looked hate at Warner and said, "Suser-punshed me."

"Sucker-punched you? Is that what you said? Of course I sucker-punched you. You're standing there with your right leg forward like you are going to pull on me at any second, and the only weapon I got is my fist. What the hell did you think I was going to do? Stand there and listen as if I liked it? Now, what the hell is your name?"

The man's face was sullen. He stared at Warner, slowly moving his jaw around, testing it. He didn't speak.

Warner said, "Listen, me and you is gonna have

a confab whether you want to or not. I can tie you up and leave you in the barn you was gonna burn down. Don't make me no never mind. Charlie, run and get some kind of cord and we'll snub this gentleman up good and tight until his mouth gets a little looser. And quit acting like your jaw was broke. If it was broke, you couldn't move it around like you're doing. Likely the hinge got wrenched a little, but that ain't shucks to what I'm gonna do to you if you don't start answering my questions. I know I look easy, but I might fool you now and again."

The man started to lift his shoulders, pushing up with his hands. Warner reached out to push him back, but the man said mushily, "Gotta spit, dammit."

Warner let him push himself up far enough that he could work his mouth around and spit to one side. It left a string of blood hanging from one corner of his mouth. He brought his hand up and spit into his palm and looked at the blood and then looked up at Warner. He said, "You sumbitch." He wiped his palm on the dried grass by his side.

"Let's see," Warner said. "I believe you've called me a damn fool and a son of a bitch about four times. You got any other good ones in you?"

"Whuskey. You got any whuskey? Jaw hurts like hell."

"I got whiskey if you got a name."

27

His face sulled over for a moment, but he finally said, "Name's Carl."

"Carl what?"

"If it's any of yore fuckin' business it's Carl Hamm."

"Like what comes off a hog. Ham." Warner jerked his head at Charlie. He said, "Go bring him a glass of whiskey. I don't want the bloody-mouthed son of a bitch drinking out of the bottle. In fact, get one of them fruit jars Rosa puts preserves up in. We'll chunk it away when Mr. Hog is through with it."

Carl Hamm stared at him, his eyes still flat and cold. He said, "Last feller called me Mr. Hog is wearin' the devil's spurs. You savvy?"

Warner cocked his head. He said, "You are just full of threats, Carl. Well, I won't call you Mr. Hog again. Not because you don't like it but because I feel a little silly sayin' it."

Carl Hamm suddenly seemed to become aware that he was wet all over his front. He put a hand toward his head. "Whar's my hat? You git that soaked?"

Warner jerked a thumb. "It's back there on the porch steps. I put it there for you, Carl. I might shoot your ears and your toes off, but I wouldn't mess with your hat. Your revolver is back there, too."

As he said it, the man suddenly clapped his hand to his side and realized his holster was

28

empty. He said, "You be a mighty lucky man, feller. You better keep that gun outten my hand you want to keep yore lights and yore liver."

Before Warner could answer, Charlie came out the back door with a bottle of whiskey in one hand and a pint fruit jar in the other. He handed them to Warner, who said, "You better shut that door, Charlie, before some dust blows into Rosa's kitchen and me and you both will pay for it."

Charlie turned back to the door, and Warner poured a little whiskey into the jar and held it out to Carl Hamm. Before he could take it, Warner said, "You better use this first bit to swish around in your mouth. Maybe it'll stop them cuts bleeding. I'm getting tired of you bleeding all over my ground."

Hamm gave him a look, but he took the jar and poured some whiskey into his mouth. He winced as it bit into his cuts as he swished it around. Finally he spit it out. Warner poured the pint jar about a quarter full and watched while Hamm sipped it down. When he was finished, Hamm held the jar out for more.

Warner squatted there thoughtfully, the bottle in his hand. He said, "Carl, we ain't runnin' no saloon here. And if we was, you'd have been throwed out long ago. You ain't exactly the kind of material I make a friend out of, Hamm. You come in here insulting me and commenting on my eating and working habits and telling me I got to run some horse races with Jack Fisher whether I want to or not. And I'm supposed to sit here and fill you up on my whiskey just because your jaw hurts? What do you say to that, Charlie?"

Behind him the young man said, "Don't see where it says we took him to raise. That whiskey costs money."

Hamm stared at Warner, not saying anything. Finally Warner poured him out the same amount, and Hamm tossed it off and handed the jar back to Warner. Without looking, Warner pitched it over his shoulder. He heard Charlie say, "Whoops!" and, when he didn't hear a crash, knew that Charlie had caught it.

Warner said, "Now, you reckon the pain is down enough where you can talk and answer some questions?"

Hamm said, "I'm going to git up."

"You start up, you're going down a hell of a lot faster than you did the first time. I like you right where you are. Now. Exactly what did Jack Fisher send you down here to tell me? And I mean I want his exact words, not some gunslinger talk you made up on the ride down here that was supposed to scare me into saying yes, sir, right away, sir. You savvy? I want exactly what he said. And I know bullshit when I hear it, so keep to the undiluted article."

Hamm's face was still sullen, his eyes mean and vicious. He said, "Feller, you got the upper hand for the little while on account of you sneak-punched me. But you be pushin' yore luck. You got a lick o' sense you'll turn me go right now 'fore I git madder'n I already am."

Warner sighed. He said, "There you go again—threatening me. I am nearly sick of you, and I know I'm sick of hearing you say I sneak-punched you." He stood up. "Maybe we can't do anything about anything else, but we can settle that question." He backed off a few steps and waved with his hand. "Get up. Get up and get your fists up. We'll see how it ends, starting even."

Carl Hamm looked up at Warner and then turned and spit on the ground. There was still a pink tinge to his saliva. He said, "Go to hell. I don't fight with fists like some schoolboy. But you gimme my iron an' we'll find out who's the better man."

Warner considered for a moment and then shook his head. He said, "You don't fistfight and I don't fight duels. Ain't no profit in it."

Hamm sneered at him. "Scairt, be you?"

"No, I'm not scared. I just don't have anything to gain. I kill you and you still can't tell me what I want to know. You got to be alive for that. I kill you and I've got a dead body on my hands, and frankly I don't want the trouble and expense of burying you and notifying the sheriff and all the other trouble it would cause. Now, you came down here making trouble for me. I don't see why I should oblige you by doing matters your way."

"You're still a-scairt."

"You believe whatever you want to, Mr. Hamm. I don't give a damn. But I do give a damn about this trouble you've brought me, and I want to find out all I can about it. If you ain't willing to tell me on your own, I reckon I'm going to have to find a way to convince you otherwise."

Hamm said, "Talk all you want to. Onliest way I got anything to say is over a gun, an' you don't want no part of me on thet."

Charlie suddenly broke in. He said, "You don't know what you're talking about, bigmouth. Mr. Grayson chased down and kilt a dozen Meskin bandits."

Hamm spit again. "Sheet," he said. "I don't even count Meskins. A old woman could kill a greaser."

Warner said, "I'd moderate that kind of talk was I you, Mr. Hamm. Two of my main vaqueros are Mexican. I might call them in and let you discuss the matter of 'greasers' with them. I think they'd take a lively interest in the subject."

Because the ranch never dealt with more than a hundred horses, Warner did not need a very large crew, though he did need very special horsemen who understood and liked to work with horses. Besides Charlie Stanton, his next first-class horse handler was a little Mexican named Pancho Martinez, who was married to Rosa. They lived in a little shack a quarter of a mile from the main ranch house.

His other Mexican hand was Raoul Garza, who was big and strong and had a touch with horses, but was still learning. His fourth hired hand was Les Russel, who'd once been a member of a five-man gang that had tried to hold up Warner on the road when he'd been driving some horses to San Antonio. Warner had killed two of them and put the other three in jail. Les had not been like the others, and Warner had seen that. Instead of having him sent to prison he'd given Russel a job, and he hadn't been sorry since.

Hamm suddenly stood up. He started to move toward the kitchen steps where his hat and revolver were. Charlie promptly moved down and stood in his way. Hamm said, "Gimme my belongings. I'm gettin' the hell outta here."

Warner said, "Charlie, go get my gun belt. It's in my bedroom."

Charlie gestured at Hamm. "What about him?"

"Take his revolver with you. He's within my reach. He moves, he'll find out what a real sucker punch is."

Hamm turned slowly and stared at Warner. He said, "So you will fight?"

Warner nodded. He said, "Yeah. The only trick for me will be not to kill you. Just hit you in the shoulder or maybe the thigh. Break the bone. Leave you well enough to talk before you bleed to death."

Hamm said, "You talk a mighty fine game."

"I'm not talking now." He glanced at Charlie. "Go on. Take his revolver and bring it back along with mine. We got room back here, and ain't no stock in the line of fire in case one of us misses."

He was staring steadily at Carl Hamm. He could see a taint of doubt begin to creep into the man's face.

2

Warner wasn't quite sure why he was doing what he was doing. As he'd told Carl Hamm, he didn't engage in gun duels. He didn't find anything particularly brave or macho or heroic about a man matching his hand speed and the speed of his aim against that of another man, not when he was reckoning his life in the results. There were too many particulars that could go wrong, too many elements of luck. Warner had been forced into situations with deadly consequences more times than he cared to remember, and he considered them serious business. When guns came into play, reason had already gone out the window, and his intent was to dispatch his enemy as quickly and as thoroughly as he could with as few risks as possible to himself and those with him. It was not a game; it was a last-resort method of defending oneself—by eliminating an enemy who insisted on a fight. Warner made no attempt to play fair. He'd never shot a man in the back and never would, but he sought and seized every advantage he could think of. His grandfather had taught him that.

Warner's parents had been taken by the fever when he was a very small boy, and he'd been largely raised by his grandfather, a man of purpose, of strict honesty, of a code of balanced fairness, and of the firm conviction that when he was right he would proceed with God's blessing. He had not gone far in school, though he'd insisted that Warner got every bit of schooling available, but he'd read every book he could lay his hands on, and his life was guided by a kind of earthly philosophy built on experience and on what he considered the divine advice of the Bible. By profession he'd been a cattle and horse trader who'd gone broke one more time than he'd made his pile. He hadn't been able to leave Warner many material possessions, but he'd left him with a sizable stack of fundamentals and one of those was the ability to think clearly. He'd once told Warner, "Boy, that six inches you got between yore ears is more dangerous to your enemy than the six inches of any gun barrel. Use yore head, boy, use yore head. Out think the son of a bitch who's trying to do you down."

Not that Warner was any slouch with a handgun. He had a very fast hand, very fast reflexes, and he was an instinctive shot, not aiming the gun so much as looking to where he wanted the bullet to hit as he pulled the trigger. But only once before had he been forced into a face-to-face situation, and he had been uncertain of himself then. His friend Wilson Young had said that a lot of men thought they could shoot another man, but then, at the wrong instant, they hesitated, and that hesitation generally cost them their lives. Wilson had said, "Warner, it ain't something you can practice for, unless you can find you a human being who's willing to stand up there and let you shoot him. You either got it or you don't, and you ain't going to find out until it's mostly too late. The sad particular of the situation is that most men don't realize they ain't got it. You put the proposition up to ten men, and ten men will tell you they won't hesitate. That's one of the reasons I ain't got no more gunshot wounds in me than I do."

Of course, Wilson Young was a special case. He didn't draw a revolver so much as it suddenly appeared in his hand, already seeming to be firing, with the bullet headed toward where Wilson wanted it to go. But there was a drawback to that kind of skill, as Wilson would have been the first to admit. Because of who he was, and because of his fame, no one with any sense would come straight at him. The only place to safely shoot Wilson Young was in the back, but that meant you had to get by Chulo first, and that was a chore that might require you to bring your lunch.

Now Warner stood there staring at Carl Hamm. They were about five feet apart, with Hamm a little closer to the kitchen door. Hamm had met his gaze at first, but then he looked away. Now and then he rubbed his hand on the thigh of

37

his pants. Once or twice he shifted his weight.

And then Charlie was standing in the kitchen door. He was holding Hamm's revolver in his right hand and Warner's gun belt in his left. He stopped, looking quickly from Hamm to Warner and back again to Hamm. He said, "How you want me to do this, Mr. Grayson?"

Warner said, "Shoot Hamm if he makes a jump at you. If he don't, throw me my rig."

Charlie flipped it, and Warner caught it before it hit the ground. He said, "Not that we don't trust Mr. Hamm, but you'd best hold on to his weapon until I get belted in and tied down. Then Mr. Hamm can turn his back and you walk over and put the revolver in his holster. That all right with you, Mr. Hamm?"

Hamm said viciously, "I jest want at you, you sumbitch."

"In good time," Warner said. He strapped his gun belt on and loosened his revolver in the holster. He used a Colt .44-.40, which was a gun chambered for a .40 caliber cartridge on a .44 caliber frame. The heavier frame made the gun easier in the hand with less barrel deviation and the .40 caliber slug would stop anything you hit in the right place.

Warner thought he detected a little quaver in Hamm's voice, despite the viciousness and the words Hamm had used. He thought the man talked a shade too much, was too free and easy with a threat. He'd known other men like that. When he had his gun rig set exactly as he wanted it, he said, "Turn around, Mr. Hamm."

"Yeah? So's you kin back-shoot me?"

"No. So's Mr. Stanton here can slip your revolver into its holster. After that, we will be at evens and we can start the game."

Hamm turned reluctantly, and Charlie came down off the steps and put his revolver in its holster. Hamm said, growling, "How'm I supposed to know he ain't fiddled with my iron? Unloaded it or somethin'?"

"Have a look," Warner said. "Just keep your back turned. You try and turn with that gun in your hand, I am going to take it as a hostile act and proceed accordingly."

He watched while Hamm took his revolver out, spun the cylinder with the gate open, and then sighted down the barrel. Finally he snapped the gate shut and slowly returned the gun to its holster.

Warner took several quick steps backwards. He said, as he moved his right leg forward slightly to make the draw easier, "All right, Mr. Hamm, you can turn around now."

It took the man a long few seconds to think about it and then slowly come around to where he was facing Warner. He had his hands wide away from his sides, making it clear he was not ready to draw. Only about seven yards separated them.

Warner said, "Charlie, you better get on back inside the house."

Charlie said, "I'm all right here, Mr. Grayson. I ain't worried."

"Do like I tell you."

"Mr. Grayson," he said, as if he'd been instructed, "if you're a-thinkin' I'm scairt he might get you and then plug me, I know that ain't going to happen. I got a good view from here."

Carl Hamm gave Charlie a nervous glance. He was still holding his hands far from his sides.

Warner had his hand hanging just below the butt of his revolver, his fingers slightly curved. He was staring at the place where Hamm's vest came over his right shoulder. He decided he would try to hit that spot, but if he missed, he intended to miss on the inside. He had already decided that Hamm was more bully than anything else and that he had a good chance to wound him severely without killing him.

Warner said, "It's your play, Mr. Hamm. I called you out, so by the rules, you start the play with your draw."

It made him almost smile to think about rules governing such an idiotic activity as two men, strangers until a few minutes before, facing each other with the intent to kill and no real complaint between them.

Hamm said in a nervous, aggravated voice, "You seem for this all of a sudden. How I know ain't a rifle er a shotgun trained on me from a winder, that'll fire first move I make?"

Warner looked past Carl Hamm toward the two big barns that were in a line. In the door of the second one, the storage barn, perhaps two hundred yards away, he could see a figure standing in the door looking their way. By the size of him, he figured it was Raoul Garza. He'd had Raoul stacking some sacks of feed they'd taken delivery on. He wondered what Raoul was thinking about what he was seeing. He was going to be a lot more curious if guns started going off.

"Mr. Hamm . . ." Warner said.

Hamm shifted nervously. "I still say you got you some kind o' edge somewheres."

It was at least ten o'clock. The sun was up good, and it was warm and pleasant with a nice little breeze blowing. Warner could faintly smell the curing hay in his big field to the north.

"There's nobody else, Mr. Hamm. Just me and you. Now draw your weapon, dammit!"

Hamm looked around and then took a step backwards. "I don't like the range," he said. He took another step backwards, but still brought his hand no closer to his gun side.

Warner took a quick step forward. "I like the range, Mr. Hamm. It's the proper range. It guarantees one of us gets killed. Hell, don't you know your etiquette on these matters?"

Hamm edged back nervously. He said,

"Etiquette? What the hell's etiquette got to do with it? This here's a gunfight."

Warner took another step toward him. He said flatly, "I'm tired of this, Hamm. Draw your goddam weapon." Warner stared at him. Hamm made no move. "DRAW, DAMMIT!"

Hamm put his left hand up to his brow. He said, "The damn sun's in my eyes. I cain't see you right clear."

"Take him his hat, Charlie."

But Hamm waved him away. He said, "Never mind. I say the hell with this. You got this rigged someways, an' I ain't gonna be suckered. You done sneak-punched me. Now you gonna sneak-shoot me. I'm walkin' out of here an' gittin' on my horse and leavin'. An' you can go to hell!"

"Draw, Hamm," Warner said, his words menacing. "Draw or lick dirt."

"You go to hell."

In a blur Warner drew and fired, the slug scattering dirt six inches from Hamm's feet. The man jumped backwards, a frightened look on his face. He shouted, "Are you crazy! You coulda shot my goddam foot off!"

Warner recocked his revolver. In the morning's quiet it made a loud *clitch-clack* sound. He said flatly, "Hamm, either draw or lick dirt. Or I shoot you in the foot. Now, will you fight?"

Hamm was starting to shake. He ran his tongue

over his lips. He said, "I'll tell you what Jack Fisher told me. I—"

Warner said, sounding furious, "The hell with that. Now fight or lick dirt."

"No, I—"

The second shot plowed into the ground right between his boots. Hamm jumped and began to tremble. He said, "You are going to maim me."

Warner cocked his revolver again. He could not see anything except Hamm. All else was blotted out by his concentration on his target. He lifted his revolver. He said, "This one goes in your ankle. You'll be walking with a crutch the rest of your life."

Hamm was visibly trembling. He said, "I'll give you the same words, the very same words Mr. Fisher sent me down with."

Warner sighted on Hamm's ankle. "In three seconds I'm going to pull this trigger if you ain't down on your knees licking dirt. One. Two . . ."

He got no further because Carl Hamm immediately dropped to his knees and put his face to the ground and put his tongue out and licked at the stubbly grass of Warner's backyard.

Warner watched him for a second. Then he said, "That's enough. Get up, but leave your revolver lying on the ground. Then walk over and sit down on the ground by the steps. Charlie, get him a half a jar of whiskey."

He waited until Hamm was seated on the

ground and Charlie had given him the whiskey before he put his revolver away. In the distance Warner saw Les Russel hurrying their way. He whistled loudly and waved Russel away. There was no use contributing even more to the man's humiliation.

He said, "Charlie, go get this man's horse. I reckon he's tied around front?"

"Yes, sir. You be all right?"

Warner smiled slightly. He said, "I reckon I can hold the fort until you get back."

When Charlie was gone, Warner watched while Hamm downed a good bit of the whiskey in one long gulp. He shuddered as the whiskey hit the pit of his stomach and then dragged in a long breath. He sipped until the jar was empty. The bottle was sitting on the steps right next to him. He reached out toward it and looked at Warner.

Warner nodded. "Help yourself."

The man took another drink and then sucked in another deep breath and said, "Who the goddam hell do you be? You supposed to be some kind of a horse handler, yit you come out with a gunfighter's rig an' you damn well act like one. Hell, I seen Wilson Young, an' he ain't no cooler'n you was."

Warner smiled faintly. "You'd better be glad Wilson wasn't here. He ain't nowhere near as patient as I am."

The man looked more unsettled. "You friends with Wilson Young?"

"I reckon you could say that."

"Sumbitch!" the man said.

Warner thought now that he had lied to Hamm when he'd said he didn't know Jack Fisher or anyone who knew Jack Fisher. At least he'd lied about the part about knowing anyone who knew Fisher. Wilson Young knew him well. Wilson was headquartered in Del Rio, Texas, which was only some fifty or sixty miles from Fisher country, and Warner knew that Wilson had raced Fisher at various times for considerable sums of money. The curious fact of the matter was that Wilson was due in the next day. There was a little railroad siding at Calallen, about two miles away, that was used as a horse and cattle loading station. But passengers could make arrangements to be let off there, and Wilson was due to arrive at Calallen around eleven o'clock the next morning.

Now Warner looked at Carl Hamm, wondering if he shouldn't detain him until Wilson arrived. Wilson knew Fisher, and he'd know more questions to ask than Warner did. Right now Warner was still confused by the sudden trouble from out of nowhere. He'd dealt with Hamm with comparative ease because he'd early on recognized that the man was only a bullyboy sent on an errand. Hamm was not the main trouble; Fisher was. But Warner didn't know why Wilson

45

would know any more about what was going on than he could get out of Hamm. He said, "You ready to tell me what Fisher has in mind?"

The whiskey was making Hamm brave again. He said sullenly, "I done told you. You cain't 'member plain words, ain't my fault. You gonna run him some races er you gonna be sorry." He shrugged. "That's all they is to it."

Warner sighed. He said, "Mr. Hamm, I have taken considerable trouble to accommodate you. You didn't want to fistfight and then you didn't want to gunfight. I'm near to being sick of all this." He turned to his left and pointed. "You see that little shack down there between the two big barns? Little building made out of heavy timber? Well, that's my blacksmithy. It's a mighty solid little structure with a good door on it and a padlock. You don't tell me everything you know, I'm taking you down there right now and I'm going to lock you in there without food or water until you decide to tell me what you know."

Hamm looked at the far-off building and then looked back at Warner. His eyes were spiteful and hate-filled. He said, with viciousness, "It would purely be my pleasure to let you know what Jack Fisher has got in mind fer you. I just thank you'd enjoy it more as a surprise."

Warner shook his head wearily. He said, "Fisher knows I have never bad-mouthed him or his horses. So I don't want no more of that

46

shit." He took a step and came to a stop in front of Hamm. Without warning, Warner backhanded him with his big right hand across the right side of his face. The blow knocked Hamm sideways, sending him to the ground. But it was a slap, not a punch, and its main result was to make Hamm's lip bleed and redden the side of his face. Warner said, "Get up. You are going to look at four walls for a while."

Hamm put up his hands. "Wait a minute," he said. "Wait a minute." He touched one of his hands to his open mouth and looked at the blood on his fingers. He spit again and stood up. He said, "That done it. That's a-plenty. Now you kin do some sweatin'." His eyes were glittering, and there was a look on his face of gloating and meanness. He said, "Mr. Jack Fisher is plenty tired of hearin' yore name. It seems a horse can't be mentioned without yore name comin' up. He reckons you are gettin' too big fer your britches, and he aims to take you down a peg or two. He's gonna put you in yore place, boy, you savvy? An' I reckon that place might jest be six foot under." Now he grinned, skinning his thin lips back from his yellowing teeth. He said, "An' I'm a-gonna be thar to watch." He laughed. "Mr. Jack Fisher don't like you, boy. An' folks that Mr. Jack Fisher don't like gen'ly comes to a bad end."

"I see," Warner said slowly. "So this hasn't got anything to do with me supposedly running down him or his horseflesh. He's plain jealous of me."

"Jealous of you, boy? Shit, don't make me laugh. You ain't a pimple on Jack Fisher's ass. He's jest tahrd of hearin' yore name, an' he reckons to do somethin' 'bout it."

"So he plans to horse-race me. And what else?"

Hamm smiled viciously. He said, "I reckon they'll be more than yore horse tryin' to do some running."

"He plans to try and kill me? Like you were going to do?"

Hamm's face flushed with anger. He said, "We'll see who does the dirt-lickin', you come up agin Jack Fisher."

Warner smiled. "I wasn't going to bring up that little part of your visit again. But since you did, how does my ground taste? I ain't never tried it."

"You sumbitch." Hamm suddenly looked to his left.

Warner turned his head slightly. Charlie was coming around the corner with what Warner took to be Hamm's horse. It was a big good-looking bay gelding. He reckoned it to be a straight American saddlebred–quarter horse cross, a popular breed for those who could afford such an animal. He reckoned the horse would be a solid six-year-old and would fetch $250 easy at auction. He also saw that there was a rifle in the saddle boot. Without giving it much thought, he decided that it might not be a good idea to let Carl

Hamm leave with a gun capable of hitting targets from a long distance, be they men or horses.

Warner said, "That's a good-looking pony. That some of Fisher's stock?"

Hamm pushed away from the wall of Warner's house and started toward his horse. He said, "That be one of Mr. Fisher's culls. But it's better'n anythang you got."

Before Hamm could walk around to the left side of his horse, Warner reached in his pocket and took out a roll of bills. He peeled off forty-five dollars and handed it to Carl Hamm. Hamm took the money, looking uncertain. He said, "What the hell's this fer? You ain't thankin' you can buy yore way outta trouble, is you? I'm still gonna tell Mr. Fisher some facks 'bout you he ain't gonna like."

Warner stepped to the side of the horse and pulled the Winchester lever-action .44 carbine out of the boot. He said, "That's forty-five dollars. That's what these cost new. But ain't anyplace close around here where you can buy one." He looked the rifle over for a second. "But I think I just took a whipping on this trade. This gun looks like it's been cared for by somebody that don't never figure to use it. Rusted up and pitted." He levered a shell out of the chamber and onto the ground. "Action is stiff as hell. Shit. I just got skinned. This rifle ain't worth twenty dollars."

Hamm said angrily, "Say! I ain't sellin' you

49

my rifle gun! You put that back in the boot, you hear?"

Warner ignored him. "Charlie, see where Mr. Hamm's revolver is lying over there on the ground? You can spot it because it's right near the place on the ground he licked clean. That place where the grass died. Well, get it and unload it and give it to Mr. Hamm. God knows I don't want to buy it, not after the bad trade I made on his rifle."

Hamm was still going on excitedly about his rifle. He said, "Goddammit, I'm a hunnert miles from home. I want that rifle back, dammit, and right now!"

After Charlie let go of the horse's bridle to pick up Hamm's gun, the bay took a wandering few steps. Warner said, "Hamm, you better get on your horse before he leaves without you. I don't plan to board you. I'm surprised that the fine animals Jack Fisher raises don't ground-rein."

"Oh, fuck you!" Hamm said. But he stepped to the left side of his horse, put a foot in the stirrup, and mounted. He instantly said, "Goddammit, my hat. I left my hat on your damn steps."

Warner smiled. He said, "What'll you give me to get it for you? Twenty-five dollars? That's what I figure I lost on this rifle trade."

Hamm said, "You sumbitch!" He rode his horse over to the steps and tried, unsuccessfully, to reach his hat from the saddle. Finally he dismounted and went around and got his hat, jammed it on his head, and stared at Warner. He said, "You be havin' yore fun now, but next time we meet, you'll lick cow shit."

While he was talking, his horse began to wander off again. Warner started to laugh, and Hamm said, "Goddammit!" and lunged to catch the animal. But his sudden movement spooked the horse, and the bay ran off ten yards and stopped with a rein trailing on the ground.

Warner was still laughing, but he said, "Charlie, catch Mr. Hamm's cull up for him and give him his revolver so he'll get the hell out of here. We ain't careful, he will be here for lunch."

Finally Hamm was mounted with his empty revolver in his holster. He said, "You thank you pulled my teeth stealin' my rifle off me, don't cha? Well, you jest might be in fer a surprise, Mr. Know-It-All goddam Warner Grayson. You'll come to wish this day never happened."

Warner was tired of it. He said harshly, "Get out of here, Hamm, before I change my mind and keep you here snubbed to a hitching post." He waved his hand at Hamm's horse and said, "Yah!"

The horse instantly broke into a gallop. Behind his saddle Hamm was carrying some overfilled saddlebags. Warner could see them bouncing up and down as the horse galloped away with Hamm doing all he could to recover himself in the saddle.

Warner and Charlie stood there watching him as he rode away. Charlie said, a touch of worry in his voice, "Mr. Grayson, you reckon you ought to have shamed him like you done? I mean, making him lick dirt?"

Warner looked at him. He said, "Why do you say that, Charlie?"

The young man said slowly, "Wa'l, a man like that, he's got meanness clean through him. He looks like a bushwhacker to me. That's the kind of man won't fight you except from the back."

"I kind of think you've answered your own question, Charlie." Warner got one of the little Mexican cigarillos out of his shirt pocket and lit it with a match, striking it on his boot heel. "The kind of a man he is is the kind of a man he's gonna be no matter how you treat him. A man like that don't ever see the fairness or unfairness of a thing. He don't care. Like you said, he's mean clean through. You might as well try and gentle a rattlesnake. All I done was get mine in to let him know he wasn't fooling me at all. I didn't make him lick dirt because I thought it would shame him or make him afraid of me. I made him lick dirt just so he'd understand that I knew he was a back-shooter and a bushwhacker and that that was what I thought of such."

Charlie got a sly look on his face. He said, "Mr. Grayson, did you know he was gonna back down? I mean, I've heared you on the subject of pistol duels, and I know you thank it's a buncha foolishness. So I's wonderin' when you decided he was bluffin'.''

Warner cocked his head. He said, "Don't get me wrong, Charlie. I didn't know for sure that he would crawl, but I thought he talked an awful lot. Men that mouth around like he was doing don't generally have any real sand in their craw. But when I challenged him I was prepared to go through with it." He stopped and smiled. He said, "You played right along, Charlie, when I told you to go inside and you acted mighty confident about me winning and said you were fine where you was. I seen that kind of take a bite out of him."

Charlie said, "I wadn't playactin', Mr. Grayson. I never had no worries you wouldn't handle him." He paused. "Besides, I had yore big old twelve-gauge shotgun right to my hand inside the kitchen. Had both barrels cocked."

Warner laughed. He said, "Well, hell, I reckon all the excitement is over. We ought to try and get a little work done." He handed Charlie the rifle he'd bought from the reluctant Carl Hamm and said, "Put this in the bunkhouse with you and Les and Raoul. I hate it that that son of a bitch skinned me out of forty-five dollars. I ought to have looked at the damn rifle before I got so free with my cash."

"You reckon he'll be back?"

Warner frowned. "I don't know, Charlie. I couldn't say. With people like him and people like I've heard Jack Fisher is, there is just no telling."

"What about Jack Fisher?"

"What do you mean?"

"How you going to answer him?"

Warner shrugged. "I ain't. But I got the feeling this ain't the last of it. I wish it was, but I can't make myself believe Fisher will let well enough alone."

"What if they start shootin' our horses?"

Warner looked grim. He said, "*That* would be the last mistake Jack Fisher—or anybody else tried the same thing—would ever make. But let's get to work. Wilson Young is due in tomorrow. Likely he can give me some information about Fisher I don't know right now."

Charlie's face lit up. He said, "Mr. Young is comin' to visit?"

Warner said, "Yeah. And one of us has got to be at the Calallen siding before eleven in the morning to pick him up off the train."

Charlie said, "Reckon he'll be brangin' any of them pretty women of his with him?"

Warner looked around. "Charlie, I think you need a night off in town. You are staying out here at the ranch too much."

Charlie said, "Say, Mr. Grayson, why you reckon they call that little siding Calallen? Like

54

it was a town there? Ain't a building at the place except for a railroad toolshed."

Warner looked around at him again. "I think maybe you need more than a night off, Charlie. How the hell you expect me to know something like that? They got to give it a name, don't they? They can't just call it 'that stock-loading siding sixteen miles out of Corpus Christi,' can they?"

Charlie looked uncertain. He said, "Well, I reckon not," but he didn't look satisfied with the answer. Charlie, Warner had decided some years back, had to know the answers to more questions than there were answers, and he felt like Warner, because of his extra years, should know the why and how and how come of nearly everything. Sometimes Warner felt the responsibility was a little too heavy for the honor of the position.

They stood there staring after the diminishing figure of Carl Hamm and his horse. The prairie was mostly flat in the direction he was riding, west, but clumps of mesquite and live oak and cottonwood trees occasionally obscured Hamm from view.

Charlie said, worriedly, "That man will be back, Mr. Grayson. You mark my words. He won't leave this country till he's got his hand elbow deep in trouble. Trouble for us. You taken his rifle, but then you turned around and give him the money to buy another one." Charlie shook his head. "I don't know as I know about that."

55

Warner laughed. He said, "Charlie, money or not, it's a good ways to where a man can buy a rifle around here. The way he's headed, first town is Annarose, and I ain't even sure they got a store there that sells guns."

"Well, you didn't have to give him no money."

"And be accused of stealing? Besides, how do you know he didn't have plenty of money of his own? I took the rifle because I didn't want him riding off a hundred yards and, while his blood was hot, turning around and taking a shot back at us. Charlie, Charlie, how many time I got to tell you, you can't spend your life worrying about everything bad that might happen or you won't get no living done. Forget about that jackass. When the next trouble comes along, we'll handle it. Until then we've got to get that black Kentucky stud of Wilson Young's mounted on those two Morgan mares. And that is going to be some kind of chore. I swear I never seen a stallion that can get as ready as he can. And when he's ready he is ready."

Warner didn't know exactly what it was that woke him up in the late night—instinct, he reckoned—because he was used to night sounds in the house. Very often the hired hands who slept in the bunkhouse would come in to get a bite to eat, especially if they'd been up late with a foaling or a sick horse. And Charlie, especially, like some teenage kid, would wake up in the night and come for biscuits and syrup or a piece of pie if Rosa had baked.

But they always lit a lantern in the kitchen and he could see the dim glow of it through the open door of his bedroom, which was closed only when Laura Pico came in from Corpus Christi to, as she said, audit the management. But this time there was no faint glow to be seen.

He lay still and listened. The sound seemed to be coming from the front room, and whoever it was was moving hesitantly as if he was not sure of his way in the dark. Warner reached up beside his pillow and took hold of his revolver. Silently he edged to the side of his bed and carefully put one foot on the floor. He didn't want to be in the bed if it was who he thought it was.

Without a sound he eased himself out of the bed and got down on the floor beside it. Before he moved again he put his revolver under his pillow and cocked it, the down pillow taking the sound the mechanism made. On his knees and moving slowly, he pulled the revolver out from under the pillow and then turned and stretched out full length on the cool tile floor, the revolver in his hand, his eyes intent on the dim outline of the door to his bedroom. He could still hear the furtive noises, only now they sounded much closer.

He shivered slightly. When he could sleep in a

bed, he slept naked, but even in south Texas the nights and early October mornings were cool, if not cold. He hadn't a guess as to what time it was, but from the look of the windows, he could tell that the moon was down, which meant it was sometime after two or three in the morning.

He was holding his revolver in both hands, his elbows propped on the floor tile and his head up. It was an awkward way to shoot, but it was made necessary by the need to be as still as possible. Warner didn't want to alert his quarry and cause him to flee, only to return some other night when he might be sleeping more soundly. Because he knew the layout of the house, he considered having a quiet look and taking his visitor unawares, but that would mean movement and movement could mean sound.

As he was debating the thought, a shadowy figure passed by his open door, heading for the room beyond and across the hall, the one that he used as a storeroom, though it had originally been intended as a small second bedroom. He thought distractedly that with Wilson Young coming the next day he'd need to warn Rosa to get it cleaned up and put some covers on the bed. Though, he thought, he didn't know why he ought to go to any trouble for Wilson Young. When Warner went to see him in Del Rio and they stayed at Wilson's ranch house across the Rio Grande in Mexico, Warner slept in a room pretty much like the one across the hall and Wilson never made any attempt to clean it up or put out fresh bedclothes in Warner's behalf. Wilson had two women, girls who'd been dancers in a Mexican cabaret show when he'd won them from their manager in a poker game, but Wilson had never offered Warner one to sleep with him. He could understand about Evita—she was Wilson's woman—but her cousin Lupita, whom Wilson wasn't allowed to touch, could have been made available. But no, that was Wilson Young for you, not a thought for anyone else's comfort. Well, maybe he'd leave the room the way it was and see how Wilson liked sleeping among old saddles and packing crates and posthole diggers that had somehow never reached the toolshed, and other paraphernalia that had been tossed into the room.

Warner heard a distinct sound. Apparently his visitor had wandered into the spare room. There was no way to walk around in such a room without tripping over something. Junk was scattered all over.

And then suddenly there was a dark figure in the doorway. Whoever it was stood there hesitantly, as if he was trying to adjust his eyes to a different kind of dark. As Warner's finger slowly touched the trigger he noticed that the man—because it sure as hell wasn't a woman, unless it was Laura, who sometimes wore riding pants—was holding something in his right hand.

It was too big to be a pistol and not long enough to be a rifle. It looked like a club of some kind. Whatever it was, the man was holding it pointing toward the ceiling. Before he fired, Warner had the thought that the man intended to come into his bedroom and knock him out with the club while he was asleep—sneak-punch him, as Hamm had accused Warner of doing.

And then Warner's revolver exploded and bucked back against his palm. Even above the roar of the gun he could hear the man gasp when the slug took him square in the chest, finding bone, and slammed him back across the hall. He hit the wall, and then the thing in his right hand went off with a huge boom, and the light that flashed out of the barrels almost lit up the room where Warner was lying. It sounded like both barrels of a shotgun going off at once.

Warner got up, automatically recocking his gun, and with familiarity, went to the bedside table and found a match and lit the kerosene lamp. He trimmed the wick until the lamp threw out a good glow and then turned and went through the door and looked down at the body on the floor.

It was Carl Hamm, all right. He had slumped over to his left so that his head was almost touching the floor. Near his right hand, but jarred loose by the blast, was a double-barreled twelve-gauge shotgun with the barrels sawed off so that they weren't much more than a foot and a half long, if that. It was, Warner reflected, the kind of weapon a man like Carl Hamm would use for his dirty work. He'd probably had it taken down, the barrel off the receiver and the stock, and stowed away in his saddlebags. Just taking his rifle hadn't been enough, and that was probably the reason he hadn't put up any more squawk than he had.

Warner saw with satisfaction that the bullet had hit Hamm exactly where he had been looking, right in the breastbone. He hadn't been able to aim because of the position he'd been in, but that hadn't mattered. Wilson Young said if you had to aim a handgun you had no business carrying it in the first place. Either you could shoot instinctively or you couldn't; there wasn't any in-between. The breastbone was your best target. It was square in the middle, so you had a little latitude, but the real value in hitting it was the bone splinters it sent shooting off like shrapnel. Only a damn fool aimed for the heart; it was off to one side and too small a target. Wilson's motto was stop your man first and then handle matters after that. Warner reflected that Wilson's advice was generally of first quality, at least about certain matters.

He also reflected that most people who knew them both thought Wilson had taught Warner how to protect himself. That wasn't true. He'd learned some valuable lessons from Wilson, but it was his grandfather, who had never fired a gun at another man in his life, who had instilled in him the principles underlying the way he chose to make his way through life. Carl Hamm hadn't made any one noise that woke him up. He had been brought awake because he had expected Hamm to try such a stunt. Hamm was that sort of man; Warner had seen that five minutes after Hamm had interrupted his breakfast. And every move after that had only reinforced Warner's conclusion about how the man was likely to act. His grandfather had taught him how to read horses, but he'd also taught him how to read men. That was a hell of a lot more valuable an asset than simply being good with a gun.

He could hear his hired hands rushing in through the kitchen door. He yelled out where he was and then called out that everything was under control. They came crowding into the hall, carrying lamps. They had arrived surprisingly fast, considering the bunkhouse was a good fifty yards away. Pancho Martinez was not among them. Perhaps he had not heard the shots, either because they were muffled by the bulk of Rosa or, more likely, because his cabin was farther away.

The hands were in various stages of hasty dress. Charlie wore only a pair of jeans and was barefoot. Les Russel and Raoul had taken time to pull on boots, but they hadn't bothered with shirts, even though it was good and nippy outside. Every one of them had a revolver in his hand. They all crowded in and stared down at Carl Hamm.

Charlie said, "I knowed it! Dammit, I tole Mr. Grayson the son of a bitch would be back, didn't I, Mr. Grayson?"

"Yes, Charlie, you did. You didn't say he'd be carrying a shotgun, though. And a sawed-off one at that."

Charlie said, "I tole 'em all about him, boss. More'n you did at supper."

Les said, "Mr. Grayson, is this more trouble?"

At the evening meal, which all of the men usually took together, Warner had told them a little about the incident, though he'd tried to downplay it as much as possible. But now it appeared that Charlie had taken up the story where he'd left off. That made him frown. His men were not gunhands, and Warner didn't want them frightened by something that really had nothing to do with them. He said, as reassuringly as he could, "No, Les, I don't think it means anything. I think you are looking at the end of the matter lying right here."

Charlie bent down so he could hold his lantern closer to the sawed-off shotgun. He said, "Mighty wicked-looking little contraption. Reckon you could cut a man in two with one of them thangs."

Les Russel, who was a little older than Warner

and who had not had many breaks out of life, was looking up at the ceiling and holding up his lamp. He said, "He blowed a hole through the roof."

Warner looked up. He could see a jagged hole almost six inches across where the buckshot had torn through the inch-thick wooden ceiling. He could only hope it had not gone on and knocked a hole in the clay of the tile roof. They were coming into a season where it rained about every other day, and tile roofing was hard to fix.

Raoul, who was big and brown, was shivering in the cold. He was of Mexican heritage, and though he had lived most of his life in Texas, he still spoke with an accent. He said, "What we do weeth theese fellow, Meester Grayson? He bleed on chou floor. I doan theenk Rosa gonna be too happy cleanin' up theese mess."

Warner said, "For the time being just lug him outside and lay him on the front porch. I don't want Rosa to come over to start breakfast and run into a dead man. Charlie, you run to the barn and get a tarp and put it over him. He ought to keep all right in this weather. Wilson Young will be here today before noon, and I want him to see this fellow. I think he might know him."

Les Russel looked worried. He said, "Damn good thang you woke up, boss. He could have blowed you all to bits, you layin' thar in bed."

Warner patted Les on the shoulder and said,

64

"But he didn't, Les. So don't go to worrying about it. It's all over."

Charlie said, "Might be all over fer this one, but what about the man that sent him? That thar Jack Fisher?"

Warner gave Charlie a cold look. "Charlie, why don't you go stick a biscuit in your mouth?"

Charlie looked puzzled. He said, "Why, thankee, Mr. Grayson, but I ain't particular hungry right now."

"I don't care if you're hungry or not. I just want you to have something to do with your mouth besides talk."

"Oh." Charlie looked down at the floor. "Yes, sir."

Pancho came in while they were moving the body, and he had to have everything explained to him. All he said was "Es preety good chou hokay, Meester Grayson. *Esta bueno.*"

Pancho didn't really worry very much. All he cared about was fast horses and Rosa. When the subject had come up at supper about Jack Fisher insisting on racing Warner, Pancho hadn't paid the slightest bit of attention to the implied threat. His only interest was in whether or not Warner would let him ride in the races. The rest of the business didn't concern him, so he wasn't interested.

Warner left his men to see to getting the body out of the house and went back into his room to see what time it was. He was surprised that it was nearly four o'clock. Hamm had planned well. The small hours of the morning were the best time to catch your quarry unawares. It had been Hamm's hard luck that Warner had expected him, or at least had had enough of a hunch so that he had slept extra light.

He decided there was no point in going back to bed. Consequently he got dressed and then directed Pancho to go down and wake Rosa up and have her come and fix them some breakfast.

Pancho rolled his eyes. He said, "Señor Grayson, you ask me a berry *peligroso* theeng. *Mi esposa* es like the sleep. Chou gonna geet me kill-ed."

Pancho had a face like a monkey when he contorted it with concern. But Warner said, "Go on down there, Pancho, and get your wife up. If she whips up on you too bad I'll see you get sent to the doctor in Corpus."

Finally he went, but he went reluctantly.

Warner put off shaving until later and dressed in the clothes he'd put on after delivering the foal. Less than twenty-four hours had passed since the time in the barn with the mare, but it seemed like a week. He came out of his bedroom to see, with satisfaction, that Charlie and Les and Raoul had put Hamm's body out in the cool area under the front porch roof and covered it with a tarp. Raoul had found some rags and a bucket of

66

water and a scrub brush. He said he would clean the blood off the hall floor before Rosa saw it. He said, "Et make her seeck and maybe she don't cook so good. When it get light I geet up on the roof and see for some holes."

Warner went into the kitchen and started a big pot of coffee. He wanted time to sit and think and decide what it all meant. He wondered what he should do with the body—bury it or ship it back to Jack Fisher. He wondered if he should send a rider in to Corpus to notify the sheriff. He wondered how long it would be before Jack Fisher sent down another man. Or maybe more than one.

But finally the coffee boiled, and he poured himself out a big cup and sweetened it with a couple of shots of whiskey. He'd wanted a drink ever since he'd shot Carl Hamm, but he'd refused to let himself have one until some of the wanting had gone away. His grandfather had not been against whiskey, but he'd more than once said it was like a loco bronc or a bad-tempered woman—nothing to get careless with.

Charlie came in rubbing his eyes and yawning. Charlie had been up with him the night before with the breeched colt, so he hadn't had any more sleep than Warner. He said, "Boy, howdy, Mr. Grayson, I wish thangs would settle out around here so's I could git me a night's sleep."

Warner sipped his coffee and whiskey and said,

67

"That's all right for you, Charlie, but I'm gonna have to put up with Wilson Young for a couple or three nights, and that man, long as I have known him, don't pay no attention to sleep. If Carl Hamm had tried to slip up on him like he done me, he'd've found ol' Wilson sitting up with a bottle of whiskey and a deck of cards playing one-handed poker and taking turns cheating himself."

Charlie said, "What you reckon he's gonna think of this here Carl Hamm?"

Warner looked at him for a long second, thinking it was very lucky for Charlie that he had a God-given touch with horses because he sure asked a lot of dumb questions. He said gently, "He's gonna think Hamm's dead, Charlie. That's the very first thing will occur to him."

3

Les Russel had found Hamm's horse tethered about a quarter of a mile from the ranch house in the closest grove of oak trees. He'd brought him in, unsaddled him, taken off his bridle, and turned him in with a bunch of mares that had just been brought up from a far pasture. The men had gone through Hamm's pockets, finding about a hundred dollars in bills plus some change and a crude map showing the directions from Jack Fisher's place to Warner's ranch. Charlie had argued that Warner should take back the forty-five dollars he'd given Hamm for his rifle, but Warner had said that a trade was a trade, even with a dead man.

All they'd found in Hamm's saddlebags was a couple of changes of clothes and some beef jerky and canned peaches and tomatoes. He'd had no bedroll, so it was clear he hadn't come cross-country but had either stayed at ranches along the way or cut through towns and stayed at hotels. He was carrying plenty of ammunition. Besides two boxes of .44 caliber cartridges that would fit either his revolver or the Winchester, there had been a dozen extra double-ought 12-gauge buckshot shells. They'd found ten more shotgun shells in his pockets. That seemed like an awful lot of ammunition for a weapon you wouldn't expect to use more than a few times.

Les Russel said solemnly, "If he'd've got you, Mr. Grayson, he'd've figured the rest of us would come runnin', an' he'd've cut us down one after the other with that damn hand cannon of his."

After matters had settled out and he'd done some thinking, Warner decided to send Charlie in to Corpus Christi to see the sheriff and report what had happened. Les Russel would have been a better choice, but it was Charlie who'd seen the whole thing and heard Carl Hamm start in threatening him almost as soon as he opened his mouth. Of course they could all testify that Hamm had entered his house with deadly intent. He sent Charlie off after breakfast with specific orders to keep his report simple and stick to what he'd seen and heard and to not get excited and go to running his mouth about Jack Fisher or anything that didn't apply to the actual killing. He was to ask the sheriff what Warner was to do about Hamm's horse and possessions, and then Charlie was to get himself back without stopping off to see the widow Pico and giving her the news or stopping anywhere to tell anybody, except the sheriff, anything.

He had thought to send Les or one of the others to the railroad siding to pick up Wilson Young, but in the end he'd had an extra horse saddled and taken it on lead and set off himself to meet his friend.

Warner was riding one of the Andalusian stallions, a horse that Laura insisted on calling Paseta. But of course, that was Laura. She had named all six of the stallions, after she and her late husband imported them from Spain at what Warner had been told was a cost of $2,000 apiece. Soon after that, Mexican bandits had raided the Pico ranch down near the Rio Grande, outside of Del Rio, where Wilson Young sometimes lived. Laura's husband had been killed in the raid. The same bandits had later jumped Warner, killed his partner, made off with all of their horses, and left Warner to die on an alkali flat. He had survived only because he stumbled on one of the Picos' Andalusians that had gotten free from the bandits. Together he and the horse had made their way out of the flat and down to the Rio Grande. It was the same stallion that Warner was now riding. He had gone after the bandits, even chasing them into Mexico, and killed the bulk of them and recovered some of his horses and all of the Andalusians. His fee to the widow Pico for recovering her five other horses had been the stallion. Warner was never quite sure how it happened, but he and Laura had ended up partners on his ranch and on the stock that was bred off the Andalusians. That had been some two years past, and the widow Pico, if anything,

71

had grown more strikingly attractive, bossier, and more winsome when she really wanted her way. He figured he'd better get the hole in the ceiling fixed as quick as he could because she was liable to show up at any time. He desperately hoped she wouldn't come while Wilson was there because sparks flew when those two were around each other and Warner was generally caught in the middle. Wilson considered Laura a stiff-necked, arrogant, smart-mouthed woman who thought just because she was rich and good-looking she ought to have her way all the time. Warner agreed with Wilson's assessment, but Laura belonged to him, and the arguments put him in the unfortunate and weak position of having to defend the woman he loved against his best friend.

Warner did not know exactly how old either Wilson or Laura was, and neither had ever offered to tell him. He guessed Laura to be about two years older than he was and Wilson a long three or maybe a short four in advance of him.

He rode along through the bright, warming morning sunshine, the country stretching out all around him in rolling prairies with the grass curing off naturally and turning the color of wheat—or the color of Laura's hair if you threw in a little light strawberry shading. He sighed as he thought of her. About the only time they didn't argue was when they were in bed or when one or the other of them was being extra nice in order to avoid an argument so they could get in bed. Warner, prior to meeting Laura Pico, had been as experienced as most young men when it came to women, but nothing had, or could have, prepared him for her. She was intelligent, devious, sneaky, mean, loving, generous, bossy, lustful, puritanical, and determined to have her way from breakfast until who had the say about putting out the last lantern. Warner fervently hoped she wouldn't get wind of what had happened at the ranch and come flying out to manage matters.

But he put her out of his mind as he spotted the railroad toolshed about a half mile ahead. He consulted his watch. It was twenty of eleven and, unless the train was ahead of time, he was early.

He wondered if he should have brought a buckboard. His friend might have a big suitcase with him, and it would be awkward tying it on behind the saddle of one of the horses. And of course it would be just like Wilson to have a big valise, because he was something of a dandy when it came to his clothes. He didn't dress fancy, but he wore only the best—silk and linen shirts and gabardine and whipcord and corduroy trousers and riding pants.

Warner hoped nobody would ever ask him to describe Wilson Young. He didn't reckon it could be done, at least not in English or Spanish, which were the only two languages he spoke. Maybe if there were some foreign lingo that had a whole lot of extra words and phrases a body might be able to capture Wilson Young with a word picture, but he doubted it.

First of all, up until a few years back when the governor had given him a conditional pardon, Wilson Young had been a bank robber. No, Warner thought, that wasn't right. Wilson himself had corrected him on that one. He'd said, "No, sonny boy, I didn't reckon it fair to the banks to rob only them. What I done was rob wherever they had enough money gathered up to catch my attention. I robbed stagecoaches, trains, poker games, payrolls, anything. The only exception I made was churches, and I only excepted them out of professional courtesy for the preachers."

No one knew why the governor had suddenly decided to grant a pardon to a man who'd been on the owl-hoot trail ever since he'd turned outlaw at fifteen. Some said it was because Wilson Young was known as a gentleman and had powerful friends, but most believed it was the lobbying of the law officers, who couldn't catch him and who'd prevailed on the governor to make him honest with the stroke of a pen. The pardon had been conditional on Wilson sticking strictly to counting his own money and leaving other folks' currency alone. Wilson had once told Warner, "Hell, they could have saved themselves the trouble if they'd only known it. By the time they pardoned me I'd been living on the quiet

74

in Mexico for the better part of two years and hadn't stolen nothing more than a kiss off a pretty girl. But they was a few impostors going around acting like they was me. Fortunately, by the time the pardon got through, they'd all been killed or caught, so that left me free to come on back over the river and act like Sunday school had just let out."

Now Wilson ran a whorehouse, casino, and saloon in Del Rio that he claimed was the biggest and best west of the Mississippi River. The truth of it was that he didn't have much to do with the running of it. His woman, Evita, with the help of her cousin, Lupita, ran the whorehouse and the saloon, and Wilson had several old Mississippi riverboat gamblers taking care of matters in the casino.

His latest love was horse racing. Del Rio was the undisputed center of match racing in the South, and that was due in no small part to Wilson Young. He and Warner were going to talk about the bluegrass Thoroughbred that Warner had charge of and lay out a breeding program that would get the black stallion's blood into stock that was more suited to running up to a half mile. The idea was to give the sprinting horses a little more bottom, a little more stretch, a little more endurance. They were also going to talk about maybe laying their hands on a couple or three Kentucky bluegrass Thoroughbreds and maybe producing some colts that could be run at the longer distances. The main problem was that no one else in Texas owned such horses, and they might have a hell of a stable of racehorses and nobody to race. Wilson had half humorously suggested that the breed would make an excellent getaway horse. He'd said, "We might tap into the bank robber trade. A good horse is nearly more important to a bank robber than good judgment." Warner hadn't been at all sure that Wilson was joking.

He'd met Wilson when he was sixteen. Wilson and three other bandits had ridden onto Warner's grandfather's ranch looking for a fresh mount for Wilson, whose horse had a hot ligament. At about that time his grandfather's health was heading straight downhill, so Warner had done the trading, all the time realizing that Wilson Young could have taken whatever he wanted without benefit of payment. But he hadn't done that, and he'd made the ruffians with him behave. Warner had traded sharp with him, but he'd traded fair. The horse he'd swapped Wilson for his lame animal had been a better horse, but not by much, and Warner had gotten a hundred dollars to boot, knowing that the ligament strain on Wilson's horse would heal up in no time. When the trade was done, Wilson had looked down on him from atop his new horse and said, "Sonny boy, for the sake of the children you might never have, I hope this animal is all you say he is. I would give him a little more going-over, but I'm a mite pushed for time right now, so I reckon I'll have to take your word."

Then he'd ridden away. Later Warner had calculated that Wilson couldn't have been much more than nineteen himself at that time, and there he was calling Warner "sonny boy." Well, Warner reckoned, a man in Wilson's line of work just thought older.

Since that day Wilson had bought or traded nearly every horse he rode from Warner. Through the years they had gradually become close friends. Indeed it was to Wilson Young that Warner had staggered, half dead from his ordeal on the alkali plain. And it was to Wilson that he'd turned for advice about how to go after the Mexican bandits. Wilson's advice had been to stick to breeding horses. Warner hadn't taken it.

Now Warner stood beside the tool shack and looked off down the track, waiting. Flies buzzed around, and the horses took turns stamping their feet impatiently. He didn't know what they were impatient for. They weren't going anywhere, except back to the ranch. But he'd always noticed how some horses, generally higher-blooded stock, got impatient when they had to stand and wait. They always acted like they had important business elsewhere and like they knew that time

77

was money. Horses were only a little smarter than chickens, but they were a lot funnier. They acted so serious about matters, as if they thought they ought to be consulted from time to time on certain decisions. Warner was of the opinion, though he'd had the good sense to never tell anyone, that horses liked to put on airs and act above their station.

Finally he saw a trail of black smoke as the train rounded a curve a couple of miles away and started in for a straight run to the cattle-loading stop. There was a pen made of heavy wooden planks for holding animals and a tilted chute so they could be driven straight up into the cattle cars. It was on the opposite side of the tracks from Warner and was, because of the time of the year, empty. Anybody who was going to ship cattle to market would have already done so. Now they'd winter them on the cured grass, sell them in February or March for a better price, and buy yearlings to feed up on the spring grass. It was a cycle the cattlemen had been following ever since Warner could remember.

The train was close enough now so that he could tell it was slowing by the way the smoke didn't stream straight backwards. In a few more minutes he heard the squeal of iron on iron as the engineer set the brakes and the train came into the station blowing out great clouds of steam as the engineer bled off pressure from his boiler.

Warner had the horses a good ten yards back, but they still had to jump around and cut up like the world was about to come to an end. They both acted like they'd never seen a train before, but Warner knew for a fact that the Andalusian had ridden on more trains than most women and children.

Then the train ground to a stop, blasting out one last cloud of steam and then seeming to sag down. It sat there going *chuff-chuff-chuff,* like a horse who'd had a hard run.

Wilson Young came clambering down the steps of the car right in front of Warner. A conductor had put a little iron stool down to make the last step easier, but Wilson jumped over it. He gave the conductor a nod of thanks and then spotted Warner and smiled slowly. Warner had always thought Wilson Young put something in his smile that was intended to make people think he knew a hell of a lot more than he did. It was a twinkling, cynical smile, the kind of smile you'd use across the table at a man who was betting heavy but who you didn't believe really had the cards and you wanted to let him know you knew that before you took his money.

Wilson came stepping down the gravel embankment. Warner was glad to see he had a set of saddlebags over his shoulder. There'd be no trouble with a valise. When he was a few yards away, Wilson said, "Well, there's a man looks like he's got the case ace and he's the only one who knows it."

Warner said, "I ain't only got the case ace, Will, I got the other three besides."

Wilson came up and they shook hands, and Wilson smiled and said, "How you be, little brother?"

Warner said, "I been better, but I been worse, too."

"Well, let's get loaded up, and you just tell your old uncle about it. If he can't fix it, it ain't broke."

"You can't know what a weight off my soul that is, Uncle Will."

Wilson threw his saddlebags over the rump of the roan Morgan that Warner had brought for him, tied them in place, and put a foot in the stirrup. He said, "You ain't sold my black stud horse, have you?"

"I thought that was *my* stud. When did he get to be yours? You gave him to me for saving your life, don't you remember?"

Wilson mounted. He said, "Huh. Boy, you better go to checking the labels on some of them bottles you been drinking out of. The only way I could imagine you saving my life would be if you got between me and Evita when she had a knife in her hand."

Warner mounted and reined the Andalusian around. He said, "Don't talk to me about Evita.

Don't tell a man that's got a mountain on his shoulders about some little hill."

"And how is the widow Pico?"

"Out of range right now. Thank God."

They sat out under the porch roof drinking whiskey and talking. On the ride back from the railroad siding, Warner had told Wilson the details of Carl Hamm's visit. Wilson had not been at all surprised by any of it. His only remark had been that Hamm wasn't dangerous so long as you weren't facing the wrong way. He'd said, "Fisher's got about half a hundred like him. He'll have him replaced before you can ship the body back. Go ahead and bury him and forget about it. Sheriff ain't going to want to be bothered."

They'd lifted the tarp long enough for Wilson to verify it was Carl Hamm, and then Les Russel and Raoul had hitched up the buckboard to haul the body off to some far reach and stick it in the ground. Russel had wondered if they ought to say some words over him, but Wilson had said, "What words? He wouldn't recognize them. If you got to say some words say 'son of a bitch' and 'snake' and 'low-down cur dog' and 'bushwhacker' and 'back-shooter.' Them are the only words would mean anything to him. You can't give a Christian burial to that belly-crawler. Lightning might strike you."

So now the body was gone, and they were

81

drinking whiskey and considering what Jack Fisher's next move might be. Warner said, "You know the man, Wilson. Was it an idle threat? Something he's gonna forget about when Hamm don't return?"

Wilson chewed on his lip in thought. He was wearing a white linen shirt and tan gabardine riding pants and polished brown boots. His hat was a light tan, like Warner's except that it had cost twice as much. Wilson and Warner were almost the same height, but Wilson was perhaps ten pounds heavier. Some of the extra weight was from easy living, but mostly it was because his frame was slightly larger than Warner's.

He said, "Tell you the truth, Warner, I don't know the man well enough to make a call like that." He took a sip of whiskey and looked over at Warner. "Mark me, I think the son of a bitch is as crazy as a bissy bug. He'd have to be to get up to some of the stuff he does. Nobody can be that mean, not naturally. A wheel fell off his wagon somewhere back in the past and he ain't ever had it replaced."

"You mean Fisher's kill-crazy?"

Wilson shrugged. "If you said that, you'd have to say he'd come at anybody. But he don't. He ain't never messed with me, for instance. If he was kill-crazy he wouldn't be careful to pick his targets. And he does pick his targets. But he made a mistake about three months back. A man name

82

of Austin Vaughn moved into our locale, and Fisher went after him. Figured to take the man's seed herd and his land and maybe his pretty wife. He lost five or six men, either killed or crippled in that little affair. Of course he was reaching out a little, about forty miles past his natural base."

"What happened to Vaughn?"

Wilson shrugged. "He walks the streets and tends to his business and keeps all four eyes open. He's got a younger brother who is part forty-four-caliber revolver. I think he was handmade by Samuel Colt himself. For the time being he is helping his big brother with matters. But I don't think this Austin Vaughn is going to need any help. Fisher ain't bothered him since. That's what I mean by I don't think he's kill-crazy. I think he's cripple-crazy, or opportunity-crazy." Wilson looked over at Warner again and said, "I think your main danger comes from ignorance. Not on your part but on Jack Fisher's part. I don't think he's done his schoolwork on you. All he's ever heard about you is your reputation as a horseman. He don't know that you are the product of years of devoted study at my knee."

Warner gave him a disgusted look. "Will you be serious? I know one of your arms is longer than the other from patting yourself on the back, but this ain't the time for it."

Wilson sipped his whiskey. "I am serious. The man does not know that you make a formidable foe. You go around with that choirboy face on you and act so quiet and unassuming that folks don't really know how fucking dangerous you are. And I'm serious about that." He gave Warner a flat look. "You don't have a reputation. Not a general reputation as to how dangerous it is to fool around with you. I know and a few other people know and quite a few that are past the talking stage know, but the point is that Jack Fisher don't know. He ain't educated where you are concerned."

"Then why don't you educate him?"

Wilson shook his head. "Too late. It would sound like I was trying to protect you after the fact, coming in to head him off like you had a weakness."

"What about Hamm? Ain't that going to tell him something? Hamm come down, but he didn't go back."

Wilson shook his head again. "Fisher would figure you had three or more hired hands. Why should he figure you kilt the man? It would be just as easy for him to figure your help jumped Hamm and done him in. Besides, he ain't gonna consider Hamm much of a score. We got one advantage: Fisher don't know, or shouldn't have any reason to, that we are friends. He'll be blind on that side."

Warner said, "Wilson, we been down this road before, and I don't want to get in the same arguments. I don't want your help. I can't take your help. You keep getting me confused with the sixteen-year-old kid you bought that horse off of so long ago. A good deal has changed since then. I don't need no nursemaid, Wilson. Thank you very much, but I'll get through this one on my own."

Wilson reached out and got the bottle that was sitting on the stone floor of the porch and poured his tumbler half full. He said, "Yeah, Warner, you are going to need some help on this one. You are badly outgunned. You haven't got a man on this place, maybe with the exception of Les Russel, who could go up against the worst of Jack Fisher's gunhands. I think you could take Fisher in a halfway fair fight, but you ain't going to get that. Fisher obviously figures if he gets your horses he gets your reputation. He wants you out of the way, sonny boy. And he don't know but one way to do that."

Warner shook his head. "I have a hard time believing a man can get away with being as low-down as Fisher is for as long as he has. How come nobody ain't killed him before now?"

Wilson shrugged. "When the opportunity was there, folks was uncertain it was a pressing and needful matter. Now it's too late. He's too well guarded, and to give the devil his due, he is a pretty fair hand himself. He likes to fight. He likes to kill people. That right there gives him an edge. Where the other man has to think on it and maybe work himself up to the deed, for Fisher it's all instinct."

"Does the man seriously want to horse-race me? Is that part of it straight? Or does he intend to kill me as easily as he can?"

"I can't see in the man's mind, Warner, but I think he wants both. I think he wants to show you up by racing his horses against yours and then pick a quarrel with you and force you into a fight. He doesn't think you'll be anywhere near a match for him. That might be his weak spot."

Warner said, "But I don't want to fight the son of a bitch. I don't have any reason to."

Wilson laughed dryly. "You will a short time after ya'll lock horns."

They were silent for a moment, each thinking his own thoughts. Finally Warner said, "Look here . . . something's wrong about all this. Carl Hamm came back early this morning to kill me. If he had succeeded, what would that have done to Jack Fisher's plans? Wouldn't have been no horse races then, no chance for him to outdo me or my horses. Just a cold-blooded murder."

Wilson said slowly, "Well, you never know when a man like Hamm is gonna run off the rail. You shamed him and pressed him pretty hard. He could mighty easy have forgot he was working for Jack Fisher." He paused for a second, looking out toward the pastures beyond a little hump in the prairie. "Or the son of a bitch might've had the idea of taking you out of your bed and delivering you to Fisher in Cotulla, probably a little the worse for wear. You get to dealing with a mind like that, Warner, and you figure him to think the way you would. That don't work. Ain't any way either one of us could follow his kind of logic, because it wouldn't be logic to us. You ever been in a big cave had a lot of caverns branching off here and there and turning back on themselves until you don't know up from down, much less north from south?"

Warner shook his head.

Wilson said, "Well, I have. Out in the New Mexico Territory. That's what the inside of a mind like Carl Hamm's looks like." He sounded a little disappointed that Warner had never been lost in a cavern, because some of his point had not been put across. But he added, "And Jack Fisher is nearly the same, though I'd have to say he is able to keep the general populace fooled into thinking he's sane. You know that insane asylum they got up near Austin for the crazy people? Well, if you wanted to have one right here on your ranch all you'd have to do was to put Jack Fisher in an empty room and shut the door. Be as authentic as anything the state of Texas could put their stamp on."

Warner smiled thinly. "Wilson, I hate to see you wearing yourself out trying to make me feel a little better. You ought to take it easier on yourself, my friend. All this encouragement you're giving me is too much, even for a constitution like yours. You are trying to paint too bright a picture."

Wilson laughed and got out a small cigar and lit it. He offered one to Warner, but Warner shook his head. Wilson said, "I don't want you getting cocky."

"What I can't figure is what the man is after. Does he plan to kill or run off all the horse handlers and breeders in Texas?"

Wilson sighed. He said, "There you go again, trying to think like Jack Fisher. I know you told me that your granddaddy said them six inches between your ears was more powerful than the six inches of any gun barrel, but, goddammit, your granddaddy never met Jack Fisher. You can't outthink him because you ain't both on the same road. Don't go straining your mind trying to figure what Jack Fisher is going to do, because you can't. Figure out what *you're* going to do."

"Wonder if he knows I got a partner."

"You mean the Queen of the Wildcats? No, but even if he does know, he's got sense enough to go after you."

"But look here, Wilson, I don't even specialize in breeding racehorses. If anything, I breed road horses, traveling animals for men with the money to afford a really fine horse to get around town or around the county on."

Wilson took the little cigar out of his mouth and gave Warner an amused look. He said, "That's bullshit, Warner. You may not breed many running horses, but the ones you do breed somehow manage to get their noses across the line first. The last meet I was at on the Mexico side in Piedras Negras, half the quarter mile horses were yours, and I've seen many a winner at six hundred yards was one of yours out of your quarter horse studs and American Standardbred mares. And the two best half mile horses in south Texas are out of our black Kentucky stud and either a straight Morgan or a Morgan-Standardbred cross. I thought you were so careful about keeping breeding books."

Warner took off his hat and scratched his head. He said, "I never took it important enough to think of it that way. I seldom know what a running horse of mine does once I sell him, because I don't go to race meets."

Wilson gave him his droll look. He said, "And you don't get no inkling when all these folks show up wanting to get a quarter mile horse off you or a six-sixty horse? You reckon they are willing to pay your prices because of that boyish grin of yours?"

"Aw, shut up, Wilson." Warner sat back tiredly in his chair. It didn't seem he'd had any real sleep for a week. And now here had come a man was supposed to be one of his best friends, and all he could do was poke fun and make light. He took a long drink of whiskey and then got up and went to the open front door. He yelled in, "Rosa!"

A voice came from the back, a high squeaky voice: "Chess, *señor*?"

"How much longer before lunch? We are nearly starvin' to death out here."

"Plenty queek, *señor*, plenty queek."

Warner sat back down. He said, "That could mean anywhere from a half hour to next week." He took another drink of whiskey, and said, "Damn! Shit! Hell! Son of a bitch!"

Wilson said, "You think I am taking this too lightly, don't you? You think, as your friend, that I ain't concerned enough."

Without looking at him Warner said, "The thought has crossed my mind."

Wilson said, "I was trying to kind of casual-like point out to you that there ain't a damn thing you can do about matters right now. You are trying to break a colt that ain't been throwed yet."

Warner looked around quickly at him. "The man has stated his intentions. He sent a man to bring me them intentions."

"They wasn't very detailed intentions."

"Well, what am I supposed to do, sit here until he starts killing my horses? You said yourself that he was a man of set ways and he apparently has decided to set his sights on me. All right, I'll go see the son of a bitch and get his intentions spelled out for me."

Wilson said, "Now hold on a goddam minute. You ain't going to see Jack Fisher because that would be suicide. And anyway, he ain't killed any of your horses yet."

"No, and I don't intend to give him the chance." He stood up, staring off into the distance. "I'm not fool enough to go riding up to his front door, but there has got to be a time when I can get at him alone."

Wilson said, "Will you sit down and quit talking like a fool? The man even shoots *at* one of your horses and we'll both go to see him and take along some people to even out the odds. But right now ain't the time to worry about it. We got lunch to eat, and we got to talk about breeding that stud and what we are going to try and get. I come down here on important business, and I ain't going to waste the trip just because you are getting spooked."

Warner stared out for a moment longer and then reluctantly sat down. Finally he said, "Yeah, I reckon you're right." He slumped back and then suddenly sat up again. "But I am going to send the bastard a telegram and ask him was the message delivered by the late Carl Hamm his true instructions."

Wilson shook his head. "That's right . . . just

on the odd chance that the man might have laid it away in his mind, you be sure and send off a wire to jog his memory. Warner, sometimes I don't know about you. You are undoubtedly one of the most single-minded men I have ever met. In some that is a virtue, but I have come to believe you have managed to work it into a flaw of the first order."

At that moment Rosa came to the door, filling it. She said, "Theese *comida es* hokay ready."

Wilson got up. "Let's go and eat. I am anxious to see you get something in your mouth besides words."

It was midafternoon when they finished looking at the black stud and the three or four mares Warner was proposing breeding him to as they came in season. They were walking back toward the ranch house. Warner was looking out across the prairie toward town. He said, "I wonder where the hell Charlie is. I sent him in to tell the sheriff about this Hamm fellow. Must have been no later than eight o'clock he rode out of here. Where is he? He's had time enough to go and come twice. Hell, he was on one of them Andalusian-Morgan crosses that would lay down in shame if it spent more than two hours getting to town."

"Maybe the sheriff took more of his time than you figured."

"Hell, what he had to tell was straightforward.

Couldn't have taken more than ten minutes to explain the whole business. If the sheriff had any questions he'd have to come out here."

"You reckon Charlie might have run into a town girl he wanted to visit with? You reckon that's possible, Warner? Are you so old you done forgot about that?"

Warner shook his head. "Charlie gets enough time off. More than he needs. Besides, he's supposed to still be sparkin' that girl in Del Rio he was so hot about when he come to work for me permanent."

"Hundred and fifty miles away? Ain't many sparks fly that far."

They went into the house and sat down, still discussing what they hoped to achieve in the breeding. Wilson thought the time was ripe to start developing speed horses that could run farther, like the bluegrass Thoroughbreds that raced up to a mile and a half. Warner's argument continued to be that there was no market for that sort of horse in south Texas—or any part of Texas. He said, "Hell, Wilson, they ain't no round tracks—or oval tracks, I think they call them—like they got in Kentucky and up in there. Of course, I've never seen 'em, but that's what I hear. You can't have a straightaway mile, mile-and-a-quarter race. How the hell would the crowd see it? What would you do, run the race around a mountain and put the crowd on the top?

Or around a fenced pasture? That ain't the kind of horse folks are used to down here. Half mile is about all they want to see. I know you are going to say you got one of them oval racetracks in Del Rio, but that's the only place."

Wilson was fooling around with a deck of cards, flipping out aces without looking. He said, "I still think we ought to get a couple of Kentucky mares and see what happens."

"Cost a power of money. Maybe a thousand dollars a mare, and they wouldn't be of the best."

Wilson flipped out another ace with two fingers, seeming to make the card appear by its own energy. He said, "Hell, I got a power of money. I don't want to keep on doing what everybody else is doing. I—"

He stopped because they'd both heard a horse come running up and get pulled to a hard stop. They looked at the door. In a moment Charlie came running in looking red-faced and worried. He said, "For God's sake, Mr. Grayson, don't blame me! I swear it wadn't my fault. I done ever'thang in my power, I swear I did!"

Warner stood up. He said, "Charlie, calm down, goddammit. What the hell is the matter? What are you talking about?"

Charlie was slightly out of breath. He said, pointing toward the east, "I rode as hard as I could. I made an excuse to go on ahead. Tried to get here so's to give you as much warnin' as I could. An' I done ever'thang I could not to let it happen in the first place."

Wilson Young said, "Charlie, what in hell are you blathering about?"

Charlie pointed again, to the east. He gave Warner an apprehensive look. He said, "Miz Pico. She be about ten minutes behind me, comin' in her buggy."

4

Warner stared at him for a moment. He said, finally, "Why in hell is she coming out here and what did you tell her?"

Charlie hung his head. He said haltingly, "She's comin' fer the reason . . . the reason that— that . . . she wadn't supposed to hear about. I mean—"

"You told her what happened here? You *told her* about what happened with Carl Hamm and Jack Fisher?" He stared at Charlie with disbelieving eyes. "You couldn't have done that, not after I gave you strict orders to stay away from her and to run if you saw her, and if she ran after you, don't speak, and if she ran after you and caught you and made you talk not to say one goddam word about *any* of what has happened out here. Don't you dare tell me you told her any of this. *This!*"

Charlie looked around like a man trying to find a door in the dark. He said miserably, "Mr. Grayson, I dunno how it happent. She seen me comin' out of the sheriff's office. It was the worst kind of luck she happened along about that time. Soon as she seen me, I was caught."

"What do you mean, caught? Did you have to tell her? Couldn't you have lied? Couldn't you have told her we'd had a horse stole or something like that?"

Charlie swallowed hard. He said, "Fact of the business is, that's the line I tried to take, but then she wanted to know what horse got stole and when and how did it happen and . . . hell, Mr. Grayson, *you* ought to know how she is."

Wilson Young laughed.

Warner gave him a glare, but then came back to Charlie. "I still don't see how she got it out of you? Why didn't you stick to your lie?"

Charlie twisted his hat in his hands. "I tried, Mr. Grayson. Honest to God, I tried like hell. But she got me so twisted around, and turned first this way and that, that pretty soon I was caught in my own snare. An' then when I told her about the man comin' in the house and tryin' to kill you in bed, I—"

Warner said, "You told her *that?* You told her about Carl *Hamm?*" He sat down heavily in an overstuffed chair. "Hell, you might as well have told her ever'thing."

Charlie took a breath and let it out slowly. He said, "I reckon I pretty well did, Mr. Grayson." He shook his head. "I'm mighty sorry."

Warner lifted a hand and flicked it. "It ain't really your fault, Charlie. Once she seen you, the game was up. She'd have found out sooner or later anyway. I just wish Wilson—" He stopped and said, "Charlie, you better go cool your horse out."

"Yes, sir." He went out the door putting on his hat.

Wilson Young flipped his wooden chair around so he could rest his arms on the back. He said, "You was fixing to say something about me in your fright and your confusion. I reckon you forgot I was here. Was you going to say anything about you wished I wasn't here to see you playing ring-around-the-rosy with the missus? That why you broke off?"

Warner gave him a look. He said dryly, "She ain't the missus, as you damn well know. But you will have your little joke, won't you?"

Wilson flipped the cards on a low table by the divan. He said, "Oh, hell, Warner, what difference does it make? Like you said, she'd have found out sooner or later. What the hell, don't pay her no mind."

Warner said, "Huh! Don't pay her no mind. Nice trick. But that's the point. Right now, right when I need to do some hard thinking with the matter fresh in my mind, she'd come busting in here like a whirlwind saying this and that and asking more questions in ten minutes than you or I could think of in a week, and pretty soon she'll have me as tied up in knots as she done Charlie."

Wilson said, "But you can't argue that this ain't her business as well."

Warner nodded emphatically. "The business end, yes. I don't quarrel with that, even though we have a clear understanding between us that my judgment is final. But it won't be about the business she'll give me the hardest time. She'll—" He stopped and shut his mouth and glanced at the door as if he expected her at that very second.

Wilson said, "She'll be concerned about your hide. I know." He looked sympathetic. He got up and stretched. "That's the problem with women. They want to solve men's problems in a woman's way, and that just won't work. I been trying for four years to get Evita to understand that, and it ain't worked yet. Only woman ever understood it was my wife, Marianne, and since she knowed what I was when she married me, there was never no need to argue about the matter. But you was a horse breeder when you and the widow Pico hooked up. She still thinks of you that way."

Warner said, "How does she reckon I got those horses back? By diplomatic means?"

Wilson said, "Oh, that don't count. Don't you understand that? That was then; this is now."

Warner sighed. "Well, it don't much matter now. I think I can hear the creak of buggy springs. We might as well go on out and help her down. I'll put her rig away, and *you* show her the hole in the ceiling while I'm at it. I want her to get all the 'that could have been you' out of her system before I come back in. I figure she'll have to say it at least ten times. Keep a count and give me a whistle."

Wilson smiled. "If she's so bad, why do you put up with her, Warner? I mean it ain't as if she was all *that* good looking."

Warner gave him a stare. He said, "You gone blind or you just trying to make me out a fool?"

Wilson said, "She taste as sweet as she looks?"

Warner said, "Well, since she and Evita have about the same cake-and-pie disposition, why don't you tell me? You ought to be an expert on barbed wire and brier patches by now. Go ahead, make another smart-aleck crack."

Wilson put up both his hands. "I give up. But I still think I got it worse on account of Evita can dress me down in that Gatling gun Spanish of hers and I don't even know I been cut till I see the blood."

"Count yourself lucky," Warner said. "The widow Pico don't never say a word ain't made clear and obvious."

When Laura came to visit they couldn't eat dinner in the kitchen. It was all right for breakfast and lunch, but not for dinner. Warner was pretty sure it was one of her ways of telling him he ought to enlarge the house.

But when she was there for dinner, the sitting room furniture had to be rearranged and the big round kitchen table worked through the door between the kitchen and the sitting room and the sitting room turned into a dining room. And the hired hands couldn't eat with them and Rosa had to serve from the kitchen and she had to cook how and what Laura directed. It was a great strain on all of them, especially Rosa.

Sometimes Warner wished Laura was not so attractive and so desirable. That way he wouldn't let her get away with as much as she did. But unfortunately he'd seen her once too often without her clothes and been in the warm, soft parts of her, and the whole effect was to make him as weak around her as a drunk with a bottle of whiskey.

Not that she was always pushy and not that Warner couldn't handle her when he set his mind to it; she could read his mood on those occasions and instinctively knew when to become suddenly loving and pliant and soft. Of course that always caused him to lower his guard, which gave her exactly the opening she was looking for. He'd once told her that she was the most plaguing, irritating, dumbfounding woman he'd ever met and that she'd better thank her lucky stars for her looks and her style and whatever it was about her that caused him to lose his resolve. Otherwise he wouldn't have had anything to do with her.

By the time they'd finished a supper of chicken enchiladas and guacamole sauce with soft tortillas and flan for dessert and were sitting around with coffee and brandy, they had the problem all talked out. Laura had come to the firm opinion that if they simply left the matter alone, it would go away. Warner had appealed to Wilson as a man who knew Jack Fisher. Wilson, wary of Laura, had said, "Well, I don't know. He's crazy as hell, and you never can tell with a man like that. I've been telling Warner all day that there is no point in trying to figure out ahead of time what Fisher is liable to do, because he is just as apt to do something that you'd never think of."

Laura said, "All well and good. But until something else happens, I don't see any point in stirring him up any more than he already is." She looked at Warner. "And that means you should not go to see him or send him a telegraph wire or anything."

Warner said, "Goddammit, Laura, as much as you want it to, this ain't going to go away. That son of a bitch sets in to shooting my horses, I'll have to do something, so I'd rather get it settled before the barn-burning or the horse-killing starts."

She said coolly, "You don't know that it will ever start. You have no idea if that man really came from Jack Fisher or not. Maybe Carl Hamm was crazy in his own right. Don't take so much for granted."

Warner looked at Wilson Young. The gambler shrugged. Warner said, "Goddammit, Laura, will you learn your place? This ain't any of your affair, and you might as well stop interfering, because I don't like it."

Her face pinked up. She said, "I'm a partner in this ranch."

"You're a partner in *part* of the livestock of this enterprise, not this ranch itself."

She gave him a look. "I have put money in this enterprise, if that's what you want to call a shack on forty acres of crabgrass."

Warner could feel his temper rising, which was the worst thing imaginable. He knew that Laura deliberately tried to goad him into anger so that she could tie him into knots with her skillful words. He said, "Now just a goddam minute! I—"

Wilson Young pushed his chair back. "I think I'll take me a little walk," he said. "Feels like it is fixing to get a little too warm in here."

When Wilson was safely outside, with the door pulled closed behind him, Laura put her soft white hand on Warner's tanned forearm. She said, "Now, dear, don't go to swelling up. You get so determined sometimes, and this is a time when I don't think you should do anything. There is a time to act and a time to wait, and this, I think, is—"

"I wish to hell you could once in a while have

103

the good sense not to trot our disagreements out in public," he said coldly. "You are a strong-willed woman, Laura, and I goddam well wish you'd temper yourself a little. Sometimes I'd like to take a pair of spurs to you."

She said, looking innocent, "But that was just in front of Wilson. He doesn't count. You and he are almost like brothers."

He said as evenly as he could, "Especially in front of Wilson Young. And you know that. I've brought it to your attention more than once. Nothing makes Wilson any happier than to have something to jab me with, and anytime you are around, you ain't never late in supplying him with ammunition." His temper slipped a little. "And you goddam well know it, too, so don't come the innocent with me."

She took her hand off his arm and picked up her tumbler of brandy and took a sip. She said, "Listen, you damn fool. You are too important to me to let you go off in one of your headstrong plunges and get yourself killed. Which is exactly what you'll do if you set off to bring Jack Fisher to bay. I know his name only too well, Warner. So we're not going to have any more talk about that. If you don't want me giving Wilson Young ammunition, as you call it, then don't give me reason."

He gave her a sour look. "My only importance to you is that you've got money invested in this enterprise—which you describe as a shack and forty acres of weeds. You are a hard-hearted, addlebrained mercenary woman, and you damn well better keep your nose out of my business."

She patted his hand and then kissed the corner of his mouth. She said, "If that is what you want to think, my darling, then you keep right on thinking that. You usually get everything by the wrong end anyway."

He was about to say something back to her with a little heat in it, but the door opened and Wilson came in. He said, "All the shooting over? I don't see no blood. Must have been peaceful in here."

Warner said, "I've been defending you against an attack on your looks, your brains, and what little character you've got."

Wilson gave Laura a wink. "Then you had the easy side of it, didn't you?"

Laura said, "Never fear, Mr. Young, I have been firmly put in my place, my woman's place, my junior partner's place. I shall not open my mouth again except to express admiration for any ideas that Warner cares to give voice to."

Warner made a slight choking sound, and Wilson said, "Miss Laura, I wonder if I could get you to come back to Del Rio and instill that same kind of virtue in Evita. It would make a world of difference in my life."

Laura said, with a glint in her eye, "I doubt if

Evita needs any help in her conduct where you are concerned."

Wilson said, "Well, now that we got the heavy work out of the way, what say we clear the table and play some three-handed poker. I know it ain't much of a game, but I can't sleep of a night if I don't get in a few hands of cards before I go to bed."

Warner said, "All right, but you ain't ever going to deal or touch the cards in any way except them in your hand, and we are going to play with my cards."

"Those are your cards."

Warner gave him a slight smile. He said, "No, those are the cards you want me to think are mine. I seen you switch the decks when you first came in."

Wilson said, "Hell, Warner, I got to cheat. It makes me nervous if I ain't allowed to cheat a little."

Laura said, "You can cheat, Mr. Young, if I can too."

"I ain't playing," Warner said.

"She ain't talking about with the cards, Warner," Wilson said dryly. "She's talking about cheating with that dress she's wearing."

Laura had arrived in riding pants and soft jodhpur boots. But, for dinner, she'd changed into a light organdy gown that was not quite off-the-shoulder but showed white skin almost down

106

to her cleavage. When she'd made the remark about cheating, she'd dipped a shoulder so that the neckline of the gown had fallen a little lower. Now she laughed and pulled the puffed sleeve farther up on her shoulder.

Warner said, "Oh," and gave her a look.

She said, "Before you ask it, no, I have no shame. Or yes, whichever is right." She smiled. "I like to win."

Warner said, "By any means. Fair or foul."

She gave him a look. "What is it you say about training horses? Some need more help than others."

"That supposed to apply to me?"

"If the shoe fits," she said. "Now, then, let's play some cards. I feel lucky."

Wilson said, "Luck ain't got a damn thing to do with it, madam. It's pure skill and character."

That night she kissed him good-night before he'd finished undressing and then got into bed and slipped under the covers. When he came in behind her he put his arm over her and cupped her naked breast in his hand, stroking her nipple. She said, whispering, "No."

He pulled back a little. "What?"

She said, "Ssssh. I said no. Go to sleep."

He reared up on one elbow. "What's the matter with you? Is it that time again?"

She whispered hard, "No! Now, be quiet. My

heavens, Wilson Young is just across the hall. He could hear us."

He frowned in the darkness. He said, "These walls are two feet thick, and both doors are closed. He couldn't hear us. And what if he did? What do you reckon he thinks we do in here, talk about horses?"

Her face was turned away from him, and her words were slightly muffled. "I wouldn't feel right about it. I feel like he's almost in the room. This place is so *small*."

"Is this your way of punishing me for something? If it is, it is foul means."

"Don't be silly, Warner. I feel shy. Maybe the walls are two feet thick. I still feel like he's right next to us."

"He's clear across the hall."

"Nevertheless, I feel uncomfortable. I wouldn't have my whole mind on it. I'd have both ears open. He might take it into his head that he had something left he wanted to talk to you about. I've told you before, this house is too small. It's a shame to have this as the headquarters for a top-quality breeding ranch."

He said with disgust, "Well, there damn sure ain't no breeding going on in here."

"That's your own fault. You could add on to this place. Knock out some walls and make some rooms bigger than closets. It's not as if we don't have the money."

"Would you move out here if I did?"

She looked around at him in the moonlight streaming through the window. "You mean to stay? Of course not. I've told you I don't want to be stuck out here in the big middle of nowhere. Sixteen miles to town? Don't be silly."

"Then what did you bring it up for? Are you trying to work me with your skirt?"

She sighed. "That's a damn silly thing to say. I like it as well as you do. It was me drug you to bed the first time. I like living in civilization. But if you *did* enlarge this place with about twice the room, I wouldn't feel so shy. And I'd stay longer when I came. Warner, I've got a ten-room home in Corpus. I can give parties and receive people in style."

"You was living on a ranch stuck out in the big middle of nowhere when I first met you. If you would do it for the late Mr. Pico how come you can't do it for me?"

She was silent for a moment. She said, "That was different. He had a lot of money, and I wasn't going to be with him for very long. Besides, I was crazy to work with those Spanish horses. I thought I had a marvelous idea for a new breed. I didn't know any better until you came along." She turned her head back to the pillow. "I wasn't going to stay with John Pico. He was too old for me."

Warner laid his head down on his own pillow.

He said, "Well, I'll give you one thing—you are honest about being a jezebel."

She put her hand behind her back and found one of his and squeezed it. She said, "You won't believe it, but I'm not a jezebel where you are concerned. I am fair with you. I don't use foul means with you."

"Hah." He closed his eyes. "When you think of some more jokes wake me up. I need a good laugh." Then he let his body relax. He was behind in his sleep.

After breakfast he and Wilson walked out to look at the horses again. As they went along, Warner said, "I'm going back to Del Rio with you."

Wilson stopped walking. "That don't sound too smart to me. Not if you're going for the reason I think you are."

Warner said, "I want to get a feel for this thing. I don't like sitting here at long range trying to figure what I think is a hell of a threat to my well-being. I'd like to go and see this—what'd you say the name of the fellow was that Fisher went after and regretted it? Austin something?"

"Austin Vaughn. Him and his younger brother, Preston. I don't know the younger brother so well, but I'd figure him about your age. I don't see what the hell you can find out from them, though. Their situation wasn't nothing like yours."

"Dammit, Wilson, in spite of what you and the widow Pico say, I am not willing to sit here and do nothing. There is a train out of Corpus tonight at six. Ought to be at the siding about six-thirty. Me and you are going to catch it."

"*You're* going to catch it if you ain't careful. What about the missus?"

Warner ignored the jab. He said, "I am going to tell her that we are going to San Antonio for the horse market, tell her I got some quarter horse culls I want to get shut of at the auction."

"Will she believe that?"

"Why shouldn't she believe it? She knows enough about horses to know I know a hell of a lot more than she does. And she doesn't know anything about quarter horses and is not interested. She only cares about the Andalusians."

"You running off after she just got here?"

"Hell, I didn't invite her down. And you and I had planned this trip back up to San Antonio even before you came. We are going to look for some bluegrass mares to breed to the black stud."

Wilson laughed. "In the San Antonio horse market? Thoroughbred mares? Hell, Warner, she ain't gonna believe that."

"What if I was to tell you that the King ranch is importing bluegrass Thoroughbreds right now and they are buying them through the San Antonio horse market?"

Wilson looked at him for a moment, cocking

his head to one side. After a moment he said, "I'd say you were bluffing. I'd say that last card you drawed busted your flush."

"Correct. But you weren't so sure at first. And that's you. Laura isn't going to question me."

"And then you are going to go on home with me to Del Rio? Just like that?"

"Of course."

Wilson shrugged. "Hell, that's all right with me. I'll be glad for the company. Del Rio don't draw the brightest of conversationalists. Seems like everybody in that place is after my money."

"Maybe you think that because you're after theirs."

Wilson smiled slightly.

Warner didn't say anything until just before lunch when he found Laura in his room. She had undressed to her chemise and was taking a sponge bath out of a basin of lukewarm water. He came in and she said quickly, "Shut that door! My heavens, this isn't a public place."

He said, "It don't matter. The house is empty except for Rosa in the kitchen. Wilson is out in the colt barn acting like he knows what he's doing."

She washed down her neck and then under her arm, lifting her arm high in the air so that it bunched her breast up full on that side. The sight made his neck get thick, but he had resolved,

112

after the night before, that it would be her did the asking the next time. He said, "Honey, what time are you going back into Corpus? Right after lunch?"

She stopped washing and looked at him. "Who said I was going back today?"

He shrugged. "Nobody. I just didn't think you'd want to be here with me gone. Doesn't matter. I can send one of the hired hands in to notify the railroad to stop at the Calallen siding."

She narrowed her eyes. "Where the hell are you going?"

"I thought you knew. I thought you heard me and Wilson talking about it last night. We're going to the San Antonio horse market looking for bluegrass Thoroughbreds to breed to that black stallion."

She rocked back on her heels. "This is the first I've heard of that."

"Then you weren't listening."

She studied him for a moment as if she had the feeling something was wrong but she couldn't pin it down. "Why would Wilson come through San Antonio and come down here only to go back to San Antonio the next day?"

He said, "Conformation."

"What?"

"Conformation. It's been some time since he's seen the black stallion, and he needed to get a fresh look at him before we went to selecting mares. You look for the same conformation—shape, height, frame, bone structure, and such—in the mare as in the stallion."

She was still giving him an odd look. "He wouldn't trust that to you?"

"Well," he said easily, "you know Wilson. He wants to have his finger in the pie. He likes to be able to talk a good game about horses. He doesn't necessarily have to know anything, just act like he does."

"This seems to have come up awful sudden. It wouldn't have anything to do with this Jack Fisher business, would it?"

"Jack Fisher's place is seventy or eighty miles from San Antonio. I thought we discussed that subject. Besides, you'll recall that Wilson Young took the same position as you did—leave well enough alone. Didn't he?"

She said uncertainly, "Well, yes, I suppose he did." She tried to remember if he'd answered her question. She had the feeling that he had not. She said, "I asked you if this trip to San Antonio, this *sudden* trip to San Antonio, had anything to do with this Jack Fisher business."

"I told you this wasn't no sudden trip. Me and Wilson have been planning this for some little time. How many times I got to tell you?"

She stopped washing and then toweled off quickly. Then she turned to look at him. The short little lace-trimmed chemise cupped and held her

114

breasts and ended at mid-thigh. Looking at her, he could feel the pulse beating in his throat. She said huskily, "Will Wilson be out in the barns for a while?"

He swallowed. He was damned if he was going to be gown-whipped. He said, "No. He ought to be back any minute. Lunch is just about ready." Then he abruptly turned around and went out the door, closing it quickly behind him.

To please Laura, Warner had left the kitchen table in the sitting room and sentenced the hired hands to go on eating in the bunkhouse while Rosa served from the kitchen. Wilson and Warner were already at the table with a first-of-the-day whiskey when Laura came out of the bedroom. She was wearing her riding pants and boots with a crisp linen blouse, but that didn't mean anything. As far as Warner knew, she might be planning on having a horse saddled and taking a ride around the ranch to look over his management.

But as soon as she'd sat down, she said to Warner, "Honey, I wish you'd have one of the boys hitch up my buggy right after lunch."

He was still cautious. He said, "You going back to Corpus?"

She said, looking at Wilson, "Well, I don't see any point in staying here unless I want to talk to Rosa or Raoul. Do you always make your visits so short, Mr. Young?"

Wilson looked wary. He said, "What visit would that be, Miss Laura?"

"Why, this one. You come down for one night and then you and Warner are off to San Antonio."

Wilson said smoothly, "Well, you can't call a visit short, Miss Laura, if it was planned that way."

"Oh?" she said. "So you and Warner had this planned. It wasn't just me showing up?"

Wilson said, looking puzzled, "Why, no, ma'am. In fact, if we'd knowed you was coming, we might have rearranged our schedule. I hadn't seen our stock in some time. That's our racing stock, Miss Laura. So I had to get my mind refreshed."

"Warner couldn't have told you?"

"Ain't nothing like seeing it with your own eyes, Miss Laura. You are a businesswoman. I'm sure you can appreciate that."

She said, looking back and forth between them, "I can appreciate how well you work together." She paused. "But do you make any money at it? Or do you just play?"

Wilson gave her his half smile. He said, "Well, Laura, a man has got to enjoy what he does, don't you reckon?"

She looked at Warner. "I know Warner always does. Or at least he seems to. Of course he can get so serious sometimes. Tell me, Mr. Young, have you ever known a man of a more set turn of

116

mind than Warner? He will not turn either to the left or the right from his path."

Wilson Young shook his head. He said, "I'm afraid I don't know what you are talking about, Miss Laura. You must know the young man much better than I do."

Laura smiled slowly, giving most of it to Warner, who had been feeling little prickles at the back of his neck. She said sweetly, "Why, I'm talking about enlarging and adding on to this little hatbox of a house. An enterprise like ours needs a more expansive and impressive headquarters, wouldn't you say, Wilson?"

But Warner jumped in. "I've already decided you are right, Laura. You don't need to drag any outside opinions in. I'll add on to the house."

She was still smiling sweetly. "And when did you decide that, darling?"

He gave her a look and said evenly, "Last night. Darling."

Wilson whistled and fanned his face. He said, "Whoooee. I feel like I'm smothering in syrup. Somebody pass the vinegar."

She said to Warner, "Shall I speak to a builder about it when I get back to Corpus? Or do you have some plans in mind?"

"I leave the project entirely up to you. You keep the books. You know how much money we got to spend. You know what we want. Use your own judgment. But remember, this is a horse ranch,

117

not a town house." He was so relieved that she had not been trying to smoke Wilson out about their plans to go on to Del Rio that he would have agreed to anything.

But he said, "Laura, when you go to the freight agent in Corpus I want you to order me out a stock car. I'm going to make a double purpose out of this trip and ship some quarter horse culls I don't think will make it. Put them in the general auction. And I want a whole car, not a half car. Don't want any other stock mixing in with mine."

She looked at him, wide-eyed. "Why, honey, where did you get the idea I was going straight back into Corpus? I don't expect to be there in time to have the train make a stop at the Calallen siding. Whatever gave you that idea? In fact I was thinking of seeing you off."

He said, "Well, goddam. Now I got to pull somebody off what the men are working on and get them started for town. Not a lot of time to waste." He pushed his chair back and got up as Rosa came through the door with a platter of pork chops and a bowl of applesauce.

But Laura put her arm up and grabbed his shirt, laughing. "I'm just joking," she said. "Sit down. I'm going back to town as quick as I've had a bite to eat. I'll get word to the railroad to stop for you. With a cattle car, a whole car."

He said, looking at her suspiciously, "What the

hell kind of a joke was that? Wasn't funny. It was silly."

Wilson Young suddenly took a coughing fit, stubbing his little cigar out in a handy dish. They looked at him. He patted himself hard on the chest. He took a breath. "Guess I swallowed some smoke wrong." But when Laura turned away, he winked at Warner and shook his head.

Nothing else got said, and as soon as he decently could, Warner excused himself and went down to the bunkhouse and told Raoul to hitch up the *señora*'s buggy and tie it by the front porch. Then he went back in the house. Laura was having a glass of lemonade with a little whiskey in it, and Wilson was drinking brandy and coffee.

Laura said, "How long do you expect to be gone, Warner?"

"Oh," he said, "not that long. Couple or three days. If I get on the track of anything else I'll send you a wire."

"I hope so," she said dryly. "I'm going to start talking to a builder as soon as I get back to town. Same one did my house."

Warner groaned. "Aw, Laura, you don't want that high-priced son of a bitch. We ain't going to make some gingerbread-covered froufrou out here. This is a ranch house, not a mansion. Besides, that guy don't know how to work in adobe bricks. He only works in lumber."

"I thought you were leaving the project up to me."

"I am, but, goddammit, I'm the one got to live here." He had the almost certain idea that he was being blackmailed somehow. "Don't do nothing certain until I get a look at the plans."

She gave him a sweet smile. "Then don't stay gone too long."

It was about one o'clock before she was ready to start. Warner stood by her side at the buggy. Wilson had gone back into the house, and Raoul, who had brought her buggy over, had gone back to his work. She sat, deerskin gloves on her hands, holding the reins of the spirited Morgan he'd buggy-trained for her. The horse was ready to go. He leaned in to kiss her good-bye, but she drew her head back. He pulled away, and she said, "You're not fooling me, you know."

"What are you talking about?"

"You're not going to San Antonio on horse business. I don't know exactly where you and Wilson are going, but I know it's got something to do with Jack Fisher."

He stared at her, his mouth tightening. He said, "Someday you are going to make me lose my patience entirely."

"You're not a good liar, Warner. And I wish to hell I could say that Wilson Young—or anybody, for that matter—was leading you astray. But I

120

know better. You don't need to be led. You've got the bit in your teeth and you are running at your own pace."

He didn't say anything.

She said, "You could get yourself killed, Warner. You wear self-righteousness around you like armor. Well, it's not bulletproof." She stared at him frankly. "I care a great deal about you, Warner, but you are starting to scare me. You've won a few fights now where the odds were against you, and you think it was because you were clean of thought and pure of motive and that right makes might and all that other cant you learned from your grandfather. Go ahead and confront Jack Fisher and a half a dozen or a dozen or twenty-five of his hired gunfighters and see how well you do against *those* odds."

"You through?" he said.

"Yes. And I'm going to try not to think about you very much, Warner. I'm not sure you're the kind of man a woman can count on being there for very long. I don't like to hurt, and you look and act like pain to me."

Her words made him cast his eyes to the ground. "I am not going to go near Jack Fisher. I assure you that I will be back here at this ranch within four or five days."

"But you're not going to look at horses, are you? That was a lie, wasn't it, Warner?"

His temper flashed. "Goddammit, Laura, you

don't have sense enough to leave a man much, do you?"

Then she was immediately sorry. She put out her gloved hand and touched his face. She said, "I'm sorry. Kiss me, and then I better hurry to get to Corpus in time to order out your cattle car."

He leaned in and kissed her briefly. It was a dry-lipped kiss, but it was better than the way they'd been going to part. She said, "Please be careful."

"I'm not going into any danger, Laura. If I do and know it, I'll wire you so you can know when to start worrying. But until then, don't."

She nodded and slapped the horse gently with the reins, and she and the buggy were off at a quick trot. He stood a moment watching as the horse led her east across the grass and up a small knoll. As her buggy began to disappear on the other side of the knoll, he turned and began walking back to the house. Before he could get there, Charlie came dashing up on a nimble little quarter horse he was finishing off. The horse didn't weigh quite a thousand pounds, but someday he was going to make someone who could afford him one hell of an all-around horse. For a hundred yards he was as fast as anything Warner had ever seen, and he was as nimble as a house cat. You could drop the reins to the ground, and he'd stand as firm as if he'd been tied to a tree and, like all of Warner's horses, he wouldn't spook at either noise or motion. Horses that couldn't be trained out of spooking were let go cheap as culls. No one could ever say about one of Warner's horses that he'd shied at a leaf or a shadow or spooked at the sound of gunfire, even if it was right by his head. Warner didn't advertise that his horses would be smarter than the people who bought them, but he was pretty sure that was the case in more than one instance.

Charlie said, staring off in the direction Laura's buggy had disappeared, "How come Miz Pico took leave so quick, Mr. Grayson? She git all upset with you about that man you kilt?"

Warner gave him a look. "When you going to learn to stay out of my personal business, Charlie? What I got to do, shoot the end of your nose off."

Charlie looked down at him from atop the quarter horse and said slowly, "Well, Mr. Grayson, you always give me to understand that Miz Pico was a partner in this here ranch, so I reckon that makes her one of my bosses. How would it be inquiring into yore personal business if I ast why one of the bosses was leaving?"

Warner searched Charlie's face for the slightest trace of humor or sarcasm. He couldn't find any. "Go put that horse up," he said. "I'm going to take him with me when I leave."

"You ain't takin' Paseta?"

"Paseta? Have *you* taken to naming horses now,

Charlie? What's the name of the little gelding you're on? You named him, too? Hell!"

Charlie said hurriedly, "It jest popped out, boss. It ain't no habit. I heard Miz Pico call him that so often that I . . ." He trailed off. "I ain't gonna do it again. But you ain't takin' him?"

"I'm going to take them both. It has occurred to me that I might need to do some close scouting around, and I don't want to do that on a stallion. Be just my luck to be slipping around Fisher's place and come on a bunch of mares in heat. Besides, that little pony you are on has got mighty quick feet. That country up around Cotulla is kind of cut up. I might need a spry little horse like him."

"He's a dandy, ain't he?" Charlie patted the horse's neck. "Sometimes I don't think his feet touch the ground, he can cut and change directions so quick."

"Well, put him up and see that he's rubbed down and grained. We'll be leaving about five o'clock. Somebody's got to go along to bring back the extra saddle. I guess that would be you. If anybody has to eat a late dinner it's supposed to be the boss."

Charlie said, "I never can think of myself as the boss, Mr. Grayson. When you're gone, I know I'm in charge, but I never feel like it." He shook his head. "You know what I mean?"

"I don't care how you feel, just get the job done

and keep this place running and don't lose no money. That's all I ask. You ain't got to make us none—that's my job—but don't lose any."

Warner went into the house and found Wilson sitting in the living room on the divan. The table was back in the kitchen. Wilson said, "You ought to quit lying, Warner. You ought to give it up, especially with Laura. You ain't no good at it."

Warner poured himself a small drink of whiskey from the bottle on the sideboard. He said, "It ain't exactly lying. It's just something we do. I tell her what she wants to hear, and she pretends to believe me. Cuts down on the arguments. And our arguments here lately have been getting a little spirited. So we do it this way."

Wilson said, "From what I heard, it didn't sound like she was playing the game."

"No, she wasn't." Warner stared at the wall for a moment and then downed his drink. He set the shot glass down on the sideboard and said, "She broke our unspoken rule this time. I don't know what's come over her, Wilson. She's sounding a little more serious than I want to hear."

Wilson got up and went to the front door. He looked back at Warner. "It happens. It happens. She ain't no woman to trifle with. I don't much like her, but I sure as hell respect her. Ya'll are going to have to quit having those unspoken agreements and get a few spoken ones laid out. I'm going to walk around awhile and have one last look at the black. I still think we got to consider the future. I hope we really do run across some Kentucky Thoroughbreds in San Antonio. And not to keep from making you out a liar, neither. Hell, why don't we take a trip up to Kentucky? Wouldn't be more than two days on the train from San Antonio. Look at some good mares."

"Goddammit, Wilson, we're going to Del Rio. Now, don't you start."

In the late afternoon sunshine they started for the siding at Calallen. Wilson said, "Let's me and you get one thing straight. I know you like to ride in the stock car with the horses, and you can do that if you want to. But the way that wind whistles through a cattle car, I'd as soon be in a tornado. All that dust and straw blowing around. I've had a bath and a shave and I got on clean clothes, and I intend to arrive in Del Rio like this, not with my hair full of straw and dust all over my clothes. I'm gonna ride in a chair car. You can ride wherever you want to. But don't act like you know me when we get off the train."

"All right," Warner said, "all right. I'll ride in the chair car with you. My God, but you are getting to be a dandy."

A little farther on, Wilson said, "You ask Laura to order that car out only as far as San Antonio?"

"Yes, I guess you could say that. I told her to order out a stock car, and I told her I was going to San Antonio. I'd figured to tell the conductor, once we got to the train, to wire ahead and have the order changed so the car would go on to Del Rio."

"I bet that's already been done."

They were riding side by side with Charlie behind them. He shot Wilson a look. "What the hell are you talking about?"

"I'm saying that Laura ordered that car to be switched in San Antonio and sent on to Del Rio."

"You are crazy as hell. She wouldn't do something like that. Hell, she might catch me in a lie, but she ain't going to rub my face in it."

"I'll bet you ten dollars that car is routed to Del Rio."

Warner gave him a grim look. "Why ten? Why not make it twenty?"

"You didn't break down and tell her you were going on?"

"Hell, no, you son of a bitch. I told you me and Laura had an understanding. I never mentioned Del Rio. Besides, Cotulla isn't Del Rio."

"No, but she knows you'll headquarter with me, and she knows that Cotulla is close enough to Del Rio to get to on horseback."

Warner looked flat faced. He said evenly, "She better not have played me like that. That would be like a slap in the face. She wouldn't do it."

"Fine," Wilson said. He was grinning his mischievous grin. "I'm a gambler, but I'm also a

127

serious student of human nature. That is one little lady who does not care for you keeping secrets. Why don't we make it fifty?"

Warner was quietly getting angry. "Hell, make it a hundred! Make it whatever you like. And you can be the one to find out. When you see the conductor about chair car seats you can ask him about the routing on the stock car while me and Charlie are loading the horses. That fair enough for you?"

"It'll be a hundred dollars I didn't have two minutes ago."

"I wouldn't count my winnings until the bet is settled."

5

Running in front of a sea breeze, the smoke seemed to arrive before the train did. Warner and Charlie held the horses well back until the train had quit screeching and belching and snapping and popping. Then they led them down the train where a brakeman was getting off the top of a boxcar to open up their stock car and put the wooden ramp in place. The railroad supplied hay and water for all the stock cars. If a shipper wanted grain for his animals he had to bring his own. Charlie had brought a half a sack of oats, though Warner doubted they'd get used. It wasn't that long a trip to Del Rio.

While they got the ramp in place and led the horses into the car, Warner could see Wilson down the track talking to the conductor. They got the horses tethered and settled down and then brought the ramp into the car and jumped down. Charlie had the saddle Wilson had been using. He'd tie it on the back of his horse. Warner, with the help of the brakeman, slid the door closed and latched it. He kept one eye on Wilson, who was still talking to the conductor. Then he turned to Charlie. He said, "I don't expect no trouble, but you know where to wire me if something happens. I ain't saying I'm expecting Fisher to

129

send another man like Carl Hamm, but if he does, ya'll don't take no chances with him. Treat him like you would a rattlesnake. Ain't none of you men being paid to take chances of getting hurt or killed."

"Yes, sir. Care of Wilson Young, Del Rio."

"That's right. And if I'm anyplace else I'll get word to you. Remember, don't take no chances. And that is an order." He gave Charlie a little salute and turned and started toward where Wilson was going up the steps of the chair car. The conductor gave him a wave and called out, "Howdy, Mr. Grayson," and then started toward the engine. Warner climbed up the steps and went through the door into the car where Wilson had disappeared. He was sitting in the last seat, facing forward. Warner was halfway to him when the car suddenly jolted and began to slowly sway as the engine ground in and began to pick up steam. Warner had to grab the back of one of the seats and wait until the train had begun to run smoothly before he could make his way back to his friend. Wilson was lighting a cigar, puffing on it slowly while he held a match to the end to get it drawing. He'd moved over by the window to make room for Warner.

Warner slid into the seat and looked out the window. The train didn't pause long to pick up a couple of passengers. Looking at the prairie flowing by, Warner guessed they were already making twenty miles an hour. Warner looked at Wilson and said, "Well?"

For answer, Wilson held out a hundred dollar bill that he'd obviously had ready. Warner took the bill and stuck it in his pocket. He said, "Ain't much to show for a lifetime, Wilson, but at least you pay your gambling debts."

Wilson puffed and then took the cigar out of his mouth. "Which I seldom have to pay. Though, truth be told, I'm glad I lost this one. If I'd been right, you'd have swole up and pouted like a spoilt child the whole trip. I know how anything concerning the widow Pico affects you."

"Keep pecking away, Wilson," Warner said. "I know how it eats at you that everybody else ain't got woman trouble like you do."

"It ain't that. I hate to see a friend of mine get himself overmatched." He looked around at Warner. "She's better than you, boy. You take the emotion out of it, put matters on an equal basis, forget who wears skirts and who wears pants, and she'll beat you at anything from checkers to colts, either kind. Don't forget that when them bandits first raided the Pico place down by the Rio Grande and killed her husband, it was her that killed two of the bandits. And you got fifteen years in the horse business on her, son. Give even experience and let's see who's got the best touch and eye."

Warner said, "Where are your saddlebags?

131

I know you brought a bottle along. I know you wouldn't never be out of reach of a bottle of brandy."

Wilson pointed at the overhead rack. Warner got up, bracing himself, and fumbled around in Wilson's luggage until he found a bottle and jerked it out and sat back down. There were only a few other passengers on the car, and most of them were sitting toward the front. Theirs was the last coach before the freight cars.

He took the cork out of the bottle, waited a moment to let some of the brandy fumes evaporate, and then took a tentative swallow. He let that burn itself all the way down, grimacing a little, and then took a real drink. It was the only way he could drink brandy, sort of sear his throat first and then follow quickly with the real drink before his gullet got over its first shock. He put the cork halfway back in the bottle and passed it to Wilson. His friend took a small drink and then corked the bottle and set it back on the seat between them. Wilson said, "You gone deaf?"

"No, I heard you. Or I heard what I wanted to."

"And you ain't got no comment?"

"I heard a poor loser grousing around. Am I supposed to comment on that? Hell, Wilson, why don't you get yourself a staff like them shepherds carry? The time you spend trying to get my goat absolutely convinces me you was meant to be a shepherd."

Wilson yawned. He said, "Still don't take away from the truth of what I said. She's too much woman for you, Warner. You're overmatched. I'm simply trying to save a friend of mine some heartache on down the line."

"I suppose you could be her match?"

"Me?" Wilson swiveled his head around quickly. "Me? Hell, I can't even manage a Mexican dancer who is ten years younger than me and ain't had half of my education in school or in the ways of the world. Why, the widow Pico would eat my lunch before ten of the morning."

"What do you do when I ain't around to make a mark of?"

Wilson shrugged. "Look for some other sucker with big ears. Some sensitive soul like you who is concerned about being a good person. By the way, good person, you'll be interested to know that the next train out of San Antonio is at one in the morning. That puts us into Del Rio at about four in the morning. We could have waited until tomorrow morning and taken that nine o'clock train and saved ourselves six or seven hours of traveling time."

"I was ready to go," Warner said.

They killed some time in San Antonio by taking a late supper. After that they found a poker game in a saloon and played until midnight and then went back to the depot and waited until it was

133

time to board the train. Warner spent a quarter of an hour going down the train to check on his horses and make sure they were connected to the right string of cars. On other occasions his riding stock had been connected to one train while he'd ridden grandly away in the chair car of another. The trainmen made mistakes, and it was hell to get a couple of horses shipped back to where you were from wherever they had ended up.

He got back to the chair coach as the train started to get under way. Dim lanterns at either end cast a little light, but the inside of the car wasn't much lighter than the outside.

Neither one of them spoke until they were an hour out of San Antonio. Wilson was sitting bolt upright in the corner with his hat tilted down over half his face and his arms crossed. Warner said, "You asleep?"

Wilson pushed his hat up an inch. "Naw. I can't close my eyes on one of these things. You ever been on a big boat out in the sea?"

"Hell, Wilson, I have spent most of my life on the coast."

"The question wasn't where you was raised, it was have you ever been on a big boat out to sea?"

"No."

"Well, I done it once. I took a paddle-wheel steamer out of Galveston to New Orleans. After about five or six or seven hours of that I was so sick I wanted to die. I got up in the wheelhouse somehow and drawed my pistol on the captain and told him to turn back or I'd kill him with the last of my strength. And I would have except he showed me we'd get to port faster going on to New Orleans. I ain't never made that mistake again, except for a trip on a little coaster when I was after a man who tried to cheat me out of a considerable sum of money. But I didn't have no choice. If I shut my eyes on one of these here trains I feel exactly like I did on that steamer. What are you planning on doing once we get to Del Rio? I hope you ain't thinking of heading for Jack Fisher country, because I ain't going to let you do it."

Warner said, "What about this Austin Vaughn? You said he done pretty good against Fisher. Who is he? How come Fisher singled him out? Or was he in the way?"

Wilson took time to light a cigar. When he had it drawing he said, "No, you couldn't say that Vaughn was in the way. As a matter of fact his situation is a little like yours, and that's what puzzles me. Up to now Fisher has contented himself with pushing his near neighbors around and stealing their land and stock. But Vaughn's place is only ten miles out of Del Rio, and that makes it at least forty miles from Fisher's southern border. Way off his range."

"Hell, I'm even farther. What's the connection?"

Wilson shook his head slightly. "Must be quality." He thought for a moment. "Vaughn is a good old boy who's been a cattleman all his life. I'd reckon him to be thirty-five or thirty-six, somewhere in there. Come to our country from west Texas, out near Monahans. I don't know if you know much about that hard rock country, but it is as near to worthless as any country I've seen. And dry? Hell, it makes our little old water problem look like nothing. I never could figure why anybody would try and make a living out there from any kind of stock except lizards or horned frogs. But Vaughn and his family apparently did it. Anyway, I think he finally got tired of riding three or four days to look at half a dozen cattle so he sold his holdings out west yonder and bought five thousand deeded acres north of Del Rio. Didn't improve his water position much; you know as well as I do that, except for a few streams and rivers here and there, we don't do so well by rainfall ourselves. I got to know him when he came to my place looking for me. He wanted me to put him in touch with Justa Williams. You've heard of him, haven't you? His outfit is seventy or eighty miles north of you, and he's doing with cattle what you're trying to do with horses, upgrading through selective breeding."

"He's got that Half-Moon outfit, don't he?"

"Yeah, in Matagorda County."

"He's more like a hundred twenty miles from me than eighty. But, yeah, I know who you mean. And I know about him upgrading his beef. Brought in some shorthorn cattle, didn't he? Hereford and whiteface and such? Hell, that's a big outfit. He ranges over about a hundred thousand acres. Didn't he cause some commotion about crossbreeding with the longhorn and almost putting everybody else out of business?"

"That's him. He's got two brothers. Norris is a whiz with a pen and paper and can make figures dance around on a balance sheet like some folks I know can handle cards. The youngest brother is Ben, who runs the horse herd and ain't no bad shakes with a revolver. I'm surprised they haven't contacted you about upgrading their remuda."

Warner said, "I think I did get an inquiry from them some time back, maybe a year, about a half a dozen Morgan studs. But I didn't have any Morgan breeding stock to spare at the time, so I priced them accordingly. Never heard back."

Wilson drew on his cigar. "Ain't no fleas on that bunch. They got it to spend, but they don't spend it reckless." He looked over at Warner and smiled slightly. "I got that black stallion off of Justa Williams. He give him to me."

"*Give* him to you? What for, robbing a bank he didn't like?"

"For saving his life."

Warner rolled his eyes. "He give you the black for saving his life? And you give him to me for saving yours?"

"You didn't save my life. I like to let you think you did. Actually, I had that situation under control. I was only giving it a quarter of a second longer to see how you reacted."

"Another quarter of a second and that old boy would have killed you deader than old Billy Hell if I hadn't fired. But let it go. I've never taken the black for my own, and I never claimed to have saved your life. The man may have been talking to you—cussing you, really—but I couldn't see which way he was aiming that gun he had hidden under his duster. All I knowed was I was sitting right close to you and he was cocking the hammer. So I fired. But why in hell are we talking about this? I asked you about Austin Vaughn."

Wilson looked over at him in the dim glow. "What's your rush? It's only two in the morning. We got all night to talk about this, thanks to you."

"So Vaughn asked you about getting in touch with Justa Williams."

"Yeah, and Vaughn contracted to buy a little seed herd of those shorthorn and Hereford cattle. Bulls and heifers both. He already had some longhorns that had been bred back to some smaller Mexican stock." Wilson shifted in his seat and got out the bottle of brandy and had a swig. He passed it over to Warner. "I thought Vaughn had lost his mind. He'd bought that five thousand acres for a song because there wasn't a blade of grass on it, just mesquite and cactus and weeds and briers. But it turns out friend Vaughn was a water finder. They were digging the ranch house well, and he got down about fifteen feet and hit an artesian spring. Well, you know how them underground springs are. They'll run along way deep under the ground and then suddenly rise to the surface for a bit and then duck down again. Vaughn apparently got lucky enough to hit one right up close to the top. But didn't have sense enough to know he'd used up all his luck. He went to digging wells all along the path he thought that spring was taking. He hit another one and then another one and then he had the thing located. Now he's got springs all over that his five thousand acres, and he's dug canals and ditches every which of a way. The upshot is he's got as lush a pasture of grass as you'd want."

"When was this?"

"Couple of years back. Anyway, he fenced off part of his land to hold that little purebred herd he bought from Justa Williams—and God only knows what they cost him. Last I heard, Justa was asking anywhere from three to four hundred dollars for a heifer and twice that for a bull. But Austin fenced off that part of his land and told his neighbors he wasn't trying to cut up the range. He'd found the water, but they were welcome to use the springs that weren't fenced off. He said he'd appreciate it if they left his fences alone, though, because he was trying to upgrade his herd." Wilson stopped to take another sip. "I don't see how he could have been any fairer. He brought water up where there hadn't been any and then offered his neighbors the free use of it. All he asked was they respect the fences he had around about two thousand acres. You'd've thought that was mighty fair of him, wouldn't you?"

"Of course."

"Well, it was. For a time. Then, human nature being what it was, some of his neighbors got to grousing about him hogging all that water—them same neighbors who hadn't been able to run one cow on fifty acres but who could now run five on fifty acres on account of the water Vaughn had provided. Go and figure that one out."

"What's to figure? I've seen the like all my life."

"Anyway, I reckon that bitching worked its way back to Fisher, and he set out to find out what was going on at this little paradise in the middle of all that worthless land."

"Where'd Vaughn get his money?"

"Oh, I reckon he had a pretty good wad when he sold out in west Texas. But, like I say, that five thousand acres didn't cost him much, maybe fifty cents an acre. His big cost was labor for digging all those wells and ditches and canals and then buying the seed herd off Justa. But the way Vaughn tells it sounds a good bit like what happened to you. He says the first thing he knew was that a man like Carl Hamm showed up and offered him some ridiculous price for the place. He run him off, but then here come another one who started talking about what a shame it would be if all Vaughn's bulls, them expensive bulls, got shot down in one night. That's when Vaughn sent for his little brother, Preston. But meanwhile Jack Fisher himself showed up and told Vaughn he'd give him one week to sell. Or else."

"Did Vaughn go to the law?"

Wilson nodded. "Yeah, he went to the sheriff in Del Rio, for all the good it did him. The sheriff is a good man, but there wasn't a damn thing he could do about it. Fisher's place is out of his jurisdiction."

"So what the hell happened?"

Wilson yawned. "Not a hell of a lot for a while. Vaughn moved his wife and kids into town. Rented them a little house there. Then he come to me and asked if I knew a few dependable guns he could hire."

"You didn't loan him Chulo, did you?"

Wilson looked around at him. "Of course not. Chulo works for me. But Vaughn and I took counsel on the matter. I rode out and looked his place over and calculated he needed to hire six men, not counting himself and his brother. Four men to a twelve-hour shift, four to be in the house and four to be out in the field looking after

141

that seed herd of purebreds. That put Vaughn to considerable expense, but I couldn't see where he had no choice. He'd built a right nice house, and there was the matter of the cattle and the fence he'd erected."

"And none of his neighbors offered to help?"

"Worthless country draws worthless people," Wilson said. "Besides, the neighbors figured Vaughn didn't stand a chance against Jack Fisher and they shore as hell didn't want it getting back to Jack that they'd helped Vaughn." Wilson took another drink of brandy. "But I'm afeared that what happened is going to work against you."

"How so?"

"Well . . . I think Fisher kind of come at Vaughn a little too casual. He's been so used to knocking over easy targets that he didn't really give Vaughn his best effort. As a consequence, he sent a half a dozen men in to do the job where he needed better than twice that many. But by the time he realized that, it was too late. The first bunch got so killed and cut up that the rest of Fisher's men, all of whom are basically bullies by nature, had gotten awful leary."

"How did it end?"

Wilson was a long moment answering. Finally he said, "Well, I don't know that it has. I ain't so sure the matter is all that settled. Vaughn has brought his family back home and let all of the gunfighters go, but his brother is still there and he's been able to hire his vaqueros back—I forgot to mention that they cut and run as soon as they smelled Jack Fisher—and he's got his cattle back at work and his ranch operating."

Warner said, "Shows that Fisher has transferred his attentions to me."

"Well, if he hasn't, I'm sure he will by the time you get through stirring him up on this trip. You have to get right in there, don't you? Is that some kind of disease with you, this jumping in feet first when other folks would sit back and rock a bit until they saw which way the wind was blowing?"

"Just because I don't want to sit back and worry I am constantly being called headstrong. What's wrong with being forward in your thinking?"

"Nothing, I guess. So long as you don't get forward of your ability. You're coming down here. What's to keep Fisher from playing havoc with your ranch while you're gone?"

Warner tried to look out the window at the night going past. But it was just light enough in the car to turn the glass into a mirror. Off in the distance he could see an occasional light. He didn't know if it was a late-to-bed or an early riser, the hour being what it was. He said, "Well, maybe that's part of the reason for this trip. I'm the only gunhand there. And I wouldn't be much good if a half a dozen men struck from all different directions. Maybe I'm thinking of doing what Vaughn came and asked you about."

"You're thinking of looking around Del Rio for some gunhands to carry back to your ranch?"

Warner said, "Where else am I supposed to find gunfighters—in Corpus Christi? If I wanted sailors or men to unload cargo off of ships, I'd go into Corpus. But if I want gunhands I am going where they live. What do they get, anyway? Five dollars a day?"

Wilson shrugged. "Not good ones."

"Double that?"

"More like."

Warner thought a moment. He said, "That would be three hundred a month per man. If I got six men for that amount of time it would cost me right around two thousand dollars time you figured groceries."

"Quite a sum."

"Not when it comes to protecting my horses. I took your meaning when you said Fisher made the mistake of coming at Vaughn too soft and how that might be bad for me. I take it you mean he won't make that mistake again."

"That'd be my guess. But remember, all we are doing is guessing right now. For all I know, you are history in Fisher's mind. Crazy as that son of a bitch is, he might have decided to run for governor since he sent Hamm off."

"Yes, and he might not have, either. I don't see nothing wrong with taking some steps before it is too late. But I ain't said I'm hiring outside help. I want to talk to Vaughn and his brother and get a firsthand line on their methods. What about his brother, anyway? You said he was half pistol. What does he do?"

Warner could see Wilson smile in the half-light. He said, "He's a trick shot in a Wild West show."

Warner stared at him blankly for a moment. "What? What in hell are you talking about? What's a trick shot in whatever that was you said—a Wild West show?"

"You don't know what a Wild West show is?"

Warner shook his head slowly. "Never heard of any such of a thing."

"You ever hear of Buffalo Bill?"

"*Buffalo* Bill? Is that a name? A body's name?"

"Buffalo Bill Cody. Used to be a meat hunter for the railroads when they were building the cross-continental tracks. Which meant he killed a lot of buffalo. And antelope and deer too, I would guess. But how would Antelope Bill sound? Or Buck Bill Cody?"

"What the hell is a Wild West show?"

The train rumbled over a crossing and then began to slow. A few seconds later they heard the long blast of its whistle. Wilson said, "Sounds like we're going through Poteet."

"We stop?"

"Not on this run."

Outside the window they could see dim shapes

145

of buildings and here and there a light. The engineer blew his whistle again, and the train began to pick up speed.

"I don't quite know how to tell you. It's kind of like a circus, I guess. Least they put it on in front of a crowd, from what I've heard. A place like the fairgrounds, where they got grandstands and bleachers and where folks have to pay to get in."

"But what do they do?"

"Well, the way Pres told me, part of it is that a stagecoach comes out with a good-looking woman hanging out the window and screaming while a bunch of tame Injuns go chasing after it, all of them moving in a circle around the arena. And the shotgun rider is firing back at the Injuns and the Injuns are shooting at him and every once in a while the Injuns lose a man and then the shotgun rider falls off the coach and then, just when things are blackest and it looks like the Injuns are going to catch the coach with the pretty woman in it, out comes Buffalo Bill on a white horse wearing a buckskin jacket with his white hair down to his shoulders and a little goatee and a pistol in each hand and the reins in his teeth, and he commences to fire at the Injuns. The ones he don't kill, they cut and run, and he saves the day. 'Course they are all firing blanks and it's all playacting."

Warner looked blank for a moment. "And people pay to see such goings-on?"

146

"Well, not down here. They'd get laughed out of town. But up north and in the East, Preston says, where folks don't know anything about this part of the country, he says it goes over big. But he says the shows stay up around Chicago and New York and Boston and such places. He said that they ventured as far south as Kansas City one time and nearly come to grief. Says there was a bunch of drunk drovers in the audience who didn't know it was supposed to be playacting and they come out with their revolvers and commenced shooting real bullets. Fortunately they were too drunk to do any straight shooting and they got calmed down in time. But Pres says the show never made that mistake again."

Warner said, frowning, "Well, that is pretty nearly the silliest thing I ever heard of. What do people want to pay to see something like that for?"

"Pres says it's all the doing of some dime novelist from New York or some such place who started writing these here made-up stories of all the bad men in the West and kind of glorifying them. Man's name is Buntline, Ned Buntline, and he's the one who kind of invented this Buffalo Bill Cody. He's written all kinds of stories about Billy the Kid, that damn fool bushwhacker out in New Mexico, and even Sam Bass and—"

"Sam Bass from Denton?"

"Same one. Him and Wesley Harden."

"That's a couple of drunken crazy men. Sam Bass ought to be dead a dozen times over. And I heard Harden got killed in El Paso. How come Buntline never wrote about you?"

Wilson shook his head. "I don't know. Guess I was before his time or I was too quiet. I heard he commissioned the Colt company to make this Buffalo Bill a pair of forty-fives with twelve-inch barrels on 'em."

"You're joking."

Wilson laughed. "I know it sounds silly, but that's what Preston said. I'd hate to have to wear a revolver like that, much less try and draw it any time inside a week."

Warner shook his head and found the bottle between them and took a swig. He held it up to the light. He said, "We are running low of firewater."

"And a good ways to go. You better kind of try and show a little moderation."

Warner said, "And this brother, Preston, was in this show as a trick shot? Did he shoot blanks, too?"

Wilson laughed shortly. "Not from what I heard. I think it was him done Fisher's bunch the biggest damage. He may playact in the show, but he damn shore don't playact when it comes to the real thing."

"You seen him shoot?"

"Naw. But I was told."

"Stories can get out of hand and kind of grow by themselves. Maybe you been reading this Buntline fellow."

"I'm comfortable with what I told you."

"And exactly what does a trick shot do in one of these Wild West shows?"

"Aw, I don't know. Preston said he would come riding out on his horse and somebody would throw crockery up—clay plates and such—and he'd shoot 'em. He done a bunch of stuff. The big finale of his act was somebody would spin a silver dollar way up high in the air and he'd draw and plug it."

Warner gave him a slow look. "A regular silver dollar? A cartwheel? Not some big outlandish-sized piece of metal?"

"Naw, supposed to be a regular silver dollar like you throw on the bar when you buy a drink."

"And how high was this silver dollar supposed to be tossed up?"

"Way high. I know how it sounds."

Warner said, "Well, that's bullshit. Out of a hundred men there's not one could hit a silver dollar from five yards with a handgun if it was sitting still on a tree stump, much less spinning around in the air."

Wilson put up his hand. He said, "I know, I know. Now why don't you wait and see for yourself? I am talked out, Warner. Talkin' is all we done for what seems like a week. I can't shut my eyes, but I want to put my head back and block the light out with my hat and rest. We got an hour to go and I want to spend that in peace. Lord, I do love to get into a town at four o'clock in the morning."

Wilson kept quarters over his saloon and casino. He stayed at his ranch on the Mexican side of the Rio Grande as a general rule, but there was a very nicely furnished set of rooms over the saloon that he stayed at when the spirit or the hour moved him. They managed to get the horses into the stable and then both went to bed, Warner in a kind of guest room where Lupita sometimes slept. Warner had slept in the same bed with her on one occasion when he'd been wounded, but nothing had happened. She'd been there as a nurse more than anything else.

He awoke alone about noon and got up, creaking in every joint as he did when he slept late in the day. It always messed him all up to get his sleeping hours turned around. He was of the opinion it was best to go ahead and stay up all night rather than sleep way later than he was used to getting up.

He found Wilson and Evita in the kitchen. Evita took one look at him and got up quickly and brought him a cup of coffee. Neither he nor Wilson said anything until Evita had prepared and Warner had eaten a plate of ham and eggs.

Then, after Warner had finished a cup of coffee sweetened with whiskey, Wilson said, "What are you planning for the day?"

Warner said, "Nearly over. But if Vaughn's place ain't too far away, I'm planning on going out to meet him."

"Little over an hour's ride. Easy to find."

"Good. I'll get started."

"Was you figuring on me going with you?"

"Nope."

"That's good, because I wasn't figuring on going even if you asked."

"I wasn't going to ask."

"Saves me the trouble of turning you down."

"You'd've never got the chance. I don't need you leading me around by the hand."

"That's good, because I wasn't going."

"Nobody was going to ask you."

"Just wanted you to know, in case you was going to."

"Well, I wasn't."

"And a good thing for you, too."

"I reckon we can agree on that. I appreciate the breakfast, Evita."

"How es Laura?"

"Meaner'n hell."

"Es not right a woman should change for a man."

"And vice versa," Warner said.

"Wha' that? Theese 'vice versa'?"

151

Warner said, "It means—" Then he stopped and got up. He said to Wilson, "You tell her."

"Want me to come down and point you out of town?"

"Nope. I figure I can find Vaughn's place on my own."

"That's good, because I ain't moving for an hour, at least."

"I am," Warner said. He went out the door yawning and trying to get the wrong kind of sleep out of his head.

Wilson yelled after him: "Don't you go no farther than Vaughn's. You get back here this evening. Don't make me come looking for you."

Warner didn't say anything, just started down the stairs, a small smile on his face. He knew that Wilson had been dying to be asked to come along and make the introductions. Well, Warner figured he could handle that.

6

Next day Warner was sitting out on the board-walk in front of Wilson Young's whorehouse and casino having a midmorning drink and watching the street traffic heading down toward the International Bridge to Mexico. He said to Wilson Young, "I don't know where you got all your information about what a hell of a fight the Vaughns put up against Jack Fisher, but they damn sure didn't impart any of it to me. Next time I go to talk to them folks I'm going to take you with me to act as an interpreter."

Wilson had his chair tipped back against the wall of his saloon. He said, "Hold on, I never said they told me anything. What I said was I *heard* they stuck Jack Fisher's tail between his legs and sent him packing. I never told you I seen anything."

"You flat-out told me that that Preston Vaughn was a ring-tailed wonder with a six-gun. You said he could sound like a Gatlin gun and shoot straighter."

Wilson nodded. "That part is true. I have seen the young man shoot. However, I never said I'd seen the young man shoot at a human target. Search your memory and see if you recollect me making any such remark."

153

Warner took a sip of whiskey. "Well, I got misled somewhere," he said. "Where, exactly, I don't know. But that was a wasted trip. I reckon we talked close on to six hours, and I don't know a hell of a lot more now than I did when I went calling. They *say* they hired some gunmen, but they won't say if they had an effect on making Jack Fisher reconsider. They say they themselves shot a few of Fisher's men, but they aren't sure how many and they damn sure won't say if their hired guns did any shooting. Said they didn't want to talk about other men's business."

"Well, that's sensible, ain't it? There are some folks around here you don't want to be telling tales on."

"But I was trying to find out if there was any point in hiring gunmen. How the hell can I figure that out if they won't tell me whether the gunfighters were effective or not?"

Wilson lowered his chair onto the boardwalk with a thump. "Look here," he said, "Fisher is leaving them alone, ain't he?"

"I guess so."

"Didn't that ranch appear to be running about normal?"

"Yeah. Far as I know."

"Then why don't you figure that whatever they done worked and let it alone?"

Warner raised a hand in frustration and said, "Because I don't *know* what they done! They are the closest-mouthed pair I ever set eyes on. I thought you knew them better than that."

Wilson shook his head slowly. "I don't remember claiming that. They come to me for help, and I give them what little advice I could. I told them that hired gunmen were generally a pretty low breed of animal and about as dependable as the weather. I told them that in the end it would more than likely come down to them and the few friends they could depend on."

"Say, Jack Fisher has got hired gunmen, don't he? Ain't that the crowd he surrounds himself with? Ain't that their makeup?"

"It's more like an army."

"Well, what makes his hired guns any more dependable than those you'd hire off the streets here?"

Wilson yawned and got out a cigar and lit it. "You are a pip, you know that?" he said. "Fisher's men ain't hired; they are part of a gang. Fisher is one of them, and they share in the spoils. Besides that, most of them are scared of him. These two-bit pistoleros around here ain't shucks to his crowd."

Warner said, "Then how the hell did ten of them or six of them run off Fisher's army, as you call it?"

Wilson shrugged and drew on his cigar. "I don't know. Why don't you go ask Austin Vaughn?"

Warner said, "Oh, hell, Wilson! You would

155

try the patience of a circuit judge. Has it not occurred to you that I am in trouble? That I got to do something? That I got a horse ranch being threatened?"

Wilson said comfortably, "You been in trouble before and got out of it. Let me do some thinking on the matter. I don't believe there is any cause to rush."

"No cause to rush? Hell, it's been three days since I killed one of Fisher's men. How long before you think he'll find out about that?"

Wilson made pacifying motions with his hands. "Will you just take it easy? This thing has got a ways to go."

"Let me just say this: you told me that Vaughn got away with eight of Fisher's horses in one of the gunfights and that Fisher was having the gall to sue Vaughn in a court in Austin. Now, I *know* you told me that."

"That's what I heard."

"And you told me you counseled him to hire gunfighters four men to a shift."

"That I did."

Warner drew his head back. "He never mentioned word one to me about that. Or about the two gunfights you said they had out there."

Wilson shook his head. "I am going to explain to you one more time that I told you what was reported to me. I was not there! Can you get that through that stump you call a head? I took it for the gospel because the man I heard it from had no reason to lie. I also know he's probably got the good sense to not go around bragging about it. I remember also telling you he ain't exactly sure that the whole matter is settled. So don't go to quoting me back to me because I know what I said. Besides, I know something you don't know and now I ain't going to tell you."

"What?"

"There you go, getting hard of hearing again. Didn't you just hear me say I wasn't going to tell you?"

"Does it affect me?"

Wilson whistled. "Is a pig's ass pork? I reckon it concerns you. At least I'm damn near certain it concerns you."

Warner stood up. "You don't know shit. That old dog won't hunt. You are pulling my leg because I caught you overplaying your hand."

Wilson nodded and puffed on his cigar. "Let's wait and see."

"That's fine for you, Wilson, but I've got other fish to fry. If you're not going to help me, I guess I'll have to help myself. I reckon I can recruit gunhands as good as you can."

Wilson looked disgusted. "Will you sit down, for God's sake? There's not any rush, I tell you. You said you got off a telegram to Charlie to see how matters were faring. Ain't you even going to wait until you hear back from him?"

Warner's voice still carried the ring of anger. "I'd like to start getting something, *anything,* organized. I got better things to do than sit around here listening to smart cracks from you."

Wilson shook his head wearily. "I have made it as clear as I can that there are no quality guns to be hired around here. All you'll find is trash who will take your money and run at the sound of the first shot."

"How come it worked for Vaughn?"

"Goddammit, I don't know *what* worked for Vaughn! I didn't have me no grandstand seat to the affair. The few men I pointed him at were good men, but I haven't seen them around."

"Fine. I'll get hold of Chulo and have him round me up a bunch of pistoleros from Mexico. They'd probably be better and cheaper."

"Chulo ain't here. He's over in Mexico trying to get his women sorted out and satisfied. Won't be back until day after tomorrow. It's him I'm waiting for. When he gets back, him and me will go and have a talk with Fisher. I'll make it clear that you are a friend of mine and that Fisher would be wise to leave you the hell alone."

Warner leaned toward Wilson Young. "That," he said, "is exactly what I don't want you doing. I don't need you to fight my battles for me, Wilson. And I ain't going to have it. Anybody goes to talk to Fisher, it will be me."

Wilson Young laughed shortly. He said, "You

reckon yourself to be bulletproof, Warner?"

"What about yourself? What's to keep Fisher and his gang from shooting you and Chulo off your horses before you can even open your mouth."

Wilson said carelessly, "Because even Jack Fisher ain't dumb enough to do that. It's pretty well understood you'd have to bushwhack me to kill me, and that's murder. Though Jack Fisher ain't above bushwhacking a man, he knows I've got a lot of friends with long memories."

Warner stared at him. As arrogant as the words were, Warner knew that they were true. Jack Fisher couldn't kill Wilson Young in a fair fight, and while he might own the law in his own county, the death of Wilson Young would draw the attention of the state authorities. For a second he gave Young a sour look and then leaned down to pick up his empty glass. He straightened up and said, "I'm going inside your lousy saloon and have one more drink, and then I'm going for some lunch. Are you coming?"

Wilson got up slowly. "I might as well. Looks like I'm stuck with your company. At least until tonight."

Warner was about to go through the batwing doors of the saloon, but he paused. "What happens tonight?"

Wilson said, "That's what I'm not going to tell you."

Warner gave him a look. "With a little work, Young, you might make a fair hand at being a son of a bitch."

They ate lunch down the street at a café called La Cocina, which means "the kitchen" in Spanish. Wilson had chili and eggs, and Warner had a steak topped with picante sauce. They drank beer. Neither one of them said much while they were eating. Warner was not so much irritated by Wilson's casual attitude toward Fisher's threat as he was worried about what he could do and how he could go about it. If a man announced he was going to burn your house down there wasn't a hell of a lot you could do about it except never leave home and keep someone on guard all the time, and that could run into a lot of money and trouble. The problem was, he didn't know for sure how serious Fisher was, or how dangerous. Maybe sending Hamm to the ranch had been a ploy to test Warner's mettle. If, with a little encouragement, he could throw a scare into Warner and collect some sort of a payoff for a little trouble, well, then fine and dandy. But if that didn't work, did Fisher mean to follow through with some heavyweight work? Did he really intend to kill horses until Warner knuckled under?

Warner sat there eating and worrying about such matters while Wilson ate and drank as if he hadn't a care in the world. Warner wondered how

160

much Fisher knew about him. Did Fisher believe that Warner was some greenhorn who'd fold his hand at the first sign of trouble? Or was he set to get into a serious fight?

Aloud, Warner said, "Dammit!" and slammed his empty beer mug on the tabletop.

Wilson looked up at him. "Don't throw a fit, Warner. They got more beer. And if you're in that big of a hurry you can finish mine."

"The hell with that! I got to have me a talk with this Jack Fisher. Surely to heaven a man can get at him some way."

Wilson said carelessly, "Oh, he ain't hard to get at. It's the getting away part that is kind of tricky."

Warner got a telegram from Charlie late in the afternoon saying that all was well at the ranch. Other than that, he didn't do much except walk around and think or sit up in Lupita's room and think. The two women who belonged to Wilson had gone to see their aunts in Monterrey and would not be back for several days, so Wilson was forced to manage the whorehouse, or at least to oversee it, as well as to take on some responsibility for the saloon. As a consequence he had left Warner pretty much on his own; a condition that was in accord with the way Warner felt.

But Wilson had said something to him that had

puzzled him most of the day. Over lunch, while Warner was still worrying the why of the matter from Jack Fisher's standpoint, Wilson had said, "Warner, that's your goddam trouble. You can't believe that some people are snake-belly mean. You can't believe that a man can be mean and do mean things just because that's his nature. You keep trying to figure out what he's after and what is making Jack Fisher do all these wrong things. It's because he's a mean son of a bitch, Warner! Mean, mean, mean! He owns half of a county and has got more money than ten men could spend in a lifetime, and you think he goes after Austin Vaughn's purebred cattle because he wants them. He don't want them. He just don't want Austin Vaughn to have them. You think he wants your reputation as a horse handler? Well, hell, we both know he can't have that. In a million years he'd never understand horses like you do—the care of them, the riding of them, the breeding of them. But he don't want *you* to have that ability either. He wants to take it away from you because he's mean to the bone, you dumb son of a bitch. So quit trying to figure out why he's doing what he's doing and figure out a way to stop him from doing it."

It worried Warner to think he knew so little about human nature that he could not judge a man like Jack Fisher. If Fisher's motives were as simple as Wilson made them sound, then that meant Warner was awfully naive about people, especially men like Fisher. The thought troubled him. He knew he was no babe in the woods, but he was hard-pressed to believe another man could be so low-down and loathsome as to wish harm to another man with no hope of gain for himself. But maybe it was so. If that was the case, he thought, he was up against stiffer odds than he'd figured on. If a man like Jack Fisher set out to ruin you, and hang the cost, he was going to be hell to beat.

About eight o'clock that evening Wilson Young found him in the bar of the saloon having a solitary drink. Young said, "Where the hell you been? I been looking all over for you to eat supper."

"I ain't hungry."

"Listen, don't talk like a jackass. C'mon and let's go to the hotel and get a bite. We ain't got much time, and you'll need all your strength."

Warner got up from the bar stool he'd been perched on. He threw back the rest of his drink and then dropped a silver dollar on the bar.

Wilson said, "You pay in my saloon?"

"Ain't I supposed to?"

"Fine with me if you're that nuts. I don't pay you for whiskey when I come see you. Now come on."

"What am I supposed to need my strength up for?"

"Let's eat and then I'll tell you."

They stepped across the street to the Greystone Hotel and took their meal in the dining room. While they ate, Warner was conscious of Wilson looking him over.

He said, "What, this place too fancy to be wearing a hat at the table?"

Wilson chewed a bite of steak and said, "I was noticing you was looking particularly scruffy. You was wearing them same clothes when you rode out of here yesterday morning. You ain't shaved, and I'd bet my stack you ain't had a bath."

Warner gave him a perplexed look. "Are we courting?" he said. "When did you commence taking an interest in my appearance? Wilson, ain't everybody rich enough to change clothes as often as you do."

Wilson was wearing an ironed white linen shirt and starched, ironed military twill riding pants. His boots were shined, and he had on a soft black leather vest. He said, "We've got to go down to the train depot and meet someone. I hate them to see a friend of mine look like he's just come in off a cattle drive."

"We're meeting someone at the depot? Who the hell is coming in? Anybody I know?"

"Eat up," Wilson said. "It's getting right on to nine, and we'll barely make it as it is."

When they were finished, they left the hotel

and turned toward the bridge and Mexico, because a railroad bridge also ran across the river. The depot was five blocks away, and the streets and boardwalks were still crowded with people hurrying about their business. As they dodged their way through the crowd Warner said, "Wilson, who the hell are you meeting at the train station?"

"You'll know when you see."

"Well, the way you seem concerned about my appearance makes me think it might be a lady. You ain't fool enough to try and sneak a woman in here while Evita is gone, are you?"

"You never know."

Warner stopped dead in his tracks. He said, "Have you lost your mind? That Mexican woman will cut your throat while you sleep. I ain't having nothing to do with this. You're crazy."

"Oh, c'mon," Wilson said. He tugged Warner along by the shoulder. "It ain't nothing like that."

"Then how come you care how I look?"

"I don't. I don't. All right? I made one simple comment and you are going to go on about it all night. Hurry up, I think I hear the train blowing for the first crossing."

They got to the depot several minutes before the train came into sight. It was the late train, so there weren't many others waiting to meet it. Warner said, "I don't see why you are so secretive."

"What did you hear from Charlie?"

165

Warner shrugged. "He said things were all right, but that was as of the time he sent the telegram. God only knows what might have happened by now."

Wilson said, "You worry too much for . . ." The rest of his words were drowned out by the sound of the engine as it came huffing and squealing and clanging into the station, its bell dinging and donging loud enough to wake the dead.

The engine passed and then the tender and then two mail cars and then the first of the passenger cars. As the train came to a stop, the second passenger car pulled up exactly opposite where they were standing on the platform. She was the first person down the steps with a porter following, carrying her luggage. She was no more than ten feet from Warner, but she hadn't spotted him. Warner turned and gave Wilson Young a disgusted look. "You son of a bitch. I will not soon forget this."

Wilson said, a little alarm in his voice, "Don't get on your high horse with me. I didn't send for her. All I got was a telegram telling me she was coming."

"You could have warned me."

Wilson laughed cynically. "Yeah, and watched you leave town and hide out until she'd left. Which would have left her on my hands. Listen, she's your woman. I got enough problems of my own."

"She ain't my woman; she's my partner. And you're still a son of a bitch for not telling me. That was the reason you took notice of my appearance."

But before Wilson could answer, Laura Pico spied Warner and came hurrying over to him. She was wearing a severely cut woman's traveling suit. But even its less than flattering lines couldn't hide what was underneath. As she came up to them, Warner thought she at least had the good grace to look slightly embarrassed. She reached up and kissed him on the cheek and put out her hand sideways for Wilson to take. Then she said, looking up into Warner's face, "I hope you haven't done anything too foolish so far."

He had been wrong. She wasn't at all embarrassed or uncomfortable. He said, "I hope you're on your way to Mexico and are getting off the train to stretch your legs, because I goddam sure don't want you here."

She put both her arms through his. "How sweet," she said. "Now tip the porter and let's get to a hotel or wherever we're staying. That was the longest goddam trip I've ever taken. Does that train stop at every cattle crossing?"

Warner gave the porter a half dollar, and then he took one bag and Wilson took the other and they started back toward town. Wilson said, "Warner, ya'll can have the room Evita and I use. It's bigger than Lupita's. I'll use hers because

I got to stay in town tonight on account of I'm keeping store."

The night was still warm, and the crowds were as thick as ever. Laura said, "Why, Wilson, do you know how to run a whorehouse? And where's Evita?"

Wilson told her about the two girls going to visit family and then said, "No, Miss Laura, I don't know how to run a whorehouse. But I got about a half a dozen young ladies who know what to do to get the money and where to bring it when they got it. Myself, I'll mainly be keeping my eye on the cash register in the saloon and watching the casino. I know it's right hard to visualize me as a workingman, but then, I'm having a hard time visualizing you as a gunfighter."

She was still holding Warner by the arm. "Whatever are you talking about?" she said.

Wilson said, "Well, Jack Fisher is a gunfighter, and since that's the only language he speaks, I figured you must be one too."

Warner, who was walking with his head down and his jaw set, said, "Oh, shut up, Wilson. The both of you shut up. I don't want to hear another goddam word out of you, Laura, until we are off by ourselves, and then you better get ready to do some fourteen-karat copper-bottom gold-plated explaining."

She gave his arm a hug. "And, yes, I'm glad to see you, too."

Laura made a mild protest about putting Wilson out of his room, but Warner could see she felt right at home in the lavishly furnished place with the big four-poster bed. He wasn't surprised when she graciously acquiesced after Wilson explained he'd most likely be working half the night anyway and that Lupita's room was plenty big enough for him. "Besides," he said, giving Laura a wink, "you're farther from the action here. Less likely to get disturbed and—oh, yeah, I remembered to tell the maid to put clean sheets on the bed."

After Wilson had left, saying he'd wait for them down in the bar, Laura swirled herself around, looking at the room, and said, "Well! I never thought I'd find myself sleeping upstairs at a whorehouse."

Warner was so angry he was speaking through clenched teeth. He said, "Why? I'd think you'd feel right at home."

Laura stopped twirling around and fixed him with a look. "What's *that* supposed to mean?"

Warner knew better than to talk up when he was angry. He especially knew it was a bad idea to talk to Laura when he was as mad as he was. But he was too angry to care. He said, "Can't see much difference between you and them except they are more honest about it."

Her eyes narrowed. "I can see you are hot and bothered about something. You better spit it out. What do you mean by that remark?"

169

He said recklessly, "Hell, you married your husband for his money, didn't you? You told me you married Pico because he was rich. Now he's dead and you got it. What do you call that if it ain't whoring? Piece of paper and a few words by a minister don't—"

Laura's hand streaked out, and she gave him a stinging slap across the face. "You son of a bitch! How dare you talk to me like that!" She drew her hand back. "I'll—"

He reached out and caught her wrist. "You slap me again, woman . . . I'm gonna let your arm go and you just go ahead and slap me and see what happens. But you better think on it real good."

He let go of her wrist and stood in front of her with his hands at his sides looking into her blazing eyes. Her shoulder twitched a couple of times, but she didn't raise her hand. Finally she said, "What the hell are you so mad about? Calling me a whore. You know goddam good and well I agreed to marry Pico with the understanding that I didn't love him and probably never would. But he wanted me just the same. You know the story, you son of a bitch! Now explain this attitude of yours."

He was still boiling inside. He said harshly, "All right. I give you a back-sided lick on the whore business. But that still ain't got nothing to do with what in the goddam hell you are doing here. And what *are* you doing here? By the way, you call me a son of a bitch again and mean it, I'll show you another use for a belt and your bare ass. Now what in hell are you doing here?"

She said stiffly, "I came to help. What the hell did you think I came for? Your delightful company?"

"Help? How you gonna help? What, am I supposed to hide behind your skirts so I can sneak up on Jack Fisher? You wet-nursing me, woman?"

"You seem to forget, Mr. High-and-Mighty, that I am your partner and I have got a half interest in this affair."

"Oh, no!" he said. "You are not my partner in the River Ranch. You are only my partner in the get from those Andalusian studs. You don't own one goddam foot of that ranch."

She flared back. "The Andalusians are the bulk of the business, you stupid man. And I have advanced money to improve that ranch. I hold *paper* on that ranch! I've got a vested interest in that ranch, and I've got a right to protect that interest. And *that* is what I'm doing here!"

"The best way you can protect your interest is to get your ass on the next northbound train and stay out of my way. I've got trouble enough with Jack Fisher without having you here to slow me down."

She gave him a hard look and went over and sat down on the bed and began to take off her laced high heels. She was wearing black silk stockings, and he knew that they ran up her soft thighs and connected to garters that came off her wasp-waisted corset. He stood there watching as she took off the coat of her traveling suit, revealing a starched white blouse caught at the collar with a cameo brooch. After that, she stood up and undid the button and let her severely cut skirt fall to the floor. He could see she was wearing only one petticoat. She sighed and sat back down on the bed and rummaged in her reticule until she found a match and a dainty little cigar that fitted into an ivory holder. She got the cigar lit and blew a cloud of smoke toward Warner. She said, "Is there anything to drink around here?"

It was a too obvious question, since she could see, if she only turned her head, a decanter of brandy on the bedside table. But Warner, looking grim, decided to humor her. He stepped over to the table, poured brandy into two tumblers, and handed one to her. They both took a drink without benefit of a toast. Finally she said, "I might could help, Warner, if you'd stop being angry long enough to think about it. I didn't come on the spur of the moment, but I knew you'd take it that way, so I came prepared to offer what I could."

He was still so angry he had difficulty talking calmly. The words came out as stiff as planks. "Laura, you and I have been together going on two years. And other than what we do in bed, I don't know that there is much that we agree on. But we've managed to make it this long because we've had—or at least I thought we had—a sort of unwritten and unspoken agreement about some lines we didn't step over. Well, you broke that agreement by coming here. You have taken to interfering in my business, and you know how I feel about that."

She straightened and stiffened her back. "What about lying?" she said. "Is that part of our agreement? I don't remember saying it was all right for you to lie to me."

His face flushed. "You better be careful with them goddam compliments of yours. You are getting a little free with your mouth. I do not recall lying to you."

"Oh, yeah?" She tossed her head so that her shoulder-length blond hair with the strawberry tinge flew backwards. "And I thought you told me you were going to San Antonio to look at horses? Isn't that what you told me? Where did I order the stock car for? Del Rio or San Antonio?"

Warner looked toward the far window, remembering his bet with Wilson. He said roughly, "Maybe I changed my mind. Maybe I decided to come straight on down here after I looked the market over in San Antonio and didn't like what I saw."

She looked disgusted. "Oh, bullshit, Warner. You were coming here all the time. If you're telling the truth, let's march down to that depot and you can prove you didn't route that car straight here." She stood up. "Come on, let's go. I just sent it to San Antonio like you told me. But let's go look at the bill of lading and see if it and you didn't come on to Del Rio the same night you left. You didn't spend any more time in San Antonio than it took you to get out. And you never went near any horse auction and never meant to. What you did was lie to me." She reached for her skirt. "I'll get my traveling clothes back on, and if you're telling the truth I'll sit in that depot and take the first eastbound train out. Hell, if you're telling the truth, I'll take the first train out even if it's going to Mexico." She stood there holding her skirt, looking at him expectantly. "Well? Shall we go?"

He was still looking into the distance. Finally he cleared his throat. "One thing ain't got a goddam thing to do with the other and you know it. You are just trying to put me in a bad light."

"Bad light? You? Mr. Pure Heart, who would never lie or steal or do anything underhanded? Mr. Do-the-Right-Thing? Mr. Fair Play? Put you in a bad light? Little old me?" She put her hand to her breast and fluttered her eyelashes. "How could little old Laura do something like that?"

He flushed. "Oh, go to hell, Laura. All right, I lied. So what? I didn't want you to worry. I was only thinking of you, and this is the thanks I get. Yes,

174

yes, I lied. A little. But it was for your own good."

She reached him in two swift strides and grabbed his shirtfront and jerked him around so that he was facing her. She was tall for a woman, and her lips were just below his chin, her eyes not quite able to see into his unless he bowed his head, which he wouldn't do. She jerked hard on his shirt and said fiercely, "Listen to me, you idiot. You worry me when you go off half cocked. You worry me when you get that machismo of yours all worked up so that you'll charge into anything. You worry me when you quit thinking because you're mad or because your pride is hurt and you are going to get even even if it kills you. Goddammit, look at me when I'm talking to you! I'm tired of talking to your neck!"

Finally, grudgingly, he looked down at her. Her eyes were still blazing. He said, "I don't like to be nursemaided, and you know it."

"And I don't want you getting hurt. I came down here to see what was going on. If you think I was going to sit in Corpus Christi while you risked your life, you're crazy. If you have to get yourself killed, I don't want to have to wait to find out."

Her eyes were softening. But he still felt sulky. He said, "Aw, what the hell do you care?"

She gave his shirt another hard jerk and said angrily, "What do I care? What do I *care?*"

"Yeah, what's it to you what I get up to?"

"Are you that dumb?" she said. "Are you really that stupid?"

He looked into her eyes. "Just what are you talking about?"

There was a fierce look on her face. "Don't you know that if you get cut, I bleed?"

It was the closest they had ever come to saying how they really felt about each other and they were both immediately embarrassed. Warner jerked his eyes away from hers and looked toward the bedside table. He said gruffly, "You better get on some fresh clothes. Wilson is waiting for us downstairs. There's a bathtub in the next room. Wilson has got piped-in water if you was to want to take a bath first."

She stepped back from him. "Yeah, I'd like that. You go on down, and I'll take a bath and change clothes and come down as soon as I'm ready. I haven't had any dinner. Will there be a place open?"

Still not looking at her he said, "I think the hotel dining room serves until late. I'll ask Wilson. We'll be able to rustle up something."

"You go ahead."

He walked downstairs with a great deal on his mind. If he'd had any sense, he thought, he could have given voice to how he felt about her. But his nerve had failed him, and the opportunity might never present itself again in such a form. Theirs was such an odd relationship that he hoped to hell he never had to explain it to anyone else. He and Laura could make fierce, passionate love, giving expression to every physical sign of caring and loving that was possible. But to actually speak of it they would have had to breach a wall that neither could penetrate or climb over or burrow under. He suspected they were both afraid to express what they felt for fear of being rejected. So instead, they contented themselves with sex and compassionate and uncivil cruelty. They were both hard, but they were also terribly afraid of being hurt. Warner, for his part, had never let himself get very close to any human being. He had friends, like Wilson Young, but he never wanted to get so close that another person's death would nearly kill him. He'd already been through that with his parents and his grandfather, and that, he'd decided, was enough.

He and Laura had never really talked of love except once, and that had been a casual conversation. She had asked him if he'd ever been in love, and he'd said he reckoned not. He'd said he'd been in heat, but he doubted that was the same thing. She'd said it had been that way for her, also, which had kind of shocked him, her having been married. It was then that she'd told him she'd married Pico for his money and not for love and that he'd understood and agreed to the arrangement. But he still felt she had a sense of shame about it because of the funny way she had of never using her late husband's given name, referring to him only as Pico. They'd both done that; it was one way of pretending he'd never existed, because Warner had once shown signs of being jealous of her dead husband. That occasion had been the closest she'd ever come to telling him how she felt. She'd gone out of her way to reassure him that Pico hadn't meant anything to her, that being in bed with him had been a chore and nothing like what she felt when she was with Warner.

He was still bemused when he entered the saloon and sat down at the table that Wilson occupied. The table stood on a little platform and gave the owner a good view not only of the saloon but of part of the casino as well.

Wilson said, "Well? You still got a mad on?"

Warner sighed and poured himself a drink out of the bottle in front of Wilson. He said, "Naw, not really. Ain't no use getting angry at her. She's going to do what she's bound to do, come hell or a prairie fire. But I know there'll be an argument about everything I want to do."

Wilson took a drink of his whiskey and said, "You can't fight women, kid. They hold all the cards. They got most of the cash and *all* of the gash. That's a hell of a pair. Beats my four of a kind."

Warner said slowly, "Sometimes it makes a man want to go out and get himself castrated."

Wilson laughed and tapped his temple. "Wouldn't do any good. You'd still have the memories. You'd be like a steer, still with the urge but not the equipment. Ain't you ever seen ol' steers trying to mount one another?"

Warner gave his friend a deadpan look. "I really wasn't giving it serious consideration, Wilson."

"Gown-whipped as you are, I don't know. Wouldn't give odds."

"Let's wait until Evita gets back and see who is gown-whipped." He stood up as he caught a flash of yellow coming down the stairs. He recognized the frock. "Here she comes. You be sure and help her tell me how to handle this matter."

Wilson got up. "Hell, why don't you turn the matter over to her? She's got plenty of money. Maybe she can buy Fisher off."

"Yeah, I can see her doing that. She's nearly as quick with a greenback as you are. But she can talk all she wants. It's not going to bother me, so long as I don't have to talk back. She can say or do anything, long as she don't involve me."

They started toward the stairs. Wilson said, "That's what I like to see, a man and his woman pulling together in harness."

Warner gave him a sideways look. "Anybody ever tell you that you are a sarcastic bastard, Mr. Young?"

"Ain't nobody around here smart enough to know what 'sarcastic' means."

7

They took Laura across to the hotel dining room. While she made a dainty meal of chicken and dumplings and salad, Warner and Wilson drank coffee and whiskey. When she was finished, she said, with a little more of a commanding air than Warner cared for, "Now tell me as much as you can about this Fisher fellow." She looked at Warner.

Warner looked at Wilson and raised his eyebrows. "Well, of the three of us, only one has had the honor of meeting the gentleman. You'll have to ask somebody besides me."

Wilson looked at him with humor in his eyes. Then he said to Laura, "Fisher's pretty quick with a six-gun, Miss Laura, but I'd put my money on you."

She gave him a look. "Do you always have to be so goddam cute, Wilson? I want to know what we're up against."

Warner laughed. "Yeah, Wilson, do you always have to be so goddam *cute?* I had never noticed it before, but you are as cute as a spotted heifer."

Wilson gave them both a sour look. He said to Laura, "For somebody who wants something, you appear not to have the slightest idea how to go about getting it."

"Then quit treating me like an interfering woman. I've got a stake in this."

Warner said, "But you *are* an interfering woman. How else do you expect to be treated?"

"All right." She pushed her chair back as if to get up. "If this is what I came all this way for, then so be it. You don't have to hit me over the head with a hammer."

Warner put out his hand. "Oh, hang on, Laura. Goddammit, if you're going to be pushy, I don't see why you're so surprised when you get pushed back."

"I came to help," she said stiffly. "I do have a brain. I might have a constructive idea, but I have to know what we're up against."

Wilson Young upended a glass and pushed it over in front of Laura. "Have a drink and cool out. I wasn't trying to be cute, if that's what you want to call it. But this ain't a real easy situation and there ain't a lot of reason to get brisk about it. If you're vulnerable and Jack Fisher sets his sights on you, you've got trouble."

Laura poured herself a drink and sipped at it. When she set the glass back down, she seemed more relaxed. "What is it he wants, exactly? Do we know?"

Warner shook his head. "Not the extent of it. The man he sent sort of indicated to me that Fisher planned to put me . . . us . . . out of business."

"Then, for heaven's sake, why don't we go see him and find out exactly what he's after?"

Warner looked at Wilson and smiled wanly. Wilson said, "It ain't all that easy, Laura. You don't go riding up to visit Jack Fisher like you would an ordinary citizen. I have spent a good deal of energy talking Warner out of that very idea. I've told him it's real easy to get into his place, but it ain't quite so easy to get out. At least it won't be for Warner."

"Then why don't *you* go see him?"

Wilson sat back in his chair and stretched his legs out in front of him. "Because I don't want him to know that I am Warner's ally. Not right now."

"Why not?"

"Because," Wilson said, "I want to be a surprise that Jack ain't got counted in the pot. If he knows in advance that I'm a surprise then I won't be a surprise no more."

"Wilson thinks it's best that we see what Fisher has in mind before Wilson shows his hand. We already know that Fisher doesn't necessarily want to fool with Wilson."

"Then, Wilson, why don't you go and tell him to leave Warner alone?"

"There is something known as pushing a man too far," Wilson said. "We don't want to put Fisher in the position of having to back down and lose face. Then there will be hell to pay, because odds are that he won't back down."

Laura looked at him for a moment, thinking. "Tell me something about this man. Anything that will give me a key to the kind of man he is. I know you think little of my opinion, but I might surprise you."

"On the contrary, Miss Laura, I have great admiration for your judgment. Your interest in those Spanish horses was enough to win my regard right there. And then you didn't fold your tent after your husband was killed and your stock stolen, and that raised you even more in my eyes. Of course, I won't comment on you going in partnership with Warner." Wilson smiled faintly. "Lot of folks have wanted to partner with him in the horse business. I congratulate you on succeeding where others had failed."

She said, with a little edge in her voice, "Warner and I went into partnership because I had the Andalusians and Warner knew the right way to use them. I'd been going at it the wrong way."

Wilson said innocently, "I never meant nothing more about your partnership than that you had the right goods for the right man. If you've taken any other meaning, you're off the trail."

Warner said impatiently, "Will you two quit nipping at each other's heels and get on with it? Wilson, if you've got some magic insight into a cold-blooded killer that will give Laura a start to do her thinking with, I wish you'd tell her."

"All right." Wilson leaned forward and took his

glass from the table and sipped at the whiskey. "I'll give you an example. It may not mean much to you, but it has stuck in the minds of quite a few folks around here. About three years ago I had occasion to be in the Lone Star Saloon, which is down at the north end of town, seeing how the competition was doing. Well, it happened that Jack Fisher and several of his gang were in there sitting at a table. I didn't pay them no mind, just went up to the bar and got a drink off the proprietor. While we was talking, an itinerant preacher come in and was going around trying to sell the boys some little Bibles for fifty cents. Them little kind that you can carry in your shirt pocket, the kind they are always telling stories about one of them stopping a bullet that was headed for a man's heart. Of course them kind of stories are generally told by folks who don't know where the heart is located."

"Get on with it."

"Anyway, this was some poor old circuit-riding preacher trying to pick up a dollar or two between tent meetings. Skinny little old man. He moved around amongst the tables and wasn't bothering nobody. In fact, a couple of fellows bought a Bible, and I was going to give him a dollar. But then he come upon the table that Jack Fisher was sitting at, and he asked Fisher if he'd buy a Bible. Well, Fisher held out his hand and told the man to give him one. Then he took that Bible and ripped out a page. Then he got his makings out of his pocket and commenced to use the page out of that Bible to roll a cigarette, said he was out of papers and that thin Bible paper was just the thing. Well, that saloon got so quiet you could have heard a cat walk. And that preacher stood there gawking at Fisher like he was expecting lightning to strike at any minute. It even kind of made the men that was with Fisher uneasy. You could see it on their faces. Finally Fisher flipped that ruined Bible back to the preacher and asked him what he owed him. He said since cigarette papers didn't cost but a nickel he didn't see no reason to lay out half a buck, but he was willing to pay for what he'd used. And of course he was grinning like the devil all the time, that Bible paper cigarette hanging out of the corner of his mouth."

Laura said, "What happened?"

"Nothing. That preacher backed out of there and took off, and Fisher had a good laugh. But he was the only one laughing, near as I could see." He glanced over at Laura. "That tell you anything about the man?"

Laura waited a moment and then looked from Wilson to Warner and back to Wilson Young. She said, "Is that it?"

Wilson frowned. "Ain't that enough?"

She looked at Warner and said, "Do you find that insightful?"

185

"Are you loco?" Warner frowned. "If I wanted to look for a dead certain way to thumb my nose at luck, I'd tear a leaf out of the Bible and roll a cigarette out of it. The man had cigarette papers in his pocket. Or he could have got one from somebody else. But he didn't do that. He *chose* to mutilate that Bible right there in front of everybody that could see him. I don't know why it don't shock you, but it shocks the hell out of me and this is the first time I've heard the story."

Laura said, "Well, Christianity aside—and I don't see how we can expect a man who goes around murdering people and stealing their property to be a Christian—what did Fisher really do? You'd think that was the first Bible ever had a page torn out of it. Did you ever see the Bibles they use in Sunday school? They look like they've been in a cattle stampede."

Warner pulled a face. He said, "Right there is why I didn't want you mixing in on this matter. It ain't the Bible, goddammit, it's the attitude the man expressed. He wanted to shock that saloon full of drunks, and he done it. Wilson is telling you he don't stick at nothing."

"Maybe so. It sounds to me like Fisher's just a showoff."

"Well, Laura," Wilson said casually, "it don't seem like there's much we can tell you about the man. Like you said, he kills people and takes their property. Then there's times he only kills

186

people. Or just takes their property. That's what makes it hard to get the man laid up to a straight edge and measured. He ain't consistent."

She said, "I know you both would rather I stayed out of this—Warner especially. But if you can't go see the man, how do you expect to find out what he wants? You've got to be able to communicate with him. I can see where it would be dangerous, even fatal, for Warner to approach him on his own ground. And I suppose I can understand why you don't want him to know you are on Warner's side just yet. But what I can't understand is how you are going to do anything about this situation if you don't get in communication. Can't you send a messenger?"

Warner said, "We are trying to think it out. I've been to see a family named Vaughn who had similar trouble. I thought I'd get some answers there."

"What did they have to say?"

With a long-suffering look, Warner outlined the substance of his visit to the Vaughn ranch. He finished by saying, "So that was a dry water hole. I don't know much more than I did before."

She looked at Wilson. "What's your plan?"

He shrugged. "To do nothing for the moment. Maybe Fisher'll come to town. I think Warner should go back home and wait."

"Wait for what? Until Fisher shoots our horses at long range?"

Wilson said, "Laura, he's not going to start out shooting valuable horses. There are a few more threats to be got through before he starts that."

"Oh? Seems like he's fast enough when it comes to tearing up Bibles."

Warner gave a slight groan. "The one ain't like the other."

"Why not?"

Warner threw up his hands. He said, "Goddammit, Laura, you are the beatingest woman I've ever seen. You know that? You beat everything. Anything. You want to shove your nose into something you don't understand and then argue about it. Hell!"

She said, "Where, exactly, is his headquarters?"

"Outside of the town of Cotulla," Wilson said, "about sixty miles northwest of here."

"Does the train go there?"

"There's a spur line. You have to change trains at some junction out of here. I'm not exactly sure what town. Why?"

"I wanted to be sure we can get at him in a hurry if we choose to."

Warner was watching her face. He said, "Laura, that's a lie. How come you asked that question?"

"What question?"

"If the train went there."

"It was a perfectly innocent question, Warner. My heavens, the way you keep that gimlet eye on me, you'd think *I* was the enemy. Have I ever

188

actually interfered in the business of the ranch?"

"Hell yes! Are you making a joke?"

She was shaking her head. "I've *tried* to interfere, yes. But you tell me one instance where I had my way. Just one. Tell me one."

He thought for a moment. "Right off I can't think of any. But it damn sure hasn't been for lack of trying."

"Do you see me arguing with you or Wilson? I'm here simply to help in any way I can. You act like you think I might do something rash."

He eyed her, but didn't say anything. Instead, he became aware of the several waiters standing around in their aprons, holding trays in front of them and directing looks their way. Warner looked around. They were the last people there. He got out his watch. He said, "Hell, it's way past eleven o'clock. I need to get to bed."

Wilson said, "I'll get the score."

"Naw, let me."

Wilson shook his head. "I'm still trying to get over you paying for a drink in my place. Besides, me and the man that owns this place swap out. And he's got quite a little gambling bill run up."

Back over at Wilson's, in his room, Warner sat down to have one more drink. There was a small dressing room off the big bedroom, and Laura had gone in there to change into her nightgown. Never before had she refused to undress in front of him. She knew he liked to watch her, and she liked him to watch her. But tonight he knew he was being punished for resenting her arrival. She'd given him the cold shoulder ever since they'd left Wilson downstairs. Now she came out in a particularly flimsy nightgown, but she got quickly into bed and pulled the covers over her. Without a word she turned her back to Warner and settled down to sleep.

He said, "You ain't hurting nobody but yourself with that attitude. If you think I'm supposed to feel like a little boy who's had his sugar-tit taken away from him you are badly mistaken."

She didn't move or say a word.

He pulled off his boots and let them fall to the floor. "Maybe you'd rather I slept somewhere else? I understand there are quite a number of rooms on this floor."

She didn't speak. He stood up and took off his shirt and then unbuckled his gun belt and hung it over the bedpost and then unbuckled his jeans and shucked them off. Naked, he crawled into bed. As he got under the covers, he happened to touch her, and she made a production of moving farther over on her side of the bed. Warner said, a touch of anger in his voice, "You better look out, you'll jerk your hip out of joint yanking around like that. And where in hell do you get off thinking I'd even be interested? I'm the one that's mad, if you will recollect. Frankly, right now, I wouldn't fuck you with a mule's dick." He

190

turned over, putting his back to her, and finally went to sleep as his anger cooled.

The next morning Warner woke at dawn. Laura was still sleeping, but in her sleep she had worked her way across the bed so that she was pressed up against him. He looked down at her for a second, wondering how someone who looked as good as she did could be so contrary on occasion.

As carefully as he could, he climbed out of bed in the dim room, slipped into his jeans, gathered up the rest of his clothes and his boots and gun belt, and let himself out of the room without waking Laura. He went down to the big bathroom, shaved, and took what Wilson called a whore's bath, washing himself off all over with a wet towel. Then he brushed his teeth and got dressed and started downstairs. His intention was to eat breakfast in peace without benefit of Laura's company and then have a quiet think about the situation. He was even hoping to avoid Wilson Young. He figured his friend had worked late and wouldn't be up too soon, so he thought to go down the street to the Mexican café and have some eggs and chorizos. He figured it to be not quite eight o'clock.

But then he met Wilson coming up the stairs as he was going down. Warner said, "Hello, sunshine. What the hell you doing up and about?"

Wilson said, "We've got an early visitor. I reckon you need to talk to him."

191

Warner's heart jumped. He could only think that it might be Jack Fisher and he said so, but Wilson shook his head. "Naw. It's Austin Vaughn. He showed up about half an hour ago. He's waiting down in my office. We'll take him across the street and get some breakfast, or some coffee at least. Damn, I could have used about four more hours of sleep."

Warner had been carrying his gun belt, and he took a moment to buckle it on. He said, "You fetch him out. I'll wait at the front door."

While Wilson went to get Vaughn, Warner stepped out onto the street. The wind was blowing from across the river and he could smell the town of Villa Acuña. It made him wrinkle his nose. He didn't know why, but that one Mexican town always smelled worse than any other place he knew of.

Del Rio was already up and about its business. He watched the traffic going by until Wilson and Austin Vaughn came out. Warner shook hands with the rancher, taking notice that his face looked worn and worried. He said, "Where's Preston?"

Austin said, "He's at the ranch." He hesitated a moment and then said, "We don't like to both be gone at the same time."

They went across the street to the hotel dining room, figuring that would be a better place to talk than the noisy café. Austin said that he'd already had breakfast but that he could do with some coffee. As they went into the hotel, Warner said, "I reckon this has got to do with Jack Fisher. Something new?"

Vaughn hesitated. "Not exactly. Why don't we all get settled and ya'll get some vittles in you before we start talkin'? I got some things to say might get your attention." He hesitated again for a second and then added, "Some things that I ain't all that proud of."

Vaughn wouldn't say any more; he sat fiddling with his cup of coffee while Warner and Wilson ate. Warner hurried through his eggs and steak with biscuits, anxious to hear what Vaughn had to tell him. But then he noticed that Wilson Young was eating deliberately, and he knew that Vaughn wouldn't talk until they were both through. He kicked Wilson under the table and cut his eyes at Wilson's plate, but the man didn't take the hint. Instead he put down his fork and said, "What?"

Warner gave him a sour look and said, "Nothing. My foot slipped."

Then, finally, they were both through. They pushed their plates away and waited until the waiter had cleared the table before they settled back with coffee and looked at Austin Vaughn. He cleared his throat nervously several times and then said, "What I got to tell you needs to be said, Mr. Grayson, but I am almighty ashamed to tell you of it. The fact is, I misled you when you was out to my ranch, and I can't let that stand. It would be dangerous for you and dangerous for me. But maybe a hell of a lot more dangerous for you."

"How so?" Warner felt a chill of bad feeling easing over him.

Vaughn cleared his throat again. "One thing . . . one thing I got to ask of you . . ."

"What would that be?"

"I . . . I got to ask that you keep what I'm gonna tell you under your hat. Wilson, I'd appreciate it if you'd do the same. I'm telling you both together because I know Wilson is probably going to help you, Mr. Grayson, so he needs to know also. But I can't have this put about."

Warner said, "I don't see how I can promise not to reveal something that I don't know anything about."

Wilson Young said, "Let it alone, Warner. If Austin says it's worth keeping mum about, he's got his reasons and they're good with me."

Warner nodded. "All right, Austin, tell away."

Vaughn nodded slowly. "I led you to believe that me and Preston and some hired guns fought off Fisher and caused him to give us a good letting-alone." He looked down at his hands. "That ain't the truth of the matter."

Warner said, "I don't understand. Did you fight him or not? I heard you killed or wounded half

194

a dozen of his people and ended up with their horses. You didn't deny that."

Vaughn nodded slowly. "That part is true. We did give them a fight at first, but it was mostly me and Pres done the fighting. My hired guns made sure they never come much in harm's way. That part ain't a lie."

"Then I don't understand what you're saying."

"Hush, Warner," Wilson said, "I think Austin is fixing to tell you that that was just the beginning to the fight."

Vaughn nodded. "There wasn't no more fight. Wilson had warned me you couldn't depend on hired guns, that they was about as loyal as a greenback dollar. He was dead right. Didn't take Jack Fisher long to either pay off them so-called gunfighters or to persuade them in some other way that they had more important business elsewhere. Hell, some of them still owed me time."

Wilson said to Warner, "A hired gun usually takes his money by the day, his profession being what it is."

Vaughn said, "And I'd paid some of them in the morning, depending on the time of their shift, and then didn't have to worry about feeding them lunch because they'd lit a shuck." His face got dark. One second he was sitting there calmly, and then the blood rushed to his face and Warner could see anger pass through the man as clearly

195

as if it were written out on his forehead. Vaughn said, "I should have killed the son of a bitch the one and only chance I had."

Wilson said, "I doubt that Fisher was alone, Austin."

Vaughn glanced at him and said grimly, "Not that bastard. Of course, his men would have killed me, but at least I'd've rid the land of that rat."

Warner said, "You have still got me confused, Austin. You appear to be rid of him."

Vaughn smiled faintly with no humor. "Yes, like a dead man is rid of his coffin." He looked straight at Warner. "As bad as this hurts me to say, I've got to tell you. I now have Jack Fisher for a partner. That was his price to leave us be. At least for now."

Warner was shocked. He pulled his head back. "What! Your partner?"

"Well, he's not a full partner yet. Right now he only takes a third of the profits. Next year he'll get forty percent. Year after that is when we become fifty-fifty partners. He kindly said he realized I needed some working capital, me being a new enterprise and all." His face flushed again, and he looked down at the table. Under his breath Warner could hear him mutter, "Goddammit, goddammit, goddammit to hell."

It was clear now to Warner why the Vaughns had been so evasive. They'd had to be. He wouldn't have wanted to admit such a thing himself. He said as much to Austin Vaughn, adding, "You had me puzzled at first, but now I understand. I wouldn't mention it around either."

Vaughn looked up at him. "It ain't just me who wants to keep this quiet. It's Fisher, too. For whatever reason he don't want the truth to get around. Can't say as I understand his reasons, but if we talk about it, the deal is off."

Wilson said softly, "I reckon it's because he's working the same proposition at other operations. So I reckon Fisher don't want to be going at a man who knows going in that he can't win. If he did that, his target would just throw up his hands and walk away. I wouldn't be surprised to hear that Fisher is a part owner of half the ranches in this part of the state. He is a slick son of a bitch. No wonder he can afford to meet the payroll he's got."

Vaughn said, "Me and Pres figured it was something like that. So you can see why I'm anxious that you not speak of this matter other than between yourselves."

Warner said, "There's no need for us to speak of it. But it does send me back to the barn to try and figure which way I'm headed." He looked over at Wilson Young. "The gunfighters was all I could think of."

Austin Vaughn said, "My experience ought to warn you off that. Wilson tried to tell me."

"He's said the same to me."

They both looked at Young. He shrugged. "I know the breed."

"Having been one," Warner said.

Wilson smiled slightly and said, "Care to step out in the street and make that remark, stranger?"

Warner might have laughed, but he was too troubled. He said, "Well, Austin, I am sorry for your trouble. I wish I could help."

"I'm sorry I didn't see fit to tell you the truth the other day. I reckon we puzzled you the way we was dodging around."

Warner sighed and shook his head. "No help from the law. Can't hire help. The gunhands know Jack Fisher better than we do and would a hell of a lot sooner stay on his good side than ours."

"That's the truth."

Warner looked around the table. "So what's to be done? Austin, I think you're delaying the inevitable. Fisher takes a third of your profits now, and he'll take more in future. How long before he takes the whole place?"

Vaughn said bitterly, "Oh, he won't do that. He needs somebody to operate the business."

"You are a sharecropper on your own land."

"And you might well be, too, if something isn't done."

Warner said, with an edge, "*I* will kill the son of a bitch before he gets his hands on my stock."

Vaughn said, "You'd see your animals shot?"

"If it come to it."

Wilson said, "Both of you, cool down. Austin, I know how hard it was for you to come in here and tell us this. It puts a whole new complexion on my thinking. Jack Fisher is a different man than I had him pegged for. I got to put on my thinking cap over this matter."

Vaughn said, looking at Warner, "Pres and I are agreed that if there is any way we can work together on this matter we are in whole hog. I'm hemmed in right now, but I'll eat dirt before I pay that robber another cent. And I got a payment coming in season in less than a month."

Wilson said, "Hell, does he have a bookkeeper? I should have thought of that when I was robbing banks. Might be a little more flush now."

Austin Vaughn stood up. "I've got to be getting back now. Deal with the devil, you don't like to stray too far from home." He shook hands with Warner. "Sorry I nearly done you harm."

"I thank you for what you did do. But don't give up. There has to be a way."

Wilson said, "I'm glad to hear about those hired guns. I was starting to doubt my own judgment, and that ain't good for a man who owns a whorehouse and a gambling casino. Either one of them concerns calls for a considerable amount of sagacity."

They left Vaughn outside of the hotel and

walked across the busy street toward Wilson's saloon. Warner said, "That poor son of a bitch. He has got himself in a bog."

Wilson stopped to light a small cigar. He looked up and said, "Him? What, you reckon yourself to be on a different side of the fence?"

Warner shook his head. "No. Actually, I'm more worried now than I was. The only difference between him and me is I don't have a family. Something was to go dead down with my ranch, I could always go back to handling other folks' horses. Lord knows I did it long enough."

They went into the dark, cool saloon. Wilson led the way toward his table in the back. "Let's have that first drink of the day."

Following him, Warner said, "I bet Laura is mad as hell, me walking out not telling her where I was going. Wonder where she is?"

"Likely still sleeping—it's a little after nine— or primping, most likely. She'll be down soon enough for a good all-day fight. Sometimes I think I ought to fix it up where I can sell tickets when ya'll get into it."

The daytime bartender brought them over a bottle of Wilson's special brand of brandy and two glasses. They poured out and then knocked them back and said "Luck," as befitted the toast.

After a moment Warner said, "Why can't we trap the son of a bitch?"

"How?"

"Vaughn refuses to pay. And then the four of us—no, Chulo would make five. I think the five of us could give him such a licking that he'd figure it was worth his while to leave Vaughn and me alone."

Wilson took a sip of his drink. He said, "You planning on sending him an invitation naming date and time?"

"What are you talking about?"

"Hell, Fisher isn't going to come when you expect him. We could sit out at Vaughn's ranch for a month while he watched us—watched us and maybe killed a few high-priced cows for recreation. What's the matter with you, Warner? Ain't you got no horse sense? You of all people. I done told you that Fisher ain't going to dance to your tune. You want him to do what you expect him to, but he is not going to do that. After all the meaness he's done, Fisher ain't stayed alive this long by being dumb."

"There's got to be a way to get at him."

"There is, but I ain't thought of it yet."

"What makes you think *I* won't? You ain't got no monopoly on thinking of the best way out of a tight spot."

"Maybe not, but I claim the experience."

"Well, yeah, I never robbed four or five hundred banks. I imagine that kind of activity might get you in a little hot water from time to time. But this is my knitting, and I'll tend to it."

201

"A minute ago you had me and Chulo in *your* gunfight. It's your knitting, but *our* gunfight. That it?"

Warner threw back his head and drained his glass. He said, "You know what I mean, Wilson. I got to quit hanging around you. I'm starting to like this damned brandy. I better go up and try and make a little peace with the widow Pico."

"Don't get so tangled up in that gown tail that I have to come up and cut you loose."

Warner gave him a sour look and started for the stairs. He halfway expected to find her still in bed, but the room was empty, as was the little dressing room. The scent of her perfume still lingered in the air, distinguishable from the other woman smells. Her valise lay open on a chair, and the traveling suit was still on the floor of the dressing room, and so was the dress she'd worn to dinner the night before. Warner stooped and picked them up and gave them a shaking-out and then folded them and laid them on a chair. He was not by nature an overly neat man, but Laura was casually messy. She said that when she was a girl growing up in Virginia there'd always been a servant to pick up her clothes, so she'd gotten into the habit of letting them lie where they fell, and she'd never bothered to change. As far as Warner was concerned her messy habits went with her messy way of thinking.

He went down to the big bathroom and knocked

on the door, thinking she might be taking a bath or whatever. A woman's voice answered, but it wasn't Laura's. He went back to the room and looked about, perplexed. Since he didn't know what she'd brought in her valise, he couldn't know what she was wearing, but there was only one blouse and skirt left, along with some underwear and toilet articles. He scratched the back of his head, wondering where she could have gotten off to. It was possible they'd missed her if she'd crossed the street to the hotel dining room for breakfast, but it was slim odds.

He went back downstairs and found Wilson still at his table. Warner took a chair and told him that Laura was nowhere around.

"Hell, she'd don't need your leave to come and go," Wilson said. "Likely she's out having breakfast or maybe shopping. Who knows what gets up in a woman's mind? More than one man has lost his mind trying to think like a woman. It's a dangerous practice, kid, and no mistake. Take a drink. She'll be along."

Wilson got up to attend to a matter every so often, but Warner sat watching the front door and the stairs for the next two hours. There was no sign of Laura. At a quarter of one Warner said, "Wilson, we got to go find her. She ain't got no business wandering around a town like Del Rio on her lonesome."

Wilson said, "Let me go upstairs and ask some

of the girls if they've seen her. They ought to be good and awake by now. You know, we got a kitchen up there for their use. Laura and them might be fixing something to eat."

"Laura and a bunch of *putas*? You're crazy."

Wilson said dryly, "Laura might be a lot of things, but she ain't no high-hat, kid. I don't reckon she would hold herself above these working girls."

Warner touched the side of his face where Laura had slapped him. "Then go right ahead and ask the girls. I doubt you will find her having tea with them."

While Wilson was gone, Warner got a drink of corn whiskey and thought about his situation. It was clear that he was going to contact Jack Fisher in some way and find out exactly what he wanted. Hamm had talked about a horse race, but after hearing what Austin Vaughn had had to say, Warner doubted that was what the man really wanted. It might be the opening bid in a complicated card game, but there was a good deal more at stake than appeared in the pot. Warner didn't know much, but he knew for certain he wasn't going to have Jack Fisher for any kind of partner.

Wilson was gone long enough that Warner got anxious. The bar was beginning to do some business, and more than one man came up and asked him if he knew where Wilson was. He answered that he expected him at any time, but it was another fifteen minutes before his friend came back.

Warner said, "Well?"

Wilson had a curious look on his face, as if he didn't quite know what to think. He said, "One of the girls saw Laura going out this morning. She thinks it was eight or eight-thirty, about the time we were at the hotel having breakfast with Austin." He was still standing up, looking at the door. He patted Warner on the shoulder. "Listen, you set here and let me go see about something. I ought not to be gone too long, and then we'll go have some lunch."

"Where you headed?"

Wilson hesitated. Warner could see concern on his face. Wilson said, "Oh, just out. I got an idea. Let me see about it."

"Couple of men at the bar want to see you."

Wilson glanced their way and half smiled. "Yeah, I know what they want. Credit." He patted Warner's shoulder again. "Just set steady. I won't be a half an hour."

Wilson was gone a little longer than he said. He signaled Warner from the door of the saloon. Warner got up and joined him on the street and said, "Well?"

"Well? A well is a hole in the ground."

"Yeah, turn it sideways and you got a tunnel. What happened?"

205

"Nothing happened. Let's go down to La Cocina and eat some grease."

They made a meal of tamales and enchiladas and chili with guacamole salad and beer. Wilson Young was unusually quiet while they ate. Warner asked him if he'd found out anything about Laura or if he'd seen her.

Wilson said, "What makes you think I went looking for Laura?"

"I don't know. But I figure to get on back to the hotel. She's been gone a hell of a long time."

"Don't worry about it. Eat up. I got something I want to show ya'll about that room you're staying in, where me and Evita usually bunk."

"What?"

"Hell, didn't I say I wanted to show you? Finish up that chili and let's go."

Wilson was quiet on the walk back to his place. They went up the stairs and into the room. Warner said, "What the hell is going on, Wilson?"

Wilson Young had shut the door and was standing in front of it. He said, "Take a seat. I need to tell you something."

Warner sat down, his heart suddenly beating wildly. "Then tell me, dammit! You been mysterious as hell the last hour."

"I went down to the depot. The ticket agent and the telegrapher are friends of mine."

"So?"

Wilson heaved a sigh and said, "Laura sent

Jack Fisher a telegram this morning care of his ranch, informing him she was on her way to meet him and that her business was important."

Warner slowly stood up.

"She caught the nine-thirty train that stops at Uvalde. It makes a connection there with a train that'll get her into Cotulla about two this afternoon. Except the telegrapher told her that Fisher has got a siding at his place about fifteen miles this side of Cotulla. She took a ticket for there and asked Fisher to have someone meet her."

"That's enough," Warner said. He started toward the door. "That goddam harebrained woman is determined to get us both killed. Well, she might have succeeded this time."

Wilson put out his hands as Warner grabbed him by the shoulders. "Hold it right there, Warner."

"Get the hell out of the way, Wilson."

"Go sit back down! I mean it! I'm not going to let you do anything more stupid than usual. Not if I can help it."

"Goddammit, Wilson, you better get out of my way. I'll put you aside if you make me!"

Wilson pushed him back a half a step. "There's not a damn thing you can do. I knew you was going to act like this. That's why I brought you up here. Now I want you to listen to me!"

Warner had not raised his hands to push Wilson

away from the door, but he was about to. He said, "You got about ten seconds,"

"She bought a round-trip ticket. If all goes well, she'll be back here on the midnight train."

Warner said, "Yeah, if all goes well. Listen, are you crazy? Don't you realize that idiot woman has gone to see Jack Fisher? God alone knows what could happen to her. I got to get there as fast as I can."

Wilson said, "If anything is going to happen to her you can't get there in time." He took a tighter grip of Warner's shoulders. "The last train that would have connected to Cotulla left while you were having lunch."

Warner stared at him for a full half a minute, the shock evident on his face. He said, "And you knew it! You kept me from following her on purpose!" The color drained from his face. "You son of a bitch!" He swung his right hand toward Wilson's face, shifting his feet to get his shoulder behind the punch.

8

Because Wilson had his arms up, gripping Warner by the shoulders, he was able to partially block the short, powerful punch that Warner threw. Still, it knocked him back against the door, and the force of the blow made him think his cheekbone had been broken. But instead of trying to step clear of Warner, he lunged forward, smothering him with his arms and pressing in close to Warner. When he could, Wilson got the wildly flailing horse trainer in a bear grip and wrestled him to the floor. Warner was still swinging with his right fist, catching Wilson in the back and the kidneys. They rolled back and forth on the floor, both yelling and swearing. Finally Wilson broke away and jumped to his feet. His gun was suddenly in his hand, and he held it threateningly over Warner's head. Heaving great breaths, he said, "Damn you, Warner, you crazy son of a bitch, I ought . . . ought to . . . to break this gun over your fucking head, and if you get up, I will!" Wilson stood over him, panting for a moment. Finally he slowly returned his revolver to its holster.

Warner rolled to a sitting position. He said, "You son of a bitch, where you get off making decisions about my woman? That ain't for you—"

"Oh, so now she's your woman!"

"Well, you ain't got no right to be making them kind of decisions for me."

Wilson reached up and touched his right cheek and winced slightly. He said, "You bastard, you would have knocked my head off if I hadn't got an arm in the way."

Warner said sulkily, "Well, it was no more than you deserved."

"Bastard. Next time I do you a favor I'm going to leave town. You could have listened before you lost your head. Where did you get that temper, anyway? I never seen you act like a schoolboy before."

Warner got up slowly, flexing his right arm at the elbow. "Did you feel it necessary to bang my arm against the floor? My right arm? I swear, I never thought I'd see the day Wilson Young was wrestling around on the floor like some barroom thug. Shit!" He turned around to the bedside table and poured them both a glass of brandy. As he handed Wilson Young his, Warner said, "I suppose you got some explanation for your meatheaded thinking, why you wouldn't tell me in time to go after Laura."

Wilson took his glass and sipped at it. "Of course I've got a reason. You ever known me to do something without I had a reason to? No, you haven't. But did that keep you from trying to knock my head off? Hell, no! Warner, you want to get something done about that temper of yours. You need to put a lip twitch or a martingale at least on it."

"You could've opened your mouth and said something."

"When'd I get a chance before you started playing recess in the second grade?"

"You ain't got no reason." Warner finished his drink and then reached out with the bottle and filled Wilson's glass and then his. "That's your problem."

"Yeah, shore. Listen, you jughead, if you'd've made that train, that *last* train, you'd've been four or five or even more hours behind Laura, depending on the connection out of Uvalde. If anything bad was going to happen to her, you would have been too late to stop it. And then I would have had two of you to go and try and pry loose from Jack Fisher. I know you think you can whip the Gulf of Mexico, including all the sharks swimming in it, but Fisher has got maybe two dozen or more gunhands, and you couldn't have done nothing. Plus, I don't think Laura's in any danger. Like I said, though I doubt you heard me, she's got a return ticket puts her back in here at midnight. Before we go to getting all bent out of shape, let's wait and see what happens. *Comprende*?"

Warner heard him out, sipping his brandy, and then turned and looked out the window at the busy street below. Finally, grudgingly, he said, "Maybe you're right."

"No maybe about it. You couldn't have done a goddam thing except get yourself killed."

Warner heaved a great sigh. After a second he said, "Well, all right. Okay, I can see your point. But I still don't like it, because you didn't tell me while there was still time and let me make up my own mind."

Wilson just stared at him for a moment. Then he said, "Yeah, sure, that's what I ought to have done. Think you were hard to hold in this room here, what chance would I have had out on the street?"

Warner looked up. "Well, the hell with you. I can be reasonable. I don't lose my temper."

"Yeah, I noticed that."

"Except with you, you sorry bastard. I swear, Wilson, you could try the patience of a Baptist preacher. You always got to be managing affairs, don't you? Goddammit, and now Laura has got herself into God only knows what."

Wilson said, "I wouldn't sell that lady short. Fisher ain't got no reason to harm her."

"He could hold her hostage."

"Hold *her?* Hell, he's already holding your ranch and your breeding stock hostage. He don't need no more to hang over you head. Besides, he don't know how it is between you two."

"What do you mean by that? She's my backer, a part-time partner."

"Oh, yeah. That's all she is. And *I'm* a Baptist preacher."

Warner looked down and didn't say anything. Then he looked back out the window. He said, "I hope she didn't wear one of them dresses she puts on when she wants her way."

Wilson smiled slightly. "Listen, Warner, the widow Pico is a hell of a poker player. She's better than you are. If it come down to making a trade between your outfit and Fisher's she'd be the one I'd want in the saddle."

"Hell, she's just a woman!"

"Only at times. Other times she might be tougher than me and you put together."

Warner set his glass down and grimaced. "Well, there's nothing we can do until midnight. Let's go see what's going on in town."

But going down the stairs Warner said, "I wish the town, the whole town, could have seen the fierce pistolero Wilson Young rolling around on the floor like an eight-year-old. Hell, how come you didn't stand up and fight back? Give me a chance to get a solid lick in on you?"

Wilson touched his cheekbone again. "Because I wanted to talk, not fight. I had things to tell you. If you'd've listened to me first, there wouldn't have never been no blows thrown. Only thing I could do was grab you. Why didn't you try and

213

get up so I could have crowned you with my pistol barrel?"

"Is that the way you treat your friends? Pull a gun on them?"

As they hit the saloon Wilson said, "I can promise you one thing, kiddo, I'm going to catch you looking yonder before long, and I'm going to coldcock you from the blind side and put a bruise on you like this one that I feel rising up on my cheekbone. I think you have done me permanent damage. You ain't big enough to hit that hard."

"How we going to kill this time? We can't get drunk."

"Let's go across the river. I got a horse I want you to look at."

Warner followed his friend out the door with a dour look on his face. He said, "Damn that woman. She don't ground-rein worth a damn. I wish somebody would explain why you can get a horse to stand still, but you can't a woman to do it. I'd like, just once, to set her down someplace and have her right there when I got back ten minutes later."

"Ain't gonna be. Not with that filly. You ain't even got her halter-broke and you expect her to ground-rein? Hell."

She wasn't the last person off the train, but it seemed to Warner that she was. He'd been holding his breath for what felt like the last six hours, his heart racing, imagining every bad thing that could happen to her. And now here she finally was. Before she got both feet on the ground, he stepped forward and took her firmly by the arm. She didn't even look to see that it was him, only said in a weary, breathless voice, "Warner honey, I know you are angry. I know I did something you didn't want me to do. And I know I'm going to hear about it. But, please, let it wait until morning. I'm dead tired, and I'm filthy. I want a bath and something to eat, and then I want to go to bed. Please let it wait until morning and then you can beat me if you want to."

He closed his mouth on the hot words he was about to say and shifted his hand from her arm to around her shoulders and started walking her off the passenger platform toward the street.

Over her head Warner could see Wilson Young, who'd heard the whole thing, giving him a sly grin that said, "See? You ain't going to win no matter what you do. She will outsmart you at every turn."

They didn't try to talk to her that night. Instead, while she took a bath, Wilson sent down to an all-night café for a meal, and they sat and watched while she fought to stay awake long enough to eat most of the steak Wilson had ordered. She was dressed in a quilted blue robe of demure enough cut that Warner didn't mind Wilson being in the room. But when it became evident she would be asleep before she could finish a cup of coffee, Wilson got up and left them to it. All she said about Jack Fisher was that he was tiny. "Little-bitty man. Struts around like Napoleon, though I doubt if he knows who Napoleon is. And what a dandy! Dressed to the nines. Black suit with a vest and a string tie and a huge white Stetson hat. Silly-looking little bastard. Tried to act courtly and only looked foolish.

"Expected me to be impressed with him. Wanted to show me his empire. And he actually called it that. I told him I was there to talk serious business, not to compare horses."

Her speech got slower and slower as she tried to finish her meal. Before Warner undressed her and put her to bed she said, "Evil little bastard, Warner. No morals. Don't bother to look for morals. Has none. Do not trust him. Evil. No morals."

She went to sleep still talking. One second she was lying under the covers with her eyes closed and her mouth talking, and the next she was asleep. Warner pulled up a chair by the bed and got the bottle of brandy and a glass to have one last drink to try and cool out and relax from all the tension of waiting. He looked at her blond hair against the white pillowcase and slowly shook his head. He was getting too damn fond of the woman. Way too fond. He looked at her lying in the bed and thought how beautiful she was.

She was getting dangerous, but it was too late for him to get shut of her. He was hemmed in and penned fair and square, and he knew he might as well get ready to take the grief she was going to deal him. But he was damned if he would ever let her know how he felt. He was damned if she would ever be allowed to feel cocky where he was concerned. He might not be as devious as she was, but he was just as tough.

He finished his drink, put out his cigar, and then undressed and crawled in beside her, pulling her sleek body over next to his. She made a little moaning noise, but then resumed her regular breathing.

Warner was up and gone by the time Laura awakened, but he waited for her in the hotel dining room, his breakfast finished, a cup of coffee in front of him. Wilson had finished and left. When Laura came in, she sat down next to him and put out her hand to take his, but he moved his hand, putting it in his lap.

She said, "Oh, it's going to be like that."

"Naw," he said, "I always like to be treated like you done me. I love it. Run off again like that sometime and see what you get. You'll get your horses tied out front of your house in Corpus Christi and a good look at the back of me."

She sighed, "I knew this was going to happen. So go ahead and get it all said. Don't drag it out.

217

I'd rather you say everything you have to say about how dumb and risky and womanish my behavior was. Say it all—that I'm just a fool woman, incapable of any intelligence or strategy, but there, I'm saying your words. Get it off your chest so I can finally tell you what I did and why."

He folded his arms and said stolidly, "I don't have a word to say."

And he left it that way until they assembled at Wilson's table on the raised platform at the back of his saloon. She was wearing the yellow frock with the square-cut bodice that she knew he liked. He figured she was wearing it with a purpose. That was one thing he could say for her: she never did much without a purpose.

She said, "That little bastard Jack Fisher thinks he's a genius because he's still alive. Well, actually, I didn't feel like I could argue that point with a toad like him."

Warner said, "What in hell come over you to do something that damn fool crazy?"

She said to Wilson, "Why didn't you tell me how little Fisher was? Struts around like a banty rooster. Hell, his hat is bigger than he is."

Warner, his voice controlled, said, "I'm still waiting to hear why you done what you did."

Still talking to Wilson she said, "He's got a big frame house. Not as big as my house in Corpus, but a great deal bigger than he needs. And made out of lumber and painted white. You never saw anything so silly. Sticks up out there on that brown prairie like a snowman or something. Not a tree in sight, and his house is made out of lumber. And so is his barn. He wanted to show me around 'Fisher County,' as he calls it. I told him I'd been on a ranch before and let's get down to business."

"I'm going to ask you one more time why you did it," Warner said, "and I reckon you had better answer me."

She said to Wilson, "Do you know, the little bastard tried to flirt with me? My God, he doesn't come up to my chin even in his high-heeled boots."

"Last chance."

She came around on Warner. "Last chance for what? To get told off? To get fussed at? To be embarrassed? To be told I stuck my nose in where it wasn't wanted? I already gave you that chance, and you didn't take it. Just folded your arms. How come you are so interested now? Because you've got an audience?"

Wilson said mildly, "Would you not pull out the knives before we get the whole story here?"

Warner sat back in his chair, his right hand twisting his whiskey glass around and around on the tabletop. "I'm trying to get a simple answer to a simple question," he said. "Why in hell did she do it? What possessed her?"

Wilson said, "All right. I feel like the fellow

standing by the fight holding the coats, but, Laura, that is a fair question. I'm a little curious myself."

She said, looking fiercely at Warner, "I did it because somebody had to find out what Fisher wanted. You couldn't go, Wilson, because you didn't want him to find out you were in with Warner. Warner couldn't go for obvious reasons. We couldn't sit back and await Fisher's pleasure. So I went. Who better than a woman? Women haven't got any sense, you know. I wouldn't be a threat to him, and he could brag to me. He could talk to me without getting his hackles up. A big-time outlaw like him wasn't going to hurt some little weak woman. So I went." She gave Warner one last defiant look and turned to Wilson. "And I think it worked."

Wilson nodded slowly, "That's about what I figured. A man like Fisher, compounded of pure conceit and vanity, would overload his mouth around a woman, even a woman who was involved. Especially if he could see she was a lady. Makes sense to me, Laura. I think it was a good idea."

Warner said, "Well, I won't wear it."

Wilson said, "Why not? What's wrong with what she done?"

Laura said to Warner, "Of course not. You couldn't. I did something on my own. I didn't ask the boss, who would have said no in the first place and the second place and the third place. Am I saying the words right, Warner? Am I leaving anything out?"

Wilson Young suddenly stood up. "I can see this ain't going nowhere until ya'll get matters settled between yourselves. I'll go over here to the bar and leave you to it. If you come to any sort of settlement that both of ya'll can wear, as Warner says, then give me a signal and I'll get on back and see where we are."

When he was gone, they both sat silent, staring off in their own direction. Warner kept his jaws firmly clamped together. A long moment passed and then another. Finally she said, "I can see you are not going to speak, that your pride won't let you. All right, I will. I'm sorry. It was a foolhardy thing to do. Warner, please don't be so angry at me. I did it for us."

It took another moment but he finally said, "You scared the hell out of me." He turned his head slowly so he could see her eyes. "I don't reckon I've ever been so scared before in my life. Waiting on you to get back was the longest day I ever spent."

She put her hand on his. "I'm sorry."

"You remember telling me that if I got cut you bled?"

"Yes."

"Then you ought to have understood what running off like that would do to me."

221

She squeezed his hand. "I knew what I was doing, Warner, and it scared me to do it. Oh, Fisher never worried me. I knew I could handle him. No, I was afraid what would happen when I got back. If I swear I will never do it again, will you forgive me?"

A faint smile tugged at the corner of his mouth. "What do you want to start making promises you know you can't keep for?"

She smiled and squeezed his hand harder. "Will you forgive me?"

"Do I have a choice?"

"I guess you'd get upset if I were to kiss you in here."

He looked quickly back toward the bar. He said, "You're damn right I would. You just save that stuff for privacy."

"Did you make love to me after we went to bed last night? Not that I remember going to bed."

"Of course not. You were asleep even before I could get you undressed."

She smiled slightly. "I guess I dreamed it, then. I know that was all I thought about on that long, long train ride back—you and me in bed."

Warner reddened slightly. "Laura, for God's sake . . . I better get Wilson back over here." He turned and waved until his friend saw the signal.

She described being picked up at the siding by a man in a buckboard. "I had to ride five miles going and coming through a dust storm," she said. "I don't think I'm ever going to feel clean again." And she told them about her reception by Jack Fisher and the subsequent difficulty she had bringing him around to the reason for her visit. Then, finally, Laura told them what Fisher wanted. She looked at Warner and said, "He wants to run you three horse races to settle who is the best horse breeder around. Warner, he doesn't like you."

Wilson said, "He doesn't like anybody. What he doesn't like about Warner is his good reputation. Sounds like he's acting not so much out of a desire for gain as out of pride."

Laura said, "Oh, I wouldn't say that. There are the stakes."

"What are the stakes?"

She had finally consented to having a glass of wine, and she took a sip. "Warner is to put up all his studs, including the Andalusians."

Warner laughed. "That man has been eating locoweed. I wouldn't bet all my breeding stock on the sun coming up in the morning."

Laura looked at him. "He said you could bet the stallions or watch them rot."

Wilson said, "Yeah, that would be something Jack Fisher would say."

"And what is *he* putting up?" Warner said.

Laura looked up at the ceiling. "All our studs, including the Andalusians."

"What? Why that's crazy."

Wilson said, "No, that's Fisher. Let me see if I got it right, Laura. If Warner loses, he loses his breeding stock. If he wins he gets to keep them."

"That's about it."

Warner said, "But I don't even own those Andalusians, except the one."

"Paseta. Yes, I told him that. He said it didn't make him any difference, that we were an outfit and he was betting against the outfit. I offered to put up ten thousand dollars in lieu of the Andalusians, but he just laughed at me."

Warner turned to Wilson, confusion on his face. "What kind of thinking is that? Those Andalusians aren't even worth ten thousand dollars."

Wilson took his cigar out of his mouth. "I done told you—Fisher's after your reputation."

"But why involve Laura? She told him those were her horses."

"Because she's part of your outfit."

"It still don't make no sense. Not unless . . ." He turned to Laura. "You didn't let on that . . . that there might be, you know, anything between us?"

"Warner, give me some credit. I went out of my way to make him think I didn't much like you. I even went so far as to say I'd move the Andalusians, take them away from you, entrust them to another breeder."

"What'd he say to that?"

224

Her eyes took on a glint, a shininess he recognized as a sign of anger. "He told me it wouldn't make no difference. I couldn't move them alive. He very distinctly gave me the impression that he's having the ranch watched."

Warner just shook his head. "The son of a bitch is crazy. What makes him so all-fired sure he can beat me? I don't think he can. What if I win?"

Laura reached out and touched Warner's cheek. "I think I can answer that. He said if you win, you lose."

Warner looked at her and then at Wilson. "Does that mean what I think it does?"

Wilson nodded over his cigar. "I would imagine so. He's saying that if you want to live, you better let him prove he's the better horse breeder."

Warner sat there for a moment, looking bewildered. Then he suddenly slammed his fist on the tabletop, making the glasses jump. "This is the craziest goddam proposition I have ever heard of! Am I dreaming? Can such goings-on happen in this day and time? This sounds like something out of one of my grandfather's books, something back in the old days when they had knights and earls and kings who could do anything they wanted. Where the hell is the law?"

"Where he lives, the law is in his pocket," Wilson said. "Local law from Corpus Christi ain't got no jurisdiction there. And you can be sure that if Fisher kills you, it will be where circumstances are friendly. 'Course, so far as shooting your stock is concerned, well, that's a middle-of-the-night proposition, and he ain't going to have had nothing to do with it. You can't prove a damn one of his threats."

Warner turned and stared at Laura. "What are we going to do?"

The words made her eyes melt. He was actually including her in whatever plans they might make. She said, "Fisher wants to run three races. He is willing to run them at the race course here in Del Rio, the one at the fairgrounds outside of town."

"Makes sense," Wilson said. "He wants a big audience, and this is the biggest and best track in this part of the country. Even got a grandstand. Word gets out about match races between you two and every brush-track gambler within a hundred miles will be here."

Warner said to Laura, "What are the terms of the race? What distance?"

"The first race is to be a quarter mile run in a straight line."

"Makes sense," Wilson said again. "He's got good quarter horses."

Laura said, "The winner of the first race decides the length of the second race. And then that winner decides the distance for the third." She paused. "If there needs to be a third. It's the best

226

two out of three. He sent you word that you'd be smart to make it two races, that he didn't want to overtire his horses."

Warner shook his head as if he wasn't hearing right.

Laura said, "We're supposed to telegraph him today about the first race. We have to respond within the next four days. He was very emphatic about that. He says he won't be kept waiting around while you make up your mind, that he has other work for his men. He says four days will give you plenty of time to send for the horses you want to race." She put her hand on his. "Warner, he already knows you're here. He knew it from the first. I didn't tell him."

"Does he know about me and Wilson?"

"He didn't say. But we're going to have to send him a telegram soon."

"Hell!" Warner said. "And what do I say in the telegram? 'Why bother with the races? Just go ahead and shoot me because I am not going to lose on purpose'?"

Wilson laughed. "Yeah, wire him that."

Warner pulled a face at him. "You think it's funny?"

Wilson said, "I think the man has made a serious mistake."

"Oh? What?"

Wilson took his cigar out of his mouth. "Racing down here. I think you can beat him. And he

227

can't do a thing in this territory, this county. The law don't think much of him here."

"Oh," Warner said, "so I win and he kills me someplace else. Is that it?"

Wilson raised his eyebrows. "Why don't we take one thing at a time. Once we get Jack Fisher down here, off his range, who is to say what might happen to him?"

"Hell, he'll show up with thirty gunhands surrounding him. You think he'll expose himself? I don't. I don't think he'd race here if he thought it would be dangerous for him."

"You never know," Wilson said. "Sometimes a man can get so cocky he forgets to look where he's walking and steps off a cliff. No, I think our good friend Fisher is getting a little too big for his britches. But, as I said, let's take one step at a time. Wire him you'll race him four days from now. That would be the eighth, if I know what day it is. Then you'll run the second race the next day."

Warner said, "He might win that first race, but he'll never win the second."

"Why not?"

"Because it's going to be a ten-mile race, and he hasn't got and can't get a horse that can stay up with an Andalusian for ten miles. Nobody else has either."

Laura said hesitantly, "But, Warner, you've got to win the first race to get to choose the distance for the second."

228

Warner slapped the table with his hand. He grimaced. "Dammit! I forgot about that. Well, we don't agree to those terms. Loser picks."

Wilson said, "He won't go along with that."

Warner let out a breath and sat back in his chair. "I'd cuss if I thought it would do any good." He looked at Wilson. "You don't by any chance have a hell of a running quarter horse, do you? One I don't know about?"

Wilson shook his head. "Every head of running stock I've got I've got from you, and you know I've been breeding up for longer races."

Laura said, "It wouldn't make any difference. Fisher says you have to show proof you've owned the horses you're going to race for at least sixty days. He says that is to stop you from going out and buying another man's runner and passing him off as one of your own breeding."

Warner's face went red. "Why that son of a bitch! For that insult alone I'd kill the bastard. Damn!"

They were all quiet for a moment, and then Laura said, "So what are we going to do?"

Warner shrugged. "Send Fisher a telegram and go to thinking. Then I guess we wire Charlie and have him bring me some racing stock. Not that it will do much good. I don't actually have a quarter horse on the ranch that is racing quality. I never bred for that. So Fisher will win the first race and name the next distance as the same quarter of a mile."

Wilson said, "That choice ought to be negotiable. Say you can't run two races in a row the same distance. Or even close. Second race has to be a half mile at least. But we'll wait until he arrives to argue that."

Warner said, "I guess I'll send for your black Thoroughbred, though I have little hope Fisher'll run a distance that that horse is bred for. He's not going to be willing to run a mile." He sat back, drumming his fingers on the table, shaking his head. "I never run into a deal like this before. I doubt if anybody else has, either."

Wilson got up. "Well," he said, "I don't see it is going to do us any good to sit around like this. We got to split up and go freshen our brains a little. I wish Evita was here; she always makes my brains fresh."

"Yeah," Warner said. He looked at Laura and smiled wanly. "You sure picked a hell of a partner."

Wilson said, "Don't go to feeling sorry for yourself yet. You better go send off your telegrams. I guess you know what you want Charlie to bring. Not that it's going to make a difference. Fisher has already got that part rigged. We got to figure us out his weak spot."

Warner said, an edge in his voice to show he was more than a little serious, "How about if I just shoot the bastard on sight. Or during the race."

Laura said, "I forgot about that. He'll ride his racehorse, and you'll ride yours."

Warner just made a wry face and looked at Wilson. "What does Fisher weigh? One thirty? One forty?"

"Maybe not that much."

"So I'll be spotting him forty pounds. Maybe more."

Wilson said, "I've still got that Mexican calvary officer's saddle. That thing don't weigh no more than a set of lady's underwear. And you can bet that Fisher will be using a big range saddle. You might get a few pounds back that way."

Warner stood up. "Hell with it. C'mon, Laura, let's go to the telegraph office. I'm worn out, and it ain't even noon."

That night Warner and Laura were lying side by side in the bed staring up at the ceiling. The air was warm enough that they didn't need anything covering them but a sheet. In the darkened room Laura said, "Goddam, I hate this horrible country." She turned her face until her lips were only a few inches from Warner's ear. She said, "Warner?"

"What?"

"Let's move. Let's get the stud stock out and ship them to Virginia. We can move the rest later. We'll go to Virginia and buy a ranch. You can breed Andalusians to Thoroughbred racing mares."

231

Warner rose up and leaned on his elbow until he could see down into her eyes. "You want to cross an Andalusian with a bluegrass Thoroughbred?"

"Yes, why not?"

"Because you'd either have a real slow racehorse with a hell of a lot of endurance or a faster Andalusian that couldn't last more than five miles. Be like breeding me to you—you'd end up with an ugly know-it-all."

She tried to punch him in the belly, but he caught her arm. "I am not a know-it-all," she said.

"I didn't say you were."

"Ugly? Are you calling me ugly? Listen, mister!"

She whirled on him, all flailing arms and legs and nipping teeth. He was laughing so hard he could barely defend himself. But then, he wasn't trying very hard.

After a time, after they were both spent and were lying quietly again, she said, her head on his chest, "Honey? Is everything going to be all right? Will this work out some way?"

He sighed. "It has to, Laura."

She said, "I feel just like I did when the Mexican bandits were swooping down on us and that fool Pico ran out into the open and got himself killed."

He found her hand. "This is not like that," he said. "I'm not Pico, and I'm not going to get killed. If anybody loses his life or his livestock, it will be Jack Fisher."

She squeezed his hand. "You sound so sure. I wish you really were."

"So do I," he said dryly.

And then, as they were both about to drop off to sleep, he said, "You done good." But he said it so softly that she didn't quite hear.

She raised her head. "What?"

He cleared his throat. "I said you done good. Going to see Fisher. It was a good idea. At least now we know what we're up against."

She lowered her head back onto his chest. "I am shocked. I never in all my days expected to hear you say such a thing."

"First time I've had a reason."

She dug her fingers into his groin until he let out a howl and swore he was just kidding. But not about her doing good. He'd meant that.

9

Warner stood staring at Charlie in disbelief. They were at the freight yards at the railroad depot. Other than bringing two riding horses for himself, all Charlie had brought in the way of racing stock was Wilson Young's black Thoroughbred. Warner said, "You just brought the black? Charlie, are you crazy? I told you to bring the two best quarter horses we had."

Charlie said, "You already *got* the two best quarter horses we have. That little gelding you brought with you? He's the fastest thing on the ranch."

"What are you talking about? That horse is as green as you are. He doesn't know anything about racing! Hell, Charlie, he's a soft three." Warner stared at his hired hand, shaking his head. "Charlie, this was no time to make a mistake. This is serious. Dead serious. Or have you forgot Mr. Hamm?"

"Boss, I'm telling you that quarter horse is the best we've got. First thing I noticed about him was his speed. Ain't you?"

Warner thought. He said, "I've never had no occasion to notice."

"Hell, he takes off like a scalded cat. I've matched him against everything on the ranch, and he's outrun every one of 'em up to a little over a quarter of a mile. The Andalusians will beat him at a half a mile, and of course he ain't going no further than that. But, boss, I don't think you know how fast that little horse is."

Warner stared at him. Charlie was nearly as good a hand with horses as he was, and if he said the little quarter horse was that fast he was that fast. "You may be betting the ranch on this, Charlie."

"Boss, I'm telling you I know what I'm talking about. You are letting his size fool you. Take a look at the hindquarters on him compared to the rest of his body. He could jump a six-foot fence from a standing start. I was meaning to tell you about him soon as I got him finished off, but then this other stuff come up and I never got around to mentioning it. I meant it for a surprise, because that little horse sure as hell surprised me."

Warner tried again to think back on his experience with the little quarter horse, but as far as he could recall, he had never had occasion to ask the horse for sustained speed. He said, "Well . . . I hope you are right."

Charlie said earnestly, "Way I figured it was you had the black for anything at a mile or over, and you got the best of the Andalusians right here in ol' Paseta for distances around a half a mile. And the only other thing we got for the quarter mile is that little button horse that I've trained. I figured I had you covered. I got the next best two quarter horses on the ranch right here, but Button has already beaten both of them."

Warner gave him a glance. "Have you started naming horses? Planning on making a pet out of that one? Let him eat sugar out of your palm?"

Charlie scuffed a boot in the dust. "Aw, Mr. Grayson, you are funnin' me. The name just popped in my head, an' I kept on thinkin' of him as that little button horse."

Wilson looked around. The train crew had all the horses unloaded. Warner said, "Well, the little button horse is at the hotel livery across from Wilson's saloon. We might as well get all the running stock gathered up over at Wilson's ranch across the river. He's got a couple of quarter horses I can test Button against."

Charlie shuffled his feet again. "Mr. Grayson, yore telegram never said what all this was about. Is it that Fisher fellow—the one that sent the man you kilt? The one that sent all them bad threats?"

Wilson said, "Charlie, don't you figure you got enough to do getting a young horse ready that's never raced before? You reckon you need to know everything?"

Charlie said, "I reckon I need to know if my job is ridin' in a horse race."

Warner looked at him, amazed. "You might be riding on smart talk if you've got anything more along that line you want to say."

Charlie blushed. "Mr. Grayson, I am right

sorry. That jest popped out. But you got to know that the rest of us been sitting back there at the ranch wondering our heads off about what is goin' on. We are pretty shore we have seen one or two strangers makin' regular visits to kind of look the place over long distance. I shore didn't mean no disrespect, sir."

Warner said, waving his hand, "Get moving, Charlie. If I had anything to tell you, I would. If you haven't had your breakfast, go ahead and get it. But then take the horses over to Wilson's as fast as you can. And I want you to limber up that little button horse, because I think we might test him this afternoon. See if what you say is true."

Charlie started nodding his head emphatically. "Mr. Grayson, I swear you are gonna be surprised. Unless something has overcome him since he left my care—"

"You mean unless I've ruined him."

Charlie looked horrified. "Mr. Grayson, I would never say a thang like that. I'd never even *thank* such a thang. Warner Grayson ruin a horse? At about the same time that Jack Fisher goes to heaven."

"All right, all right," Warner said, "I won't hold you accountable for a smart mouth. I guess it has been a chore for ya'll sitting back there at the ranch not knowing what was happening. But get moving now. We got less than three days until that little horse has got to earn his feed."

• • •

That afternoon Warner and Wilson Young were sitting in the shade on the front porch of Wilson's whitewashed adobe ranch house on the Mexican side of the border. Even though Wilson's pardon was clear and irrevocable, he said he still felt comfortable having a place in Mexico. They were drinking lime juice and water with a little tequila in it. Neither of them planned to do any heavy drinking in the immediate future.

They sat there looking out over the broad, flat pasture that ran by Wilson's barns and came up to the house. The grass was so cropped down by Wilson's cattle and horses that it was almost nonexistent. Earlier they had paced off four hundred forty strides and called it a quarter of a mile. Then Wilson had had his workers walk the straight stretch looking for holes, soft spots, rocks, and anything else that might hurt a horse. As they watched Charlie astride Button, two of Wilson's vaqueros rode out of the barn on Wilson's two best quarter horses and began to limber up the horses. Warner and Wilson watched, both of them instinctively casting a critical eye at the little horse Charlie was riding.

Wilson said, "Hell, Warner, he don't weigh over nine hundred and fifty pounds."

Warner took a drink of his fortified limeade. "I'd be surprised if he weighed that much. But Charlie's right. Look at the hindquarters on him in proportion to the rest of his body. He looks like he slants downward from back to front."

"I can't see how you'd have failed to notice if he had speed."

Warner looked over at the ex–bank robber. "I never ran him, Wilson. Is that a good enough reason, or am I supposed to tell how fast a horse is just by looking at his droppings?"

"To hear you tell it, you are."

Warner got up. "Let's go on down there. I don't want to get them too warm. Which horse you going to run against Charlie?"

"That blaze-face."

"You never got that horse from me."

"Warner, I know this will shock you, but there are other people in the world who sell horses."

"Yeah, like Jack Fisher. How much does that vaquero you got up weigh?"

"I'd reckon about the same as Fisher. He's just a kid."

"But he can hold a horse straight?"

"If Fisher would let you have a jockey he's the one you'd want."

They started walking down toward where the riders were circling their horses. Charlie had the little horse in a slow lope. Warner watched him critically for the first time, noticing the easy motion of the animal as he lightly drove off his hind legs and pulled in ground with his front, an effortless drive.

"I'm going down and start them," Warner said. "We'll just run two. Maybe I'll run the Charlie horse twice today, but I doubt it."

"He looks hard as nails to me."

"You stay at the finish and position yourself so you can see if the horse runs in a straight line or wanders all over the place. I know we ain't got no fences on both sides like the racetrack, but I want to see how he does instinctively."

He caught up with Charlie about fifty yards from where they had planted a stick with a piece of cloth on it. There was a similar flag at the finish line. As they walked along, Warner looking over the light cavalry saddle, Charlie said, "Mr. Grayson, you are going to notice this little horse has a queer way of doing. When you start us, he is going to take off like his tail was on fire. And he is going to keep getting faster for about two hundred yards. Then it's going to seem like he slows down. . . . Well, actually he does. But what he's doing is hitting a gait I never found in no quarter horse before. It seems like he kind of shifts himself, sort of stretches out and commences taking longer and longer strides. When he gets going good in that gait, you won't think you were running fast before. So don't lose heart if that other horse seems to come up on us." Charlie patted his horse on the neck. "I guarantee you ol' Button here will make you see a new light."

Warner was not about to get his hopes up. He said dryly, "Charlie, quit trying to sell me the horse. I already own him."

Then both horses were near the start line. Warner said to Charlie and the vaquero, "Circle your horses and then bring them back to the finish line." He took off his hat and held it at shoulder height. "When I think you are even I'll drop my hat."

They turned their horses, and Wilson watched as Charlie leaned forward on the quarter horse and ran his hands down the reins on either side until they were almost below the top of the horse's neck. He could see Charlie take a firm grip of the horse's mane, a grip that would keep him from being thrown backwards by the sudden start of the horse and would also keep him from pulling back on the reins. Warner had taught Charlie that trick. A lot of riders confused their mounts by spurring them into a sudden run and then offsetting that by being thrown back in the saddle so they were also pulling back on the bit at the same time.

The horses walked toward the finish line. Warner was pleased to see that the button horse was alert but calm. He was switching his ears back and forth, but he wasn't mouthing his bit or stamping his feet, which would have been a sure sign of a nervous horse wasting energy.

The horses were aligned. Warner dropped his

hat. There was sudden motion, and even Warner was startled by the way the little quarter horse suddenly exploded. Within fifty yards he had a five-yard lead on Wilson's horse and was beginning to lengthen it. Warner started walking up the track, watching the animals as they went. Sure enough, just as Charlie had said, at about the halfway point or a little farther on, the button horse seemed to slow down. Warner could see the other horse gaining on him. The trailing horse crept up until there was only a yard or so between them. And then Charlie's horse seemed to hunker down lower to the ground, to stick his head out farther, to stretch out into a different stride. Within a very few yards the horse had regained his lead and was lengthening it. Warner shook his head, marveling. He'd never seen a quarter horse run like that. He seemed to start like a quarter horse and then, like a chameleon, transform himself into a Thoroughbred.

The horses swept past Wilson Young, and he started walking toward Warner. Warner kept watching as Charlie carefully slowed the little horse, pulling him down into a gallop and then a lope and then a trot and finally a walk. He'd walk him slowly for five minutes under rein and then dismount and lead him for another ten.

Warner met Wilson about fifty yards from the finish line. Wilson was grinning. He said, "Give you a thousand dollars for him."

"How much did he win by?"

"Oh, I don't know. Plenty. Four or five lengths. Maybe more."

"Did he run straight?"

"Like he was on rails. But what is that funny gait change he done about right there in the middle? He wasn't even running like a quarter horse when he came by me. What the hell kind of horse *is* that?"

Warner shook his head. "I honest to God don't know. I've never seen anything like it. You'll have to ask Charlie."

Charlie came walking up on the button horse. Warner took a critical look at the animal. No more than a minute or two had passed since he'd run a quarter of a mile as fast as Warner had ever seen it done, but his flanks were barely heaving. Charlie said, "We going to run him again, Mr. Grayson?"

Warner shook his head. "No. Cool him out real good, Charlie and then rub him down before you give him any water or hay."

Charlie gave him a hurt look, like he'd just been told his ABCs. He said, "Oh, I reckon I can handle that."

Wilson said, "Hadn't we ought to get another look at him? I want to see that gait again that he ain't supposed to have. I ain't kidding about that thousand dollars."

"I know you ain't. But what am I supposed to run against Fisher?"

Wilson got out a little cigar and lit it. He cocked an eyebrow at Warner. "Have you forgot? You ain't supposed to run to win."

Warner gave him a look and started for the porch where the tequila and limeade was. As he walked, he caught sight of a buggy leaving the little road that ran by Wilson's place and turning toward the house. He saw a flash of color and a skirt and knew it was Laura. He wondered if she was bringing news or just coming to see what was happening. He and Wilson sat down and poured themselves another drink while they watched her approach.

Wilson said, watching the buggy, "Well, if you plan to win, I hope to hell you got a plan that includes us getting out alive."

As Laura pulled up, Warner went over to take her reins and hitch the buggy horse she'd rented from the livery. She was wearing a lime green skirt and a white blouse. The combination of that green skirt and her lightly tanned complexion and her butter-colored hair with the strawberry tinges made Warner think of spring or of a flower garden in early summer.

They got her settled, and Warner fixed her a drink and said, "Here, this will go with your skirt."

Laura took the drink and said, "We have received Fisher's return wire. He wants to run the first race on Saturday at the fairgrounds racetrack at one o'clock."

Wilson laughed. "Saturday. Naturally. He wants to be able to draw as big a crowd as possible. I wouldn't be surprised if he wasn't having flyers nailed up around the countryside advertising the event. Warner, he has got it seriously in mind to rub your nose in horse shit."

Warner was looking off into the distance. "Saturday. And this is Wednesday. Yes, he's taking time to draw a crowd. Well, we might just give him a little surprise. He might not want a crowd."

Wilson said, "Oh, he'll bring a crowd with him. And they'll all be wearing guns that shoot his bullets."

"Wilson," Laura said, "maybe you can explain something to me that I don't understand. Why is it that the hired guns will work for Fisher but they wouldn't be loyal to Warner or to that Mr. Vaughn you told me about? Can you explain that? All money is green. Why is Fisher's any better?"

Wilson yawned. He'd been up late the night before overseeing the saloon and whorehouse. The absence of Evita and her cousin was seriously affecting his sleep habits. And the lack of Evita's body was making him uncomfortable in an area he wasn't used to being unsatisfied in. He took his hand away from his mouth and shook his head. "Got to wake up," he said. "It's this damn tequila." He looked at Laura. "This is going to be hard to understand, but money really hasn't got much to do with it. Oh, the gunmen wouldn't work for Fisher if he didn't pay them, but they'd rather have his money than yours because he's magic."

"He's what?"

Wilson laughed slightly. "Well, 'magic' ain't the right word exactly, but it was handy to my mind. All these gunhands are mean to one extent or another. If they weren't, they wouldn't be in the trade they are in. Some of them like to skin a man alive before they kill him; others are content to just put one between a man's eyes right away. But ain't none of them ever going to come close to being anything resembling a respectable citizen. Now Fisher, well, he's a whole different kettle of fish. He's evil. I mean he is plain evil through and through. And these gunhands can sense it. It's like he's wearing one of those medicine shirts the Indians used to believe would stop bullets. Laura, you weren't far off when you said he thought he was a genius just because he was alive. By rights he should have been killed a long, long time ago. He is selling a line of bullshit, and all the gunslingers are buying it. Until they met Jack Fisher they thought *they* were mean. But Fisher, it's like he's the head honcho of flat-out evil meanness. That man will stop at nothing. He's got no brake. So they look up to him. They're afraid of him."

Warner said, "That's kind of hard to believe."

Wilson shrugged. "Hell, Fisher isn't the only one. What about that fool in New Mexico—the one they called Billy the Kid? He run around free and having his own way until the price got high enough for that Garrett fellow to take a sheriff's job and shoot him down—though, from what I've read in the papers, it took him a good long time to do it. And what about Wes Hardin up in the Waco area? That son of a bitch is as crazy as they get. Or Sam Bass from over at Round Rock. That bastard holds up *railroad* trains and has no trouble getting gunhands to take potluck with him." Wilson yawned again. "Hell, Jack Fisher ain't no isolated example. Unfortunately, though, he's our example."

Warner said, with a half smile, "How about you, Wilson, back in your salad days when you thought you owned all the banks?"

Wilson nodded. "Yes," he said, "I had men riding with me who thought nothing could happen to them because I was getting away with murder. Not for real, of course, but I was damn lucky. They didn't know it was luck; they thought I had some kind of charm. Well, that's why the guns would rather work for Fisher than for you. They've seen him pull stuff should have got him killed, and he's still alive. He's one of them. Warner is not. Neither are the Vaughns. Yep, they don't believe Fisher can be killed. And as long as they are with him, they think they can't die either. Don't try and make anything complicated out of it. It's real simple. Remember, we are not talking about boys who set attendance records for showing up at school. The pack of them are dumb and deadly and vicious. But their most dangerous quality is their dumbness."

Laura shook her head. "How reassuring that sounds. This is like dealing with some big savage dumb beast."

"Now you are getting the picture."

She stood up. "I'm going to rest for a few minutes and then go back to town. Warner, you are coming back over, aren't you?"

"Oh, yes. I'll leave Charlie here to look out for the horses. I'm going to borrow a get-around-town horse from Wilson and leave the Andalusian here. I want all three of those running horses to get rested and exercised regularly."

After she'd gone into the house, the two men sat smoking and drinking and thinking. Finally Warner shook his head and said, "Boy, that son of a bitch has got me pulling at my hair. He is blocking me every which way I turn."

Wilson said, "It is frustrating. And I mean frustrating. I feel like some ol' boy who's about to get in bed with a good-looking woman and suddenly realizes he's left his dick in his other pants."

Warner smiled slightly, but he said, "Fisher's

not that smart, Wilson. He can't be smarter than you and me and Laura. It's not possible."

"He's anticipated your every move. He's set you up to humiliate you in a profession you are famous in. But two horse races are going to change that. You can be sure he'll manage that part—getting the word around."

"He's not going to beat me, Wilson."

Wilson looked up at the underside of the porch roof. "Then remind me not to stand close to you after the race is over. In fact, was I you, and I won, I'd just keep on riding. You don't want to slow down for anything. And you better hope your horse can outrun a bullet. I'll still give you a thousand dollars for that little button horse, and you can use one of my nags to lose to Fisher with."

Warner studied the ground. "We better take the horses over to the racetrack tomorrow afternoon so they can start getting used to running in formal conditions. Maybe we can take along some of your boys to yell and holler, get that little button horse used to a crowd."

"If you plan to win, you don't need to take no more than the button horse, because I got a feeling there won't be but that one race."

"Look here . . . we'll be racing in your county," Warner said. "Don't you reckon we can have the sheriff on hand with a couple of his deputies? You claim to be friends with the man. Now would sure be an ideal time to prove it. Maybe we could even talk him into making folks check their guns before coming into the fairgrounds."

"That's a noble thought in theory, but I can't see it working out on a practical basis. There is about a hundred ways to get into the racetrack without coming through the main gate. Still, it is a thought. I'll speak to Ryan about it."

"What's his name?"

"Ryan Shank. Good ol' boy. Likes to come into my saloon and casino and relax a little."

"I bet I won't be surprised to find he generally wins at cards."

Wilson shook his head. "Ryan's not that way. I don't charge him for his drinks, but when he plays poker—and he only plays in small games—he's strictly on his own. But I don't think we'll need to urge him to be on hand Saturday. He'll hear that Jack Fisher will be coming in with a crowd, and that's all it will take to get his interest. This ain't no easy county to manage, and Ryan don't waste his time on folks who spit on the sidewalk. But Jack Fisher is serious business. Ryan don't care how many big guns or no-brains kill each other, but he plans to keep the peace for the honest citizen. It would be mighty easy to be crooked in a border county, and most of the sheriffs who occupy such offices generally are. But not Ryan. We are friendly, but he has made it clear that if my place of business—any part of it—goes to causing trouble, he'll close me down."

"Well, you've got Chulo to handle that part of it."

"Yes, and Chulo was supposed to have been back this morning. The later he is, the more hung over he is, and the longer it takes to get him cleaned up and back to work. I swear, that black Meskin can find more ways to wallow in the mud, figuratively speaking, than any man I've ever known. When he takes off on one of his visits down into Mexico you can depend on the fact that he will try and drink all the whiskey and tequila he can get his hands on and fuck every woman he can reach. He won't shave and he won't bathe and he won't change his clothes. He gets back, you do not want to get downwind of him—that I can promise you. And moan and groan—Lord, you'd think he was dying."

"Well, I'll be glad to see Chulo." Warner saw Charlie coming out of the barn. "Is it all right with you if Charlie bunks down in your spare room?"

"Yeah. Ought to be plenty to eat around the place in case he gets hungry. One of the vaqueros can cook for him. But what about that girl he left behind when he joined up with you?"

"Don't bring it up. I think she got married on him."

Charlie came up and saw they were talking and went on into the house.

Wilson called after him, "Charlie! Help yourself to anything you find. All kinds of drinking material in there all the way from tequila to brandy. But hold down the noise. Mrs. Pico is taking a nap."

Warner said mildly, "Not after hearing you shout, she ain't."

They were silent for a moment, each with his own thoughts. Finally Wilson said, hesitantly for him, "Warner, you are not letting Laura influence you in thinking to win that horse race, are you? You wouldn't be taking a stand on account of her, would you?"

Warner looked annoyed. "Hell, no! Why the hell would you ask me a question like that? Do I look or act like some schoolboy taking a dare?"

"No, but I hope you understand what women want as a general thing."

"And what would that be?"

"Pan-fried ice."

"That's crazy. There ain't no such thing."

"I know," Wilson said softly, "but that don't keep women from expecting it."

Warner gave him a glance. "Wilson, I don't dispute you about guns and robbing banks and such, but when did you get to be this big expert on women?"

Wilson gave him a slow half-wink. "Almost from the cradle, kid. It's an instinct, like you have about horses."

Warner stood up. "I'm going to tell Evita you compared her to a horse." He started toward the side of the house.

Wilson said, "Now, wait a minute. Don't be going and telling her anything. There are remarks you have made that the widow Pico might be interested in. Where are you going?"

Over his shoulder Warner said, "One of us has got to take a piss, and I think it's me. I'll be right back."

"Well, take one for me while you are at it. All that limeade has got my back teeth near to floating, but I'm too lazy to get up."

The next day they took the button horse over to the racetrack along with the blaze-faced quarter horse that belonged to Wilson Young. Wilson and Charlie and two vaqueros came, as did Laura in her rented buggy. The racetrack was about two miles north of town. Warner rode his Andalusian and led the quarter horse. They brought the Mexican cavalry saddle.

It was a pleasant day with the temperature in the seventies and almost no wind. North of town the land was dry, with very little vegetation and few trees except for the stunted post oak and mesquite that dotted that part of the country.

They went in a little procession with Warner and Wilson riding in front, Laura in her buggy

253

in the middle, and then Charlie and the Mexican cowboys who worked for Wilson.

They passed the fairgrounds with its cattle barns and booths and a little show ring with a small grandstand circling it. They turned in at the racetrack and covered the quarter of a mile to the gate that would let them into the track. The track itself was a one-mile oval with a half mile straightaway that ran in front of the rickety grandstands that would hold perhaps five hundred people. On this day the place was almost deserted. A couple of horsemen were working their mounts on the backstretch with a few spectators watching them, but on the Fourth of July and other important race meet days, the place would be thronged with several thousand people. Looking the place over as he dismounted, Warner had the feeling that he would have more eyes watching him on Saturday than he cared to have. And he wasn't so sure about his goal concerning the outcome. He had talked bold to Wilson about racing to win, but his mouth had been saying words that his mind and his nerve were not so sure about. This race was a hell of a risk and a dangerous situation, and he couldn't be sure that he wouldn't instinctively pull the little horse up enough to barely lose. Of course there was always the chance that Jack Fisher might have a horse that could beat his, but he very much doubted it. Warner had a timer built into his head, a gauge of speed. He could watch two horses run independently two hundred miles apart on two different occasions, and he could tell which was the faster of the two and by how much. And he knew that the little button horse was very, very fast, even with that peculiar slowing up to change gaits that looked so odd. In fact, he had to think well back in time to remember another horse he'd seen run a quarter of a mile as fast. There hadn't been many, and he'd seen a lot of running horses in his time.

He walked down the track for a hundred yards, looking at the surface. It was a good one, loose-packed dirt that sloped slightly toward the inside of the track so that it would drain well. The fences were board, once painted white but now peeling and needing a fresh coat. Some weeds grew along the edge of the infield, but nothing that would spook a horse. He walked back, thinking that it would be better to be on the grandstand side of the track, the high side, so that, toward the end, a rider could let his horse bear down the slope and gain an extra little bit of momentum.

That is, if he was racing to win.

He got back to the gate as Charlie was leading the button horse onto the track. He had the Mexican cavalry saddle strapped on the back of the little horse. Warner inspected it. It was nothing more than a padded piece of leather about the width of the horse's back, just long enough to accommodate a rider. It had short skirts on either side, and the stirrups were small dangles of shiny steel held in place by slim leather straps.

Charlie said, "You better get up, Mr. Grayson, so I can adjust these stirrups to you."

Wilson put a boot in the small stirrup, having to hold it in his hand to get the toe of his boot in, and then swung astride the little quarter horse. The stirrups felt fine to him. They were short enough to give him some break in the knee where he could lean forward and get most of his weight spread toward the horse's withers rather than plopping it all down on his back. He said, "Charlie, this ought to be all right. I'll trot him a little; that walk from Wilson's place ought to have limbered him up plenty. Tell Wilson to have his man get his horse ready. We don't want to be over here long enough to draw a crowd. I am not interested in having visitors."

Charlie positioned Wilson and Laura at the finish line. Warner took the little horse in a circle and brought him to stand near the white post that marked the start line. Like Charlie the day before, Warner leaned forward and ran his hands down the reins, then took a grip on the horse's mane with his right hand. He toed up slightly in the stirrups and watched Charlie's upraised hat out of the corner of his eye.

And then the hat fell. Warner shoved slightly forward with his hands and his weight, intending to tap the little horse with his spurs. But it was like the little horse had been watching for the signal himself. Before Charlie's arm could complete its downward sweep, the horse exploded under Warner, driving instantly down the track. It took Warner so by surprise that he almost fell backwards in the saddle, saving himself only with the grip on the horse's mane. He never touched the animal with his spurs.

In five jumps the other horse had fallen behind his vision and he could feel the button horse accelerating under him. To his right the white fence and the grandstands flew by in a blur. There was almost no motion to the fluid pace of the horse except the rhythm of his head reaching and bobbing, reaching and bobbing. Ahead of him Wilson and Laura were rapidly growing in size as they stood at the finish line.

And then there came that queer sensation under him that felt like the horse had gotten confused about his stride and didn't know how to get back on it. He could feel the horse slowing, sense the blaze-faced horse coming up on his left to where he could see him out of the corner of his eye.

It was unlike any sensation he'd ever experienced in his years as a horseman. Even though Charlie had warned him about the gait change, he felt his hopes sinking as the horse almost seemed to quit running.

And then the horse somehow got closer to the

ground. With the blaze-faced horse almost even, the button horse began to pick up speed, and Warner could feel nothing but the smooth flowing power between his legs as the horse lengthened his stride and then lengthened it even more, leaving the blaze-faced horse behind faster than he had been at the start. In another few seconds they swept by Wilson and Laura, with Warner feeling that the horse could very easily have run another quarter of a mile at the same or a faster pace.

Warner brought the animal down slowly until he had him in a slow trot and then down to a walk. He turned the horse around and took him back up to a trot until he was close to Laura and Wilson. As he came up to them, he dropped the horse to a walk.

Laura looked stunned. "My God," she said, "that is a very fast horse."

Warner looked at Wilson. "Well?"

Wilson smiled. "Give you twelve hundred. Better take it before Fisher takes him away from you."

10

On Saturday they had an early lunch and then
hurried out to the fairgrounds so as to be there by
half past noon. Warner had interpreted Fisher's
wire to mean that they would meet there at one
o'clock and run the first race some time after.
If that was the case, Warner wanted to be there
early enough to watch Fisher and his men arrive,
to have the chance to make an early assessment
of their strength and general appearance. He had
wanted to leave Charlie in town to watch the noon
train arrive, expecting Fisher and his party and
horses to arrive on that one, but Wilson Young
had said he figured Warner would be wasting
Charlie's time. He'd said, "Listen, Fisher ain't
going to put himself depot-deep in an unfriendly
town and county with the train station, which
ain't that far from the jail, his only way out. The
county auction barn is five miles north of the
fairgrounds, right at the county line and right on
the railroad. I figure Fisher will pay for a stop
and unload at the siding there at the auction. That
way, if he gets chased, he ain't got far to go to get
over the county line and away from our sheriff.
Hell, Vaughn's place ain't but about two miles
from that same siding. At first, Vaughn thought
Fisher and his men had rode cross-country from

259

Cotulla, but I convinced him that didn't make no sense. So he watched, and shore enough, Fisher was using the train from his ranch siding to the auction barn siding. And that is the way he'll be coming to see you. He's going to want you to think him and his horses come overland sixty or seventy miles and ain't broke a sweat yet."

Now they stood waiting, looking to the north. Warner said, "What is an auction barn doing at the far end of the county? That ain't exactly handy."

Wilson said, "It's set at the corner where three counties come together. They call it the Tri-County Auction House. You get right down to it, it's the only one around. Ain't a single one of the three counties produce enough livestock to supply one auction house to each county, so they kind of all three use the one big one, except for some little one-horse traders here and there. It's set for the benefit of all the counties, not just this one."

"Uh-huh," Warner said, looking to the north. He had asked the question, but he hadn't really been interested in the answer. He said, "Where is that son of a bitch?"

"Hell, Warner, it is only twenty of one. Give the man time."

"You reckon he'll camp over there? Beyond the county line?"

"I know he ain't going to stay in town. If he

plans on racing tomorrow I would reckon he has made some sort of plans for laying over in safety. He knows this county ain't safe for him. Austin Vaughn's bad luck was that he was just over the county line. Otherwise Ryan Shank could have helped him. But that next county over is friendly to Fisher. The man picks his targets, I'll give him that. You'll notice he didn't offer to come down to Nueces County to run this sham race. Too many unfriendly sheriffs in between."

"This race ain't no sham. Not unless Fisher don't try."

Wilson looked at him. "You're serious."

"You're damn right I am. I ain't giving that snake nothing. He wants a fight, I'm ready."

"What if me and Chulo and Charlie ain't ready?"

"I'm not asking for any help."

"But you'd take it?"

Warner spit and then ground the spittle into the dry dirt with the toe of his boot. "I might take help from a carefully selected few, depending on the quality of their character."

Wilson laughed. "Hell, you'd take help from Laura right now. You get her a gun?"

Warner gave him a look. He wasn't scared, surprisingly, but he was tense, anxious to meet Fisher, size him up, make his position clear, and then get on with the horse race, if there was to be one.

He looked behind him toward the filling grandstand. He and Wilson were standing in an open space some fifty yards from the gate that led to the road, and twenty or thirty yards from where Laura had parked her buggy in the shade near the wooden stands. Around her, Charlie and two of Wilson's vaqueros were sitting on the ground. All of the horses, including the button horse, were tied nearby. Warner had not brought his Andalusian. If there was going to be trouble he didn't want such a valuable horse exposed to flying bullets.

A little ways from the others, Chulo was leaning against one of the posts that supported the grandstands. He had his sombrero off and his head hanging. Wilson said he'd gotten in the day before and there'd been some question whether he'd live or not. Now he was suffering through a monumental hangover—a *crudo*, as he called it. Warner thought the word was much more descriptive in Spanish than in English.

But hangover or not, he was still the biggest, meanest, ugliest man Warner had ever seen. He'd first encountered Chulo at the same time he met Wilson Young, when the bank robber came hurrying into his horse yard looking for a fresh mount. That had been twelve or thirteen years ago, but Chulo didn't look much different. And, *crudo* or not, Warner was glad he had made it back from Mexico in time to help with Fisher.

262

Chulo was a little over six feet tall and weighed about two hundred pounds. His skin was leathery and dark. He had a huge hooked nose and a big drooping mustache. He wore a black patch over his left eye, and an ugly knife scar ran down one cheek from the outer corner of his eye to the corner of his mouth. He had huge hands and arms, and the only thing he was scared of was Wilson Young. He would do anything Wilson told him to except not get drunk and not consider every woman fair game.

Wilson said, "I see horsemen coming down the road. From the north."

Warner whipped his head around. The men were still better than half a mile away, but he had no doubt they were Fisher and some of his men.

He said, "Can you get a count?"

Wilson laughed. "Boy, you are tighter than Dick's hatband. You better loosen up, boy. You start unwinding all of a sudden, you are liable to reel yourself around this track like a runaway chicken."

"We ain't made no plan."

"How can you make a plan about the unknown? We got a plan: we handle whatever comes up. Listen, Fisher ain't going to start nothing here. You go ahead and win your race. Won't nothing happen here, not in this county. You'll need to start worrying when you get home. Or on the road home."

Warner said tensely, "No. It is going to be settled here and now. I ain't got no intention of going back to my ranch to wait for that son of a bitch to hit me in the middle of the night. Him and me is going to reach an understanding on this very dirt we are standing on. And in the not too distant future."

"Boy, you better calm down. Wait and see what the man has to say."

"I've already heard him. He sent a man with a shotgun to give me a message." Warner looked around. "Where is your ol' buddy, the sheriff?"

"Oh, he's around, I would reckon. He ain't going to make no entrance until it's time. And then he will come sauntering along." Wilson turned his head and pointed. "See them little buildings there on the fairgrounds? I reckon that is Ryan Shank and a few of his deputies. I saw some horsemen arrive there about five minutes ago."

Warner said, "Probably Fisher's men. Boxing us in."

"By the way, the sheriff said to tell you he ain't going to stand for any trouble from nobody, and that includes you. So don't go to losing your head and starting trouble, Warner. You'll wind up in jail."

"Me start trouble?" Warner stared at him with his mouth open. "*Me* start trouble! Is your friend the sheriff a little dim-witted, or don't he understand the situation?"

264

Wilson said primly, "I'm passing along a message, not passing judgment."

"Well, you and the sheriff can both go to hell! You act like this bastard is coming down here for a barn dance instead of to put me out of business. And maybe kill me. You forget I got Laura's interests at heart here. He is after those Andalusians is what he's after. Well, he is not going to get them."

"I knew it. Knew it all along." Wilson nodded. "You are the hero protecting the little woman. I been smelling it. Well, you have now admitted it."

"Go to hell, Wilson. Just go to hell." Warner peered at the riders coming down the road from the north. "I make it ten, with about four horses on lead. What do you count?"

"That's about right."

Warner looked around at Wilson Young. "I expected him to bring more men. Hell, we can take that bunch."

"I done told you he ain't going to fight here. If you defy him, he'll come at you later. Why can't you get that through your head? Have you seen any sign of Austin or Preston Vaughn?"

Warner had sent Charlie to invite both of them to the racetrack. He had especially hoped that Preston would come. "No," he said.

"That ought to tell you something. They know nothing is going to happen here except a horse race. And I don't imagine they much want to socialize with Fisher. You can bet that Preston, if he thought there was the slightest chance for an honest shot at Fisher, would be here with both guns."

"I had hoped he would." Warner watched the men coming on. Now they were only about a hundred yards from the entrance to the racetrack. In the front was a small man on a big horse, or a horse made bigger by the man's small size. He was wearing a big white hat. Warner had no doubt the man was Jack Fisher. He said, "Well, if you are so sure there ain't going to be any trouble today, how come you and Chulo are here, not to mention your friend the sheriff?"

Wilson shrugged. "Maybe we like to watch horse races."

"Aw, yeah."

Wilson put his hand on Warner's arm and jerked his head back toward the grandstands. "Let's go bunch up with the others. Make Fisher come to us. It will look better."

They turned and started walking toward Laura's buggy as the ten men came sweeping through the entrance.

They stood as two groups about fifty yards apart. In the shade near the bleachers Warner and Wilson stood with Laura and Charlie and Chulo. The ten men of Fisher's group sat their horses and stared, obviously assuming that Warner would walk the distance and place himself at Jack Fisher's disposal. The standoff was rapidly becoming a test of wills. Several moments had passed since Fisher raised his hand and brought his gang to a stop. Warner had expected him to keep on coming toward them, but it quickly became evident he had no such intention.

Warner stood there staring at Fisher. He was not close enough to see the man in detail, but it was clear that he was wearing a black suit with a vest and a string tie. The big white hat looked ridiculous on him, but Warner could see he was a thin-featured, pinched-face man. He could not see what armament Fisher was carrying, because the waist and tails of his black suit coat hid his weapons from view. He was surprised that a man who rode in such fine clothes didn't bother to wear a linen duster to protect them. But then he reckoned that Jack Fisher made so much money giving other folks misery that he wore a suit of clothes just once and then threw it away. He said to Wilson, "If that son of a bitch thinks I'm coming over there like some dog being called, he can sit out there in the sun until his horse takes him to water."

Laura said, "This is ridiculous. What does the man want?"

Wilson said, "Take it easy. We'll wait awhile."

A few more minutes passed, and then four men came riding from the direction of the fairgrounds.

267

One man was slightly in the lead with the others behind.

Wilson said, "That's Ryan Shank. He'll get the party started."

The sheriff halted his horse halfway between Warner and Jack Fisher. He turned his animal so that he was at an equal distance from both of them. With his hands, his right toward Warner and his left to Fisher, he made little motions for them to come forward.

Wilson said, "Get on a horse, Warner. Fisher ain't going to dismount, and you don't want to be looking up at him."

But Fisher did dismount. Warner almost smiled at the long step it was for him from the stirrup down to the ground. It also interested him to see Fisher pitch his reins to one of his men to hold. If he was such a hell of a trainer he ought to have been able to get a horse to stand.

Fisher took a moment more to brush idly at his suit, and then he started walking toward where the sheriff was waiting.

Warner said, "Laura, you stay here. What about you, Wilson?"

Wilson said, "I reckon it's time he found out. I'm right behind you."

Warner walked toward the sheriff and Jack Fisher. The sheriff looked patient, but his horse was stamping a hoof as if to ask what the waiting around was all about.

And then Warner was face to face with Jack Fisher. He stared steadily at the man, looking him up and down, while Fisher just kept his eyes fixed on Warner's face, trying to lock gazes.

Warner almost laughed at the silver tips on Fisher's black boots. But then he looked on up, seeing the huge silver belt buckle and the gold watch chain that crossed his vest. Finally he could see Fisher's revolver. The handle was either ivory or mother-of-pearl. He couldn't see the rest of it because of the holster, but he bet the gun was either gold- or silver-chased. It looked like a weapon more for show than anything else, but Wilson had assured him that Fisher knew how to use it and would do so at the slightest provocation.

Warner guessed the man to be no more than five feet six inches tall. Laura was taller than him by an inch, and they might have weighed the same except that Fisher had surprisingly wide shoulders. Warner finally looked into Fisher's eyes. They were a cold washed-out greenish blue. For a second Fisher tried to stare him down, but then Warner smiled and said, "I hear you have business with me, Fisher."

But then the sheriff was talking. He said, "I understand you men are gathered here for a horse race. Is that right?"

Warner looked up at him. Ryan Shank was a lean man in his early forties with a no-nonsense appearance. Warner said, "I've been invited to race by this man under conditions you might say went a little further than an invitation."

Behind him, Wilson said, "Keep it shut, Warner."

The sheriff looked to his left. "What about you? You're Jack Fisher, right?"

Fisher said, "You know who I am."

"Yes," the sheriff said, "unfortunately I do."

Fisher said, "I have no business with you. We've broken no laws."

Warner was surprised at how deep his voice was. The low pitch that came out of him should have belonged to a man a foot taller.

The sheriff said, "And I'm here to see that none get broken. Savvy?"

Fisher said, "I don't understand why you are here, Sheriff." He turned his flat eyes on Warner. "Unless this young man here requested your presence."

"Nobody *requested* my presence, Fisher. You have all the horse races you are of a mind to. But keep it in mind that this is my county and I won't have trouble."

Warner looked at Fisher. Wilson had never told him Fisher's age, but he'd thought of him as being in his early thirties. This man looked older. "I'm here to race," he said. "I'm not looking for trouble."

Fisher stared straight back at him and said,

without unlocking his eyes from Warner's, "We'd like to get on with our business, Sheriff. If that is okay with you."

The sheriff reined his horse backwards. "You do anything you want to do as long as it don't break any laws. You might not see me, but I'll be around. Keep that in mind."

Then he wheeled his horse and rode back toward the fairgrounds, his three deputies in behind him.

They waited half a minute, and then Fisher looked over Warner's shoulder and said, "What are you doing here, Young?"

Wilson said, "Maybe I like horse racing, Fisher. What the hell business is it of yours?"

"You taking a part?"

"Mr. Grayson is a friend of mine, Fisher. A very good friend."

Fisher studied him over Warner's shoulder. "You sayin' what I think you are sayin'?"

Before Wilson could answer, Warner said, "You don't worry about Mr. Young, Fisher. I'm the one you are doing business with. Now let's you and me discuss the details of that business."

Almost as if he was annoyed at the interruption, Fisher jerked his eyes back to Warner and said, "I thought you already *knew* the details, Grayson. They were given to you twice't. The last time by your partner. If that's what she wants to call herself."

271

Warner stepped back, almost bumping into Wilson Young. "You want to start it right now, Fisher? You make another remark like that one and we won't have no trouble getting matters settled in a hurry."

Fisher gave Warner what passed for a smile by pulling his lips back from his stained teeth. Warner had not noticed before that he was chewing tobacco, but Fisher pursed his mouth and spit close to Warner's boots. He said, "I don't know what remark you are referring to, Grayson. But I reckon you know what is at stake here."

When Warner and his party had arrived they had not been surprised to see almost a hundred people in the grandstands and standing around along the fence. Ever since, they had been trickling in in ones and twos and threes until he guessed there were already several hundred people there, with more coming. He said, "Must be something important, Fisher. You seemed to have invited enough people to the party. I know *I* didn't invite any."

Fisher made the same effort at a smile. "You wouldn't have any reason to, Grayson, unless you enjoy showing your ass to the world."

"I reckon that gets decided after the race. It ain't been run yet."

Fisher's face hardened. "Are you right sure you understand the stakes, Grayson? Maybe they ain't been explained to you real good." As he said the last, he seemed, to Warner, to rise up on his toes. "Was I you, boy, I'd git somebody to explain them real good."

Warner smiled. "What are you calling me 'boy' for, Fisher? I don't have to have somebody hand me down the jam off the high shelf in the kitchen."

The skin seemed to go suddenly taut over Fisher's thin face. He said, his voice taking on an edge, "You will wish you'd never said that."

Warner said, "Let's just get the race details down. I understand you want to run a quarter of a mile for the first race. That's fine with me. I understand the winner gets to pick the distance for the second race. But I say that the second race cannot be the same distance as the first. I understand we are racing the best two out of three. That's fine. But that second race has got to be for an appreciable distance farther than the first."

Fisher pulled his head back. "How much farther you mean, and what the hell do you care anyway?"

Warner didn't answer for a second. In tilting his head back, Fisher had lifted the shadow of his hat from his face enough for Warner to see that he was wearing a mustache. But it was such a thin line that it almost looked as if it had been drawn on with a pencil. Warner stared at it, fascinated, wondering how this dandy had succeeded in making so many men afraid of him.

Fisher said coldly, "I asked you a question, boy. What the hell do you care?"

Warner smiled. "Just worrying about you, horse handler. I want to make sure you have some kind of chance to win. You ain't got no chance at a quarter of a mile."

"You don't seem to understand the stakes."

"Oh, I reckon I do. You're the one seems confused."

Fisher narrowed his eyes. "You got one way to win, boy. Lose. You can always get more horses and make another start."

From behind Warner, Wilson said, "In his delicate and sensitive way, Mr. Fisher is trying to tell you that if you let him win and look like the big shot he ain't, he won't sic his bullyboys on you."

Warner said, still smiling, "Oh, I understand Mr. Fisher well enough. It appears to me he's the one got the stick by the shit end. Mr. Fisher wins, he gets to keep his horses. He loses, he loses his breeding stock. He don't understand that I'll come and take his horses if he loses two out of three races. And judging by them hides he's got on lead over there with that bunch of oafs he's brought along, I don't give him much chance. I reckon I could outrun a couple of them horses in high-heeled boots."

Fisher turned his head slightly and, without taking his eyes off Warner, said, "Quince!"

Warner watched as a big man at the front of the group of nine horsemen immediately got off his mount and came hurrying over to Fisher's side. He was a man with a three- or four-day growth of whiskers, wearing a weathered gray hat with lanyards hanging down under his chin, held together with a slipknot, eyes too close together and dull except when they lighted up as he spoke, and shoulders and hands as big, if not bigger, than Chulo's. Warner reckoned the man to be over six feet tall and at least 225 pounds. He had a small, cruel mouth. As he spoke, his upper lip bounced up and down, reminding Warner of the way a rabbit ate. "Yessir, Mistuh Fishuh."

Still staring at Warner, Fisher said, "Quince, tell Mr. Grayson what will happen to him if he wins a race."

The light came on in the big stupid face of the man. He said, "I'll git the chancet to make his last little while on this heah dirt plumb miserable. Tha's wha'll happen."

Warner said, his voice even, "Fisher, that sword will cut both ways. And I think I'm going to have the opportunity to remind you of that in the not too distant future. Now, have you got a big enough crowd on hand to suit you or you want to talk a while longer? I thought we came here to race."

"We race. My men will handle the start and finish."

Warner shook his head. "No, Fisher. It's not going to be that way. I'm going to ask Wilson Young to pick two people out of the crowd to act as starting and finishing judges. You can send somebody with him if you're a mind. But it's not going to make any difference."

Fisher looked at him for a second. Then he said, "You're right. It's not going to make any difference." He made a motion with his hand. "Quince, send Dupree with Wilson Young to pick starting and finishing judges out of the crowd." He glanced at Warner. "I'll see you at the start line in fifteen minutes."

As he started to walk away, Wilson Young said softly, "Fisher . . ."

The small man stopped and looked back. "What?"

"No sidearms during the race. Take your guns off. I'll be at the start line, and there ain't going to be a race if you are wearing a pistol. Understand?"

Fisher stared at Wilson for a second. It seemed to Warner that Fisher couldn't speak unless he first spent some time staring at the person he was going to talk to. For answer he unbuckled his gun belt and handed it over to his man Quince. Then, without another word, he walked toward his men and his horses.

Wilson said to Warner, "I'll see you at the start line. I reckon you better have Charlie and Chulo at the finish. I'll be getting down there as fast as I can, but I shore ain't going to be there when you arrive. If anything happens, it will be at the finish line."

Warner walked slowly toward the place where Laura had parked her buggy. He swung up into the shade, able to see now that the bleachers were almost filled. Chulo and Charlie were standing near the buggy while the two vaqueros had wandered off toward the end of the grandstand.

Laura was dressed in a white shirtwaist and a white skirt that stopped just above her ankles. It was a daring outfit to wear out in public, and to complete it, she'd chosen to wear shiny red pumps. She was carrying a frilly little parasol of white silk. Warner came up to where she was sitting in the buggy fanning herself with a folded newspaper. "Well?" she said. "Are you two horse experts agreed you are finally going to run a horse race?"

"Oh, yes," Warner said. He looked at Charlie. "You better get the little button horse saddled. Limber him up a little, and then I'll take over. Chulo, Wilson Young said for you to go to the finish line. Go inside the track."

The big Mexican said, "Chure. *Ahora?*"

"Might as well." Warner watched him turn away and start toward the end of the stands in his shambling gait. He was looking considerably better than he had that morning, and Warner

277

figured he'd looked inside a bottle and found some hair of the dog that had bit him.

As Warner unbuckled his gun belt and laid it on the floorboards of the buggy, Laura said, "Where can I watch from?"

"Same place as Chulo, I reckon. It ought to be safe enough inside the track, but stay by the fence next to the grandstand. That's the side I'm going to try and take. It's a little higher than down near the inside rail. But the track is wide enough."

She said, "I don't guess I have to ask you, do I?"

He shook his head. "No."

She sighed. "For a change, Warner, I can't fault your obstinacy. I'll be damned if I'd give in to that little toad, either. Warner, don't just win—embarrass the bastard. If there are to be consequences, we'll deal with them as they come."

He was taking off his spurs and putting them with his gun belt. He wouldn't need them with the button horse. He even considered taking off his boots to save weight, but decided against it. Laura was drawing all the footwear attention that needed to be. He leaned into the buggy and kissed her softly on the corner of her mouth. "We'll be all right," he said.

"Wilson says the trouble will be at our place—I mean, at your ranch."

"It's our ranch, Laura. When I said what I did,

it was in anger. That ain't supposed to count."

She gave him a smile. "All right. At *the* ranch. We'll find help in Nueces County, or we'll send for it. Send someplace they never heard of that little toad. Did you see his mustache? Have you ever seen anything sillier?"

Warner said, "I got to go."

She got out of the buggy and stood close to him, looking up into his face. "Are you afraid?"

"A little. Now I wish that I had made you stay in town. Wilson can say all he wants, but that son of a bitch is crazy, and he's brought at least one other crazy man with him. Anything can happen. You hear a gunshot, just one, you get in amongst as many people as you can. I figure the sheriff ain't far off, so any shooting won't last long."

She stood on tiptoe in her red slippers and kissed him on the lips. "How would you have made me stay in town?"

He laughed without much humor. "I knew I couldn't, so I didn't try. But someday, Laura, I am going to have to school you. You are the only unbroke animal I own. Damn, you are a handful!"

"Go ride your race," she said. She quickly kissed him again and then twirled her parasol and went off in a swirl of white.

Warner walked over to where Charlie was walking the button horse back and forth. He took the reins. "I got him. You go with Miss Laura and keep her from walking out into the middle of the track."

Charlie said, "Good luck, boss."

Warner put the tip of his boot in the small stirrup and eased himself up onto the cavalry saddle. "Luck ain't going to have nothing to do with it, Charlie," he said. "You found this horse, and you made him. Ain't no luck in that."

"Yes, sir. I'll look after Miss Laura."

One of the town bankers was acting as the starting judge. He was dressed like a banker even on a Saturday. He stood at the starting post with a narrow-brimmed Stetson in his hand. The straightaway began behind the fourth turn of the oval track, blended in with the home stretch in front of the grandstand, and finished the quarter mile about a hundred yards before the oval bent back to the left at the first turn. Most of the race would be run right in front of the spectators. Warner did not think the crowd or its noise would bother his little horse. They were on the track, circling around, waiting for starter's orders, and the button horse seemed calm but alert. His ears were flicking around and his head was up, but he felt relaxed between Warner's legs.

As they circled, Warner watched Fisher. He was glad to see that the man was indeed riding a big range saddle. That did a little to even out the difference in their weight. Fisher had taken off

280

his hat, coat, and string tie and was wearing just his unbuttoned vest and a blue shirt with sleeve garters. Something was sticking out of one of his vest pockets, but Warner couldn't see what it was. It was round, or so it appeared, and Warner reckoned it to be the man's watch, though it was an uncommon big one. He was also wearing very big gloves.

Fisher glanced over at him as they turned to circle back toward the starting line. "You riding a lady's saddle, boy?"

Warner didn't say anything. He decided his hat would probably blow off during the race, so he took it off and pitched it to Wilson Young as he came up to the starting line.

The banker said, "All ready? Both you ready?"

Warner slid his hands down the reins and grasped the button horse's mane. Out of the corner of his eye he could see Fisher leaning over his horse like a jockey. Warner had noticed, as they warmed their horses up, that whatever else the man was, he appeared to be at home on a horse. Once again he noticed the big gloves. They were like gauntlets, with the cuffs sticking up over his wrists. Warner guessed he must have awfully tender hands and wondered how he could feel a horse's mouth through so much leather.

They were inching into line. Beneath him, Warner could feel the button horse beginning to tremble slightly. It was almost as if the horse knew he was in a race. The banker had his narrow-brimmed hat in the air. He said, "Ready . . ."

At that instant Fisher said, "You ought to be riding sidesaddle, boy."

It distracted Warner. While the words were registering on his brain and he was trying to think of something to say back, the banker dropped his hat. Again, as he had before, the little horse anticipated the start and exploded beneath Warner. But Fisher's words had caused Warner to lose his intense concentration and he had carelessly slackened his grip on the horse's mane. The first jump took him so off balance that he was thrown backwards, interfering with the horse's start. As a consequence it was five or six strides before he could get into rhythm with the little horse, who was badly off stride. He had expected to leave Fisher at the starting post, but Fisher, thanks to Warner's mistake, had moved out in front. But then, as horse and rider merged, Warner could see and feel the little button horse moving up on Fisher, then coming abreast of him, and then passing. Out of the corner of his eye Warner saw Fisher cast a frantic glance at him, and it seemed as if the man took his right hand off the reins, but by then, Warner and his horse were on by.

Once again he was stunned by the effortless acceleration of the little horse as the blur of the stands rushed past. They had gone a hundred yards and then two hundred, and Warner got ready for the unusual slowing-down to shift gaits. It didn't come when he expected it, and he glanced down the track to see how far it was to the finish line. He could see a little knot of people standing just past the white finish post and thought he could see, amid the group of people, a flash of white that could only be Laura. He could hear the noise of the crowd even above the muffled hoofbeats of his horse and Fisher's. He didn't know how far back Fisher was, but he didn't think he was ahead by much, because of his careless error at the start. By now they were past the point where the button horse should have begun to stretch out, but Warner could tell he was still accelerating and guessed the delay was due to the bad start and the horse being thrown off stride. Even as he moved in rhythm with the horse, he couldn't believe he'd been suckered so easily—fooled by a childish distraction at the starting line with the starter ready to set them off.

They were fast eating up the quarter mile, and if the horse decided to go into his gait change, which required him to slow down, there wouldn't be distance enough left for him to stretch out and get into that flying gait of his. Warner cursed himself. Hell, the horse didn't know how far a quarter of a mile was. He didn't know where the finish line was. All he knew was to go as fast as he could with that bunched-up starting gait and then stretch out and get settled into that driving, ground-eating stride that was more Thoroughbred than quarter horse. And Warner had managed to foul him up on that by delaying his normal start for five or six strides.

Then he felt that seeming confusion beneath him as if the horse had gotten his legs all mixed up. He felt them slowing, slowing so much it almost seemed as if he could pick out individual faces in the crowd to his right that before had been a blur.

He felt rather than saw Fisher coming up on his left. Then he could see him out of the corner of his eye. Fisher came up and edged past. He could see Fisher's bared teeth as if he were sneering and snarling all at the same time.

But then came that mysterious shift. The button horse seemed to go nearer to the ground as he got himself stretched out and began reaching out farther with his front legs and tucking his back hooves up higher to drive off like a coiled spring.

In what seemed like slowed down action, Warner caught a glimpse of Fisher looking back at him, the triumph on his face turning to astonishment as the button horse began coming back up on him, and then the surprise turning to fury as he realized the button horse was going to retake the lead with a driving finish. As they got even, Fisher took his right hand off his rein and reached out toward the head of Warner's horse.

To Warner's amazement, he seemed to be about to try and reach out to grab his horse's bridle or his halter, even though he knew they were too far apart for that to happen. Then—and he doubted his own eyes—he could see the inside of Fisher's big glove, and the little man's fingers came right through the glove, as if it had been split. Warner wasn't looking directly at Fisher's hand because of the necessity of concentrating on holding the little horse on a straight path as they neared the finish line, only some fifty yards away. He was seeing what was happening peripherally, aware of it but not noticing details. But it did seem to him as if the fingers that had so suddenly come through the glove were grasping something.

The next thing Warner knew, he heard the faint sound of an explosion and was amazed to see smoke shoot out of Fisher's glove. The explosion didn't sound so loud because of the wind rushing past his ears and the noise of the crowd. His first thought was that Fisher had set off a firecracker in order to spook his horse, because Fisher had been reaching out toward the button horse's ear. But he immediately dismissed that possibility and wondered if Fisher had fired a small gun, most likely a derringer, near his horse's ear for the same reason.

It made Warner want to chuckle in a distracted way. The damn fool ought to have realized that any horse trained on Warner's range would never shy or spook at a gunshot. They were trained to expect it, so that they never turned a hair. And Fisher, by letting go of the rein and distracting his own horse in order to fire the gun, had slowed his pace as the button horse went into that last stage of his fastest speed. Warner was almost laughing as he swept down upon the finish line and then flashed past it. He tried to see Laura as he went past, but the spectators were all knotted together.

He started slowing the horse immediately as he passed the finish line and looked back to his left to see how badly he'd beaten Fisher. He still wanted to laugh at the idea of the man hiding a gun in his glove, firing it near his horse's ear, hoping to scare him and run him into the fence or make him veer and break stride. He knew Fisher hadn't been trying to shoot his horse because he had seen that Fisher's hand was aimed up the track, had seen the smoke come as Fisher had tried one last desperate trick when he realized he was about to be beaten.

Looking back, he was amazed to see that Fisher had split off at the first turn and was taking the curve of the oval track, heading for the backstretch. The man didn't want to face him in defeat. Warner imagined he was seething and plotting revenge, but for the moment he was beaten, and there was nothing Fisher could do about it.

He noticed, as he rode, still in a lope, that Fisher was looking back toward the finish line as if something of interest was going on there. By now Warner had the button horse pulled down to a trot and was easing him into a walk. Beneath his legs he could feel the little horse's flanks heaving gently. Well, that was to be expected. The horse's damn jockey had made the race a hell of a lot harder for him than it should have been.

When he turned the horse to head back down the track, he was about a hundred fifty yards from the finish line. Warner was puzzled to see Fisher still loping his horse, going around the far turn, heading for the gate that led off the track. Then he became aware of the little crowd of people near the finish post. And he could see Wilson Young running hard in the loose dirt toward that group. He could see some of the crowd leaning over the end of the grandstands and looking down. He said, "What the hell?" And almost instinctively urged the button horse into a trot. As Warner neared the knot of people he could see that they were bending over something or someone on the ground. Then he saw Charlie come out of the group and start running toward him, beckoning to him. Warner put the horse into a lope, his heart starting to rise slowly toward his throat. He was fifteen yards away from the crowd when he met up with Charlie.

"Mr. Grayson!" Charlie said. "It's Miss Laura!"

But by then Warner didn't need to be told. He could already see, even through the crowded bodies, a splash of white lying on the ground. With the horse still in a trot he let go the reins and vaulted out of the saddle, landing on his feet and running. But the soft dirt grabbed at his boot heels and he stumbled a few steps and went to his knees. As quick as he could, he was back on his feet and running forward. He shoved his way through the crowd, pushing people left and right. "Let me through!" he said. "Goddammit, let me through!"

And then he was there, standing right over Laura. She was lying flat on her back with her hands up near her sun-bright hair. There was a spreading patch of red on the left side of her dress, made all the redder against the white material. Her eyes were closed. Wilson Young was kneeling by her side, carefully pulling the dress material back from the blood, trying to see the wound. He looked up as Warner knelt down. "She's been shot, Warner. That son of a bitch shot her when he tried to spook your horse. Chulo is fetching the buggy. I don't know how bad the wound is, but she's losing blood. We got to get her to a doctor as fast as we can."

Warner was too stunned to speak. And then Laura's eyes fluttered open. She looked at Warner. "Did you win? For God's sake, get me a drink. Something is hurting like hell."

He took her hand. "Honey, we got to load you in the buggy," he said. "I'll give you a drink on the way into town."

She squeezed his hand. She looked so pale and frail that it almost unnerved him. "You did win," she said.

"Yeah, yeah. Now be quiet and let us get you to town." He looked across at Wilson. His friend grimaced and shook his head. Then Warner stood up and yelled, "Chulo! Chulo! Get over here with that buggy, goddammit!"

As he looked across the grounds around the racetrack he saw, well in the distance beyond the grandstand, a group of horsemen heading out through the big gate and turning their horses north along the road toward the county border. He could clearly see the oversized white hat that the man in the lead was wearing. Behind him he heard the voice of the sheriff: "What's going on? What happened here?"

Warner looked at Wilson and said, "They're getting away. I don't know what to do."

Wilson said, "You've got to stay with Laura. They can wait. Somebody will tell the sheriff. Let's get her in the buggy. We got to make tracks, kid. She's bleeding bad. You're going to have to ride beside her—how, I don't know, in that small buggy—and take some kind of a pad and try and keep the bullet hole closed."

"You and Charlie lift her. I'll use my shirt." But

while Warner was hastily ripping off his shirt and wadding it up into a ball, his eyes followed the white hat until a little dip in the road obscured it from view. He quickly knelt and pressed his wadded-up shirt to Laura's side as Wilson and Charlie lifted her carefully and carried her through the crowd to the buggy and laid her lengthwise on the seat. Warner crowded in behind her and knelt on the floorboards while Chulo, mounted on his own horse, took the buggy horse on lead. They started out of the fairgrounds with Charlie racing ahead to alert the doctor.

To Warner's eyes Laura was growing paler by the minute. He yelled at Chulo, "Faster, dammit, faster!" He didn't reckon he'd ever been so afraid in his life.

11

The doctor at the infirmary in downtown Del Rio was the same young one who'd treated Warner's burned and bloody feet after his four-day ordeal on the alkali flat where the Mexican bandits had left him. He was waiting for them when they came flying up in the buggy, and he helped them hurry Laura into his surgery. He forced everyone out while he made his initial examination and then came out after a sweaty hour with some news.

Laura, he said, had been extremely lucky in that the wayward slug had caught her in the side and passed through without damaging any vital organs. But the lead .41 caliber bullet had made a large wound, and she had lost a great deal of blood and had suffered a severe shock. The young doctor said, "It is extremely fortunate that the lady is young and strong and obviously in good health. Otherwise I fear she would have expired before she arrived here. And if the bullet had struck her another inch to the left, medical science would have been of no avail, for it would surely have damaged her liver beyond repair. As it is, she will need the most intense care and will be some time on the mend."

The doctor did not sew up her wounds. Instead

291

he cleaned them out and doused them with denatured alcohol and inserted strips of cloth that served as wicks and kept the wounds draining while they healed from the inside out. He was uncertain if he would stitch them later. He said, "And with a lady I must be conscious of the effects a scar could have. We'll wait a few days. The wounds are cauterized with a solution of permanganate and are no longer bleeding. Now we must nurse her back to health. I've given her a heavy dose of laudanum, and she's sleeping." He looked at Wilson. "Mr. Young, is this lady under your protection?"

Before Wilson could answer, Warner said hoarsely, "She's mine. I mean, she's my partner. I want to see her. Right away."

The doctor gave him a wry smile and motioned with his hand. "Then you may go right on in. In fact, you can be her chief nurse."

Whatever relief Warner had felt that the bullet from Fisher's derringer had not done more damage to Laura than he'd feared immediately left him when he entered the doctor's surgery and saw her pale, wan face and her figure modestly covered with a sheet up to her neck as she lay on the doctor's combination bed and treatment table. Warner's first thought was that he'd seen corpses that had more color in their faces. But the doctor assured him she'd be all right with rest and nourishment. He said, "The worst is over. All we need to do now is have patience and let nature take its course."

So, even though his mind seethed with hate and bitterness and thoughts of revenge against Jack Fisher, Warner had resolutely set himself to the task of helping to take care of Laura. The doctor had an elderly lady, a Mrs. Hopp, who cooked and cleaned for him and whom he'd taught the rudiments of nursing. So it was she who made the broth that Warner laboriously tried to feed to his doped-up, half-asleep, very weak patient. It took most of the day and half of a night to get a pint of beef broth into her. Then, as she became more alert, Warner worked to feed her soft mashed potatoes with little bits of vegetables mixed in. Wilson brought her valise over, and Mrs. Hopp put Laura's nightgown on her while Warner waited outside with Wilson.

During the wait, Wilson said, "The sheriff chased Fisher and his men to the country line, but he never got them in sight. He sent one of his deputies on ahead to scout and found them camped across the line, obviously waiting for a train to stop at the siding at the county auction barn. You can bet Fisher sent one of his lesser-known men into town to arrange the stop. Right now you can bet he's home and wondering where you got that horse and what happened."

"I saw him looking over at Laura after he shot her, and I saw him never pause in making his getaway. You reckon he knew who he hit when he tried to spook my horse?"

Wilson nodded. "I'd reckon. Not much gets by that snake. I hate to say it, but he ain't lived this long by not being able to tell run from fort up and fight."

"You leave him be. You understand me? Leave him be."

Wilson looked at him. "Don't you reckon you got enough on your plate right now? This ain't no time to be thinking of Fisher. I've sent Chulo and two of my other men up to your spread with Charlie. I don't think Fisher will get after your place right now, but there ain't no harm in being ready. You can't go home now, so you just worry about Laura and leave the rest to me."

Warner said, almost as if it passed belief, "The son of a bitch shot Laura! The low-down bastard shot the woman I—He shot Laura!"

Wilson patted him on the shoulder. "Plenty of time to think of that later. Right now you better get back to your nursing."

He thanked Wilson for thinking to see to his other business and then devoted himself exclusively to Laura. He stayed right by her side the rest of Saturday and all day Saturday and Saturday night and then Sunday and Sunday night. They brought him in a cot so he could catch catnaps by her side, but he slept very little and only snatched a bite or two of whatever Mrs.

294

Hopp put in front of him, barely noticing what he was eating.

Early Monday morning they moved Laura out of the treatment room and into a regular bedroom, since the infirmary was part of the doctor's own house. Warner moved right along with her. Later that same morning she woke up clear-eyed but weak. She had a little fever, but it broke and Warner was wiping the light sweat off her face when her eyes opened fully and she looked at him and then at her surroundings.

"Where am I?" she said.

"You're in the doctor's house. You stay right still. You are not supposed to move about." He touched her forehead. It felt cool. Then he leaned down and kissed her lightly.

She wrinkled her nose. "Have you been sleeping with the hogs?"

That made him feel a great deal better. He said, "No, but I ain't exactly had a chance to take a bath or shave or even brush my teeth."

"You smell like it. What is today?"

He told her and she looked around the room. "Isn't there a woman here?"

"Yes. Mrs. Hopp. She helps the doctor."

"Well, send her in. And you go get cleaned up."

He was reluctant to leave her side. "You sure?"

"Yes, and hurry. I'm about to pop."

"Oh. Oh, I'm sorry! I'll get Mrs. Hopp right now."

"Tell her to bring a pan. She'll know what you mean."

He stopped and looked back at her. "I'll be outside."

She took her hand out from under the covers and made a weak gesture at him. "No. Go get cleaned up. You look awful." Then she smiled faintly. "I'm not going to die on you. You still owe me money. But for God's sake, tell the lady to hurry up!"

With a great sense of relief, he went to their room at Wilson's and took a bath and shaved and washed his teeth and put on clean clothes and felt considerably better. After that he went down to La Cocina and ate eggs and chili and enchiladas and drank mugs of beer as fast as the waitress could bring them to him. In his opinion, Mrs. Hopp's greatest value to the doctor was as a cook. He reckoned he didn't know of anything that would make a person want to get well faster than a steady diet of that woman's cooking. He was convinced she boiled everything, even steak. At first, in his worry about Laura, he hadn't cared, but once she'd come out of danger he had longed for something with some taste to it.

By Tuesday morning Laura was able to sit up and feed herself. But after breakfast she managed to get a look at her wound, where the bullet had gone in at the front, and she was outraged. "That son of a bitch!" she said. "I'll kill that bastard! I will cut his goddam balls off and make him eat them!"

It had scared Warner, her getting so upset, and he'd tried to quiet her, but she'd have none of it. She lay there, the covers thrown back and her gown pulled up. "Would you look at that?" she said. "Would you, for God's sake, just look at that? And the one behind has got to be worse. Do you have any idea what kind of scars these wounds are going to leave?"

"Honey," he said, "don't worry. I'm the only one who will ever see them, and I don't care."

"The hell with you!" she said. "Who cares if only you see them. *I'll* see them! I won't be perfect anymore!"

He stared at her for a long second. Then he said, "I'd laugh, but I'm damned if I don't think you are serious."

She was in a fury. "Serious? I'm as serious as a burning building. That little toad! He can hide behind his sheriff in his own county on criminal charges, but by God, I'll sue his tiny ass off in civil court! I'll slap so many lawsuits on him he'll stay in court forever. I'll keep the bastard occupied for the rest of his lousy life! I'll teach him about firing a gun into a crowd. You wait until I get started on that toad. You leave him the hell alone, Warner. I'm the one with the most against him."

"No," he said, "you're not. Now, you calm down."

She gave him a look. "Don't do anything any dumber than you usually do. I mean it, Warner. I don't like the way you are looking. What are you planning?"

"Nothing now," he said. "But he made me bleed. And that will not be allowed to pass."

"Warner, I'm the one he shot. And it was an accident."

He nodded. "Don't forget what you said about if I get cut, you bleed. It works both ways."

Her face got anxious. "Warner, don't do anything until I'm up and around. Please. Promise me. Promise?"

He got up from the chair beside her bed. "I've got to go out. The Vaughns have sent word that they're coming to see me. I'm supposed to meet them over at Wilson's saloon at eleven o'clock. It's pretty close on to that right now."

"You didn't promise me."

He stopped at the door. "I forgot what the request was."

"That you wouldn't do anything until I was up and around."

"Hell, Laura, I got to do some things. A man has got to eat and sleep and tend to business. I can't not do *anything* while you lay around in bed."

She yelled after him as he was closing the door, "You son of a bitch, you know what I mean!"

Warner met with Austin and Preston Vaughn at

Wilson's table in his saloon. Wilson was across the river tending to some business. Sending two of his vaqueros back to Warner's ranch with Charlie had left him shorthanded.

After the Vaughns had expressed their regret about Laura's misfortune and sympathized with Warner and congratulated him on his good luck that she was getting better, Austin said, "Now you can see what a hard bargain the bastard can drive when you've got loved ones at stake."

"Yeah," Warner said.

Preston said, "Warner, something has got to be done. That's what we come in to talk to you about. There's got to be some way of getting at that man. I don't know what it is, but we've got to flush him out."

Austin then said that they had seen Fisher and his party arrive at the auction barn before the race. He said, "You know, that auction barn siding ain't that far from our headquarters. One of the few riders I got left saw the train stop there and saw who got off. For all he knew, they were coming for us again. So he rode like hell for me and Pres. That's one of the reasons we didn't come to the fairgrounds. We knowed he was going there to race you, but we couldn't be sure he might not drop in on us on his way back, so we stayed pretty tight to home."

He went on to confirm what Wilson had guessed, that they had taken time to make a camp just over the county line before riding for the racetrack. Preston said, "Fisher had his getaway organized in case they was any trouble. It is that kind of thinking that makes that man so hard to hem up. No matter what meanness he's up to, he's always got his eye out looking for the back door. The son of a bitch is good at what he does. He's a sorry low-down dog, but he's good at it."

They went on talking, waiting for Wilson Young. When it became clear he wouldn't be coming across the river for lunch the Vaughns got up with the excuse that they'd stayed too long. Austin said, "Just because you might be at the front of Fisher's mind, it don't mean he's forgot us, especially with some money coming due. At least he thinks it ought to be due him."

Preston shook hands and told Warner earnestly that he and Wilson should come out to their ranch and they should all make some kind of a plan. "We've got to do something about Fisher before we suffer further losses. He's got to be put a stop to. I think we can do it together."

Warner agreed with them and walked with them out to their horses, but inside his own mind and heart was the certain feeling that Fisher belonged to him. Before Laura's shooting, accidental though it was, he would have gone in with the devil himself against Jack Fisher. But ever since that exact second when he'd known she'd be all right and he hadn't needed to focus every ounce of his concentration on hoping and praying her back to health, his thirst for vengeance had risen up and nearly consumed him. He didn't know how or when he was going to get to Fisher or what he was going to do to him when he did, but he knew that day, that hour, that moment, was coming when he would have Jack Fisher at his mercy and he could decide his fate on the same whim of chance that had nearly taken Laura from him. And for that reason he did not want to act in concert with the Vaughns or Wilson Young or anyone else who would have a say in the final disposition of Jack Fisher. Warner would agree and he would discuss and he would appear to go along with any plan, but meanwhile a fine white-hot fire of vengeance burned in his belly like molten steel, and he intended to temper that steel in the reputation or the property or the body of Jack Fisher—and quite possibly all three. It was simply a question of sitting down, now that Laura didn't occupy his every thought, and making a plan that would work, then putting it into effect.

He ate lunch with Laura in the infirmary, but that afternoon she was cross and restless and told him to go off and bother someone else for a while. It was the clearest sign he'd seen thus far that she was really on the mend. She was tired of being in bed and perfectly willing to take out her displeasure on anyone at hand. She was acting like her old self.

Warner dawdled away the afternoon playing in a small-stakes poker game at Wilson's casino. Wilson came in late in the afternoon looking like he'd had to actually do some work in his fine clothes. He said, "That's what I get for helping out a friend—dirt and cow shit all over me."

Warner went upstairs with him while he washed up and changed clothes. Then, it being near on to six o'clock, they went across the street to the hotel dining room and had steak and potatoes and biscuits with gravy for supper. Warner said, "Laura don't know what an act of faithfulness it has been for me to stay with her and eat that food that woman puts out over there. But she's better now, and there ain't no use in us both suffering. That Mrs. Hopp makes mush out of whatever it is she is given to cook. Don't make no difference—steak, beets, watermelon, old fence posts—she turns it into mush. Mush without any salt or pepper. Larrupin' stuff, I tell you."

"When you reckon she'll be able to travel?"

"The doctor said in two or three days. She has talked him into sewing up both wounds in hopes of minimizing the size of her scars. He doesn't hold out much hope it will help, but she insists. Wilson, that is the vainest woman God ever made. I'd tell you what she said, but I'm too ashamed."

"My friend, there ain't no such animal as the

vainest woman. They are all tied for the lead in that department. A woman can worry more about her appearance in five minutes than me and you and every other man who ever drawed a hand of poker can do in a lifetime."

"I guess you asked when Laura could travel as a sideways way of asking me when I'm going to let you have Chulo and your two vaqueros back. Well, I—"

"I had no such intentions in mind."

"Don't lie, Wilson. It is not good for a man's character, and yours is mighty shaky at best. What I was going to say—now that she's all right, I reckon I can go on home ahead of her and she can follow when she's strong enough. You can bring her down, if you're a mind, or hire somebody to travel with her. Ain't no need for me to be hanging around here. She's already getting cranky about being in bed, and I can assure you her disposition ain't going to improve the longer she is confined. I pity that poor young doctor whose most tasking trials have come from hardened criminals with gunshot wounds. Before Laura is through with him, he will beg her to leave and will probably detail Mrs. Hopp to accompany her home just to get rid of her."

Warner spent that evening in Laura's company, and it was not a pleasant time. She complained about the bed, she complained about the bed linen, she complained about the food, the

303

temperature of the room, the fact that the doctor would not let her have a drink of spirits, not even wine. She complained about Warner's absence, and she complained he was constantly underfoot and watching her like some ghoul at a deathbed. She complained that her life would never be the same, that Warner would never want her again, having seen her perfection shattered, that God only knew what was happening at the River Ranch and what was happening at her home in Corpus Christi and she had to get out of this place before that goddam woman came in again with either a thermometer or some more of that uneatable food or an extra blanket when the room was hotter than her temper.

Warner listened, and when he could, at about nine o'clock, took his leave as quietly as he could. He kissed her on her lips and said Mrs. Hopp had decreed it was her bedtime and he had to leave. She said to hell with Mrs. Hopp, but she settled down and let him lower the lamp before he left. When Warner paused at the door she said, "You bring me a drink of brandy tomorrow. I don't give a damn what that doctor says. Who ever heard of not giving a gunshot patient a drink every now and then?"

"All right, honey," he said. He stepped out of the room and closed the door behind him, shaking his head and putting on his hat. He reckoned Mrs. Hopp earned her wages. He reminded himself to give her a gift of money before he left to go back to his ranch.

It was a dark night as he stepped out of the doctor's front door and onto the boardwalk. Wilson's place was about five blocks to the left, heading north. He walked along in the dark, headed up toward the main street where he would turn north. He figured to have a few drinks with Wilson and then go up to his room and turn in for an early night.

The boardwalk quit at the end of the doctor's block, and Warner was forced to pick his way along in the dark, there being no lights except for the few houses that were scattered around. He was coming up to the main street when he passed an alley behind the buildings that fronted on the street. He thought he heard someone say his name. He stopped and looked into the gloom of the alley and said, "What?"

Someone said softly, "Grayson?"

He took a couple of steps into the alley, thinking the voice sounded like someone he knew, but couldn't place. He said, "What? Who is it? Is that you, Wilson?"

He took another step, and all of a sudden someone had him in a bear grip from behind and was lifting him off his feet. He struggled, but his attacker had caught him so unawares that he had both of Warner's arms pinned. He jerked and snatched himself around, but whoever it was—

and the man was uncommonly strong—had his feet off the ground and he couldn't get a purchase to use any leverage. He let out a whoop and desperately tried to reach for his gun, but there was no way he could get his hand up to it, not the way his arms were pinned.

And then the man, whoever it was, was whirling around and around, carrying Warner with him, shaking him like a sack of rags. All of sudden he threw Warner across the alley. It came so sudden that Warner had no chance to do anything except let his momentum carry him. It was a short trip. He smashed hard against the side of a building, hitting it at full tilt with his left side. He struck the wall so hard the air whooshed out of his lungs and he started to sink down to the ground, gasping. But he never made it to the ground. A hulking figure was suddenly over him, hauling him up again, whirling him around and around, and then flinging him against the same wall, only harder. This time he hit face first and thought he was knocked out as lights burst inside his head and a sort of gray mist descended before his eyes. He started to sink down to his knees, but those same huge hands grabbed him again and hoisted him up and slammed him into the wall again. This time he did slide to the ground. But then the man was on him, flipping him over, straddling his body, pinning down his arms with his knees. Warner's head was ringing and his senses were floating somewhere over his head, but he felt the man's hands go around his neck and start to squeeze into a choke hold. A low, mean voice came out of the man's face. He said, "Mistuh Fishuh wants you to hev plenny time to know this'n is yourn. You unnerstan'? I'm gonna kill you slow."

Part of Warner's brain recognized the voice and the frame as that of Fisher's man Quince. But the other part of his brain said there wasn't anything he could do about it so what difference could it make? As the grip tightened, he tried to struggle, but he was powerless in Quince's grip and weakened by the beating he'd taken. He struggled and struggled as the choke hold tightened. Finally a dark curtain seemed to drape his eyes, and he could feel himself getting weaker and weaker and feel his head growing light.

Then some of the darkness faded and he could feel and hear a faraway throat gasping and grasping for air. It was his own. As he slowly returned to consciousness the voice above him said, "Thought you wuz gone, din't ya? But ah ain't ready yit. Mistuh Fishuh wants you to go down a few times before ah let you all the way to the bottom. He wants you to have a real good pitchuh what it gon' be like."

Warner gasped and coughed. He tried to move his arms, but the man had them pinned down with his knees on Warner's biceps. He could see the huge frame of the man looming over him. His right hand reached for his holster. With the tip of his finger touching the leather of it just below his belt, he could tell it was empty. His revolver had obviously been jolted out as he'd been whirled around and slammed again and again into the wall.

Above him the voice said, in that southern white trash dialect, "Heah it come 'gain."

Warner instinctively spread out his arms to get purchase on the ground and tried to shake the man off of him as he felt the big hands once more close around his neck. Quince's grip was beginning to tighten, and he could feel his breath being slowly constricted, but at the same instant the tips of his fingers touched something cold and hard. With all the effort he could muster, he threw himself to the right, his fingers reaching desperately for the hard round object. He didn't know what it was, but thought it might be of something he could use as a weapon. He could not turn his head to see—even if he could have seen in the dark of the alley—but he hoped it might be a small piece of pipe that would allow him to dig at the man's ribs or hit him.

Then his fingers found a grip and pulled the object toward him. He put his palm down as the grayness began to take his brain. It took him a second to realize he had found his revolver. He groped for it frantically, hoping to get it into his hand and make use of it before the blackness came again. Quince might not mean to let him come back up this time, or he might make a mistake and drop him all the way.

Warner grasped the revolver in his hand and slowly, almost drunkenly, brought it up, feeling for Quince's body, his belly, his chest, any part of the man he could reach. His brain was screaming at him to hurry, but his muscles were becoming very heavy. He could feel himself beginning to slip away. He tried to jerk his head back and forth, his lungs feeling like they were about to explode, but Quince's grip was like a vise.

Then he felt the muzzle of the revolver touch something solid. He knew he had the revolver pointed inward and upward. He couldn't wait any longer. He thumbed back the hammer and fired.

For an instant nothing happened, and then Warner dimly heard a sudden intake of breath. With the last of his strength and consciousness he moved the barrel of the revolver slightly and fired again. This time he heard a moan that seemed to come from a long way away. He felt the grip around his throat loosen slightly. A little air leaked into his lungs. The grip loosened more, and he opened his mouth and sucked air out of the darkness. He could feel the black syrup that had clogged his brain slowly dripping away. His eyes had been open, but he hadn't been able to see. Now gradually the black he'd been trying to look into was revealed as just the dark of night, and he could make out the form above him, see the barrel of his revolver. His arm was bent at the elbow, and he could see he'd shot Quince too low. He raised the barrel and shot the huge man in the chest. With that same sharp intake of breath Quince received the bullet and began to fall slowly sideways, his hands leaving Warner's throat as he fell.

Warner heard him flop onto his side as he hit the ground. His big left leg was still sprawled over Warner, but for a moment or two Warner did nothing but lie still and gasp for air. He put his left hand to his throat. It was sore. If there'd been any bones there they would have been broken. He wondered if Quince had crushed his windpipe or his larynx. He tried to speak, but the only sounds that came out were hoarse squawks.

After another minute or two he slowly sat up and leaned back against the wall that Quince had battered him against. He pulled up his leg and, with his boot heel, shoved Quince's leg off him. The movement caused Quince to flop over on his back. Warner could barely see him in the dim light. He debated shooting him again, but the man hadn't made the slightest movement since he'd fallen. Warner just sat there, his mouth open, breathing. The air tasted better than anything that had ever crossed his lips before. He was reflecting on what a close call he'd had when he put his tongue out to lick his lips. They tasted salty. He put up his hand and it came away wet. Well, of course, he thought. His nose was probably broken, and who knew what else? The son of a bitch had slammed him face first into the wall at least half a dozen times. Maybe more.

He felt like there was a ton of lead resting on his shoulders, but he couldn't stay in the alley all night. Working slowly he got to his feet and stood there for a moment, using the wall for a support. He looked down at Quince. The man was lying on his back, his eyes open, his arms flung wide. Warner didn't figure Quince would be going anywhere for a while. He holstered his revolver and then, lurching and holding on to first one wall and then another, made it to the main street and turned left and started toward Wilson's place. Nobody paid him the slightest attention even though he was now back among lights and people. To them he was just another drunk staggering along the boardwalk using the walls and fronts of the stores for a plumb bob to tell which way up was.

At the saloon he gave a boy a half a dollar to run in and fetch Wilson Young. The young boy looked at his face strangely, but the half dollar took most of his attention. He said, the words barely audible, "Tell'm's Warner. Hurt. Go."

There was another way up to Wilson's quarters, but it led up a staircase that opened from a door on the main street. The door was kept locked, an innocent-looking door in the side of the saloon that didn't seem to go anywhere. Warner didn't want to go through Wilson's saloon, not because of the way he looked but because he suspected that if Fisher had sent one man, Quince, he might have sent another who would be on lookout at the place Warner was known to stay. If there was another man, Warner didn't want him to know that Quince had failed at his job. He wanted Fisher to find out in the fullness of time.

In a moment Wilson Young came cautiously to the batwing doors and looked out, holding the boy by the shoulder. Warner was leaning against a porch post. He made a motion with his hand, and Wilson saw him and came hurrying through the doors. He took one look at Warner and said, "What the hell happened to you?"

Warner made a floppy motion with his hand toward the door down the boardwalk. In his croaky voice he said, "Upstairs."

Wilson got a shoulder under his arm and helped him down the boardwalk. He leaned Warner against the wall of his saloon while he fished out a key. He said, "I don't know what got ahold of you, but I'm glad it was you, not me." He unlocked the door and helped Warner through it, and together they started up the long stairway and down the hall toward Warner's room. Wilson said, "Let's get a drink into you first and then you

312

can tell me all about it. You don't seem to want to talk right now."

"Get docta . . ."

"Yeah, yeah, I'll get the doctor. But let's get you in a good light so I can tell him what all tools he needs to bring. And get a drink in you. Goddam, Warner, I let you out of my sight for more than five minutes and you can get in some of the damnedest messes of any boy your age and size I ever saw in my life."

"Fuh you."

"Fuh me? What's 'fuh me'? Is that some new kind of nastiness your evil mind has invented? You ain't got enough trouble now, you want to go around fuhing folks?"

Wilson opened the door of the room that Warner and Laura had slept in. As he let Warner down on the bed he said, "This keeps up, that doctor is going to be in the horse and whorehouse business. Warner, you ever thought about maybe hiring yourself your own doctor? Just for you and the ones unfortunate enough to be around you? Pay him by the month—might work out cheaper that way."

Warner sat on the side of the bed with his head hanging down. It was the only position that seemed to ease the soreness in his throat. He said, "Fuh you."

Wilson said, "There you go again. Is that some new sport you've picked up in your travels? You been hanging around that Chinese whorehouse in Galveston again? I hear they get up to some mighty strange stunts in that place."

The doctor had come and gone, and now Wilson and Warner were sitting in the room drinking brandy and talking about the incident. The first drink of brandy had burned Warner's throat like fire, but the doctor had given him a small dose of laudanum, and it had eased his pain and also allowed him to talk almost normally. His head was pounding in spite of the laudanum, and his body showed him a new pain every time he moved, but he was feeling considerably better than he had been an hour before. The doctor had sworn that he would not upset Laura with the news, though he'd been curious how Warner expected to come visit her without her taking some notice of his condition. He'd said that he didn't intend to visit the next day, that Wilson would stop by with some cocked-up story to cover the short period it would take him to heal. The doctor had expressed the opinion that Warner would have to be the fastest healer in the history of medicine not to be still showing the effects for at least three or four days. He'd said, "You've got a broken nose, your lip is split in three or four places, the rest of your face is raw and scraped, and I've dug about half a dozen wood splinters out of your forehead. By tomorrow this time you are going to look like you tried to stop a train with your face. I don't know what happened to your neck, unless you got cut down before you were hanged, but it's going to look a nice shade of black-and-blue. You say a horse threw you? I thought you were this famous Warner Grayson who could ride anything that you could get on?"

Wilson said, "You actually told that doctor you got thrown into a woodpile to explain those splinters?" Warner nodded. "Boy, you ain't going to have no reputation at all when that story gets around."

"Naturally you are going to see that it does."

"Seriously, what are you going to do about Laura?"

Warner took a sip of his brandy and tried to light a cigar, but it was hard to puff because of his throat and because of the rolls of cloth that the doctor had shoved up his nostrils to act as inside splints for his broken nose. They made everything he said sound nasal. He said, lying, "I'm not going to do anything about Laura, because I don't want her to think I'm in danger here. I'm going to take that noon train tomorrow and you're going to go over to the infirmary and tell her I've had to take a quick run up to the ranch to see to some business and that I should be back in twenty-four to thirty-six hours."

They had decided, against Wilson's strong objection, not to notify the sheriff about Quince's body, but just to let him be found naturally. If nobody had noticed him by the time Warner left town, Wilson would slip around and give the lawman the word. In any case, Wilson would tell the sheriff the story once Warner was out of town. Warner said, "I ain't got no objections to reporting the matter to Ryan Shank, but I don't want to be delayed."

Wilson said, "Ryan ain't going to like it, but I can't see any harm coming of telling him after you've gone. God knows, me and the doctor can both testify that something mighty bad got hold of you. Boy, you have been lucky in your life. But the way you're using up that luck, you are likely to start running short quicker than you need to. You are burning your lucky candle at both ends, and you are going to end up with a mighty short wick. Do you know what the odds are of your revolver ending up where it did? Not very damn good."

Warner said, "You still got that antelope rifle, as you call it? The Colt that you had the barrel lengthened on?"

Wilson pulled his head back and looked at him. "What do you want with that?"

"I don't know," Warner said, lying again. "Listen, send somebody over to fetch it tonight. Unless you have it here."

"It's across the river. But I still want to know what you want it for?"

"I'm going to take it to one of my men—Les Russel. He's a good shot, and I know that rifle of yours will reach way on out there. If Fisher has men scouting my place, I want to put that rifle in Les's hands so he can reach out and pluck one of Fisher's men out of the saddle when he thinks he's out of range."

Wilson looked at him narrowly. Finally he said, "I'll get it in the morning before you leave."

"No, send for it tonight. I need to know how much ammunition you got to go with it. As I remember, it is a thirty-two caliber and that brand of bullets is hard to find. C'mon, Wilson, I don't feel like going across the river myself. Besides, I need my Andalusian tonight. I want to take him back to the ranch with me, and I may not be feeling so chipper in the morning. Hell, do a friend a favor, will you? It ain't like I never accommodated you."

Wilson got up, looking at Warner warily, "All right. I'll go myself. But I got the feeling that one of us is not exactly telling the truth, and I ain't said that much. What are you up to, Warner?"

"Nothing! What is this? Ask a friend to fetch your horse and lend you his gun and all you get is a fish-eyed look. What could I be up to in the condition I'm in? Hell, I can barely walk."

Wilson shook his head. "I don't know," he said. "I'll do what you ask, but I don't know. I'll put your Andalusian in the hotel stables."

"Bring all the ammunition you got for that rifle. Hear?"

"Yes, yes, yes. Warner, you are going to make me lie to Laura, aren't you?"

"I never made you do anything in your life. And neither has anyone else."

"We'll see." Wilson went out the door, closing it behind him.

For half an hour after Wilson left, Warner sat in an overstuffed chair and drank brandy and smoked a cigar. He did not think much, because there was nothing much left to think about. At some point he had arrived at a decision, and a plan had followed, almost fully developed, in his mind at very nearly the same time. It was a simple plan, a direct plan, and either it would work or it wouldn't. It wasn't the sort of plan that needed much revising once he'd made up his mind to it. He'd simply go and do it. Or try to.

After he was sure that Wilson was out of the way, Warner got up and let himself out through the back stairs and the door onto the street. It hurt to move, but he thought it better than sitting around stiffening up.

He went down to the railroad depot and, for twenty dollars, bribed the telegrapher to let him know if anyone wanted to send a telegram to Jack Fisher. Telegraphers were difficult and expensive to bribe because they had a sort of official job, but Warner had done it before, and he counted the results well worth the cost. It was because of the scrupulous honesty of telegraph operators that he hadn't wanted Wilson to tell the sheriff about Quince. If Quince had a confederate about town somewhere he'd hear about the killing quicker if the news of it became public, and he would most probably wire Fisher. And Warner didn't want Fisher to get that wire. Or to be warned. Or to be put in the way of any information. If he'd had the strength he would have tried to hide Quince's body, but he'd barely had the energy to make it to Wilson's place. He couldn't ask Wilson to go and hide the body because then Wilson would want to know why, and Warner didn't want to tell his friend his plan. As he limped back to the saloon he thought about going by the alley and trying to hide the body. But Quince was a big man, a huge man, and anyway, Warner didn't want to be seen about the area again. Or to risk being connected with Quince.

That night Warner lay in bed unable to sleep because of all his aches and pains. The doctor had left him a small vial of laudanum, but he reckoned to save that for a time when his hurts might prevent him from carrying out some part of his plan. At least he no longer had to worry his mind trying to work out the matter with Fisher. Jack Fisher had made this business personal with his mistake at the racetrack, and Warner intended to handle it personally.

12

He ate breakfast with Wilson Young the next morning. Warner had finally seen himself in the mirror in a good light, and his face was not a pretty sight. He'd planned on shaving, but his jaw was much too sore to bear the edge of a razor. His injuries didn't make him angry at Fisher, though, because his mind and his determination were well beyond such trivial emotions as anger.

He'd gotten a key to the street door, the private entrance, from Wilson Young so that he was able to go and come without having to pass through the saloon. So far as either he or Wilson had heard, there had been no report of Quince's death. They'd eaten breakfast in the hotel dining room, and Warner had made it short, eager to be about his errands. Wilson had wanted to know what he was going to do until train time, but Warner said he'd just rest and for Wilson to go on about his business and not bother seeing him off.

After that he'd gone down to the depot and ordered out a stock car for the noon train, specifying that it be dropped off at Fisher's siding. The car was to be picked up by the next southbound train, since Warner was only hiring it for a one-way trip. He had not heard a word from the telegrapher the night before. A new one was on duty, and Warner considered approaching him, but with time as short as it was, he'd decided that it didn't matter if word was out already.

After that Warner went back into town and hunted through hardware and general merchandise and gun stores for more thirty-two caliber ammunition. Wilson had only brought him fifty rounds, and he wanted much more than that. After some hard looking, he was finally able to buy another hundred eighty rounds and decided he'd have to be satisfied with that.

At a mercantile store he bought a ground cloth and a blanket and a two-gallon canteen and some soda crackers and canned goods. Then, with his purchases slung over his shoulder in a tow sack, he located a horse lot and bought a small donkey for twenty dollars. Leading the donkey, he went back to the general mercantile and bought two five-gallon cans of kerosene. He also bought a leather strap and rigged it so each end was attached to one can of kerosene. He took the kerosene cans outside, the weight painful to his sore back, and draped them over the donkey's back in a pack arrangement that seemed agreeable to the donkey. Then he led the donkey over to the hotel stables, got his Andalusian, gave the stableboy a half a dollar to saddle and bridle the animal, and then mounted the Andalusian and rode down to the depot, leading the donkey. He spotted his car where he'd been told it would be, and he got a couple of railroad employees to help him load his two head of stock. After that was done, he closed the door of the stock car and went back to his room. It was only about an hour to train time.

In the room he took a small valise and put a bottle of brandy and a bottle of whiskey in it, along with two extra boxes of cartridges for his revolver. He added a couple of fresh shirts, mainly to keep the bottles from banging together— he certainly didn't expect to be worrying much about his appearance on the trip—and then put in the little vial of laudanum. He felt bad enough to look at it longingly, but he contented himself with a long drink of brandy and a cigar. His face was already starting to turn black-and-blue, and he reckoned it would be purple and green before this ordeal was all over, but it was his throat that hurt him the most, that and his back.

Lastly he took Wilson's strange-looking rifle in one hand and his valise in the other, left the idea of leaving a note to his good intentions, and went down the stairs and out into the brilliant sunlight of the day. As he walked along, people glanced at him and his face, and he didn't much blame them. But all they did was give him a glance. Violence was too common a commodity in a border town to draw much interest.

At a quarter of noon he climbed into the stock

car and settled down to await departure. His Andalusian turned around from the little hayrick and gave him a look, pricking his ears forward. Warner said, "Ain't no use asking. I'm not sure myself what is going to happen, but I can guarantee that you may well earn your keep in the next twenty-four hours if things go as I hope."

The Andalusian turned around and went back to his hay. The donkey didn't seem interested one way or the other. The minutes went by, and soon Warner could feel and see his car being hooked into a line of other stock and freight cars. Shortly thereafter he felt a jolt, and the train started slowly north.

Wilson's rifle was an adaption of a Colt limited-production 1882 model. It was a nine-shot repeater, but instead of having the shells in a chamber like most rifles, the gun had a cylinder just like Warner's revolver except that, because of the size of the cylinder and the smaller caliber of the cartridges, it held nine bullets. But it fired the same as Warner's revolver. You cocked the hammer and the cylinder revolved bringing a new cartridge under the firing pin.

But it had been remodeled by a genius of a gunsmith in Fredericksburg, Texas, to Wilson Young's exact specifications. Wilson had more guns for more purposes than any man Warner had ever known, but to have an antelope gun was, in Warner's opinion, piling it on. Wilson

Young loved antelope steaks, but as the country had become more settled, the wild members of the goat family had become harder and harder to stalk. It had gotten to the point where a man could not hope to get within a quarter of a mile of an antelope, the usual range of the Winchester lever-action carbine that most men carried as a saddle rifle. You could reach them with a Sharp's .50 caliber buffalo gun, but the big bullet tore the meat all to pieces. Wilson had had the blacksmith take his Colt revolving .32 caliber rifle and stretch the barrel from thirty-two inches to forty-one. The modification had made the steel of the barrel a little thinner, but the gunsmith had decreased the chance of the barrel getting too hot with repeated firings by porting it and strengthening it with long, slender steel shims that were brazed in place. The result was an octagonal barrel that had once been round and now had rifling inside, added during the lengthening process so that the rifle was even more accurate than before. Wilson had ended up with a rifle that was accurate up to eight hundred yards and that fired a deadly shell that would drop the ninety- to one hundred–pound animals in their tracks at that distance. A spyglass sight had been mounted on top, but it had got knocked out of true so Wilson had simply used it with the iron sights, not having much trouble except when he was firing at a moving target. Warner had used it several times before and had irritated Wilson by how well he could hit with the gun. Wilson had said, "Dammit, guns are my business. Horses are yours. Do I go around making myself out to be as good a horseman as you? No. Then, dammit, don't be shooting as good as me. Especially in front of folks."

But now the train was rolling good, and Warner sat back against the side of the car and contented himself with watching the country go by. They passed the auction barn and then what he thought was Vaughn's ranch, though he couldn't be sure because he couldn't see the ranch house from the railroad, and the gate flashed by so quick he didn't get a good look at it.

He just rested, now and again taking a nip of brandy. He figured the train would reach Fisher's siding somewhere around three o'clock, so just before two he made himself a lunch of crackers and cheese and some cold beans. He sucked a can of apricots dry for dessert and considered himself well fed.

After that he had a drink of brandy and lit a cigar and settled down for the relatively quick ride. He wished the trip back could be as speedy, but he knew it couldn't. He just had to hope there would actually be a trip back to Laura by any conveyance. Or at least any conveyance except a hearse or a horse on which he was strapped sideways, face down.

• • •

Warner stood watching the train disappear down the tracks, heading north to San Antonio. He was at Fisher's siding, and there was even a railroad sign to prove it. The car switching at Uvalde had gone smoothly. The only delays had occurred when the spur-line train made several unscheduled stops to load cattle destined for market in San Antonio.

Now he stood in the big middle of nowhere with choppy prairielike country all around him in varying shades of brown. There were cattle, but they didn't look to be in as good a shape as they might. He didn't know if they were Jack Fisher's cattle or not. He didn't exactly know where Fisher's land began and ended, but he had the feeling he was mighty close to it. West, it was sixty miles as the crow flew back to Del Rio. It was a hell of a lot farther than that by train and maybe by horse, too, if the country stayed as chopped up and cut by ravines and washouts and little cliffs and hills here and there. There were trees, but they were the same old post oak and cedar and mesquite that south Texas was full of.

Jack Fisher's place was some ten miles to the southwest. Or at least that was where his headquarters ranch was. Warner knew that from questions he'd asked Laura. If the land he was standing on was Fisher's, the man owned a lot of land. Miles of it.

To get to Fisher's place he would ride south and then cut to the west, to approach the ranch from the best direction, according to how Laura had described the layout. Of course, when she was talking about the ranch and its features she'd had no idea she was describing it to him for the purposes of a visit. At the time, neither had he.

He took out his watch and studied the time. It was almost a quarter to four. The train had been late, but Warner had plenty of time. He looked up at the sky, calculating it would get dark around six o'clock. He didn't want to do any traveling until then. So, instead of turning south, he mounted the Andalusian and, with the donkey on lead and bearing the cans of kerosene, turned northeast and crossed the tracks. He rode for about a mile until he found a creek meandering through the broken-up land. It was very nearly dry, but there was enough for the animals to water. He let them drink their fill and then loosened the cinch on the Andalusian and relieved the donkey of his burden of kerosene cans and tow sack of groceries and cartridges and the other things he had brought along. He picketed the animals and then got the ground cloth out and spread it over as smooth a place as he could find. He put the blanket down over that and then took off his gun belt, loosened his pants belt, and lay down to take a nap. He willed himself to sleep no more than two hours, but it didn't really matter. He had time to kill before he showed up at Fisher's place, and he figured the ride wouldn't take more than two and a half, maybe three hours, even in the dark.

When he awoke, it was good dark with the moon just coming up. The moon was not as full as he would have liked for the one matter, and a little too full for the other, but it seemed a nice compromise. At least the greater light would make the going easier on the ride to Fisher's ranch. He got up, rolled up his ground cloth and blanket, and tied them on behind his saddle. After that he loaded the kerosene cans and the tow sack on the donkey and tightened the girth on the Andalusian and climbed aboard. He took the donkey on lead and started, without further ado, southwest toward Fisher and the solution to the problem Fisher had brought him. One way or the other, before too many hours had passed the mess would be settled.

The donkey was trouble at first because whenever they came to any bush or tree he invariably wanted to go on the opposite side from the Andalusian, causing confusion and cursing. Warner solved the problem by snubbing him up so tight next to the Andalusian that he couldn't have gotten a matchstick between them. But of course that slowed their pace, which was already dictated by the speed of the donkey, who didn't seem to be in any hurry to get anywhere.

Finally they came to a stretch of flat grassy plain without a bush or tree in sight, and Warner let the donkey back out on a longer lead and then hurried the Andalusian along, forcing the donkey to either strike a trot or get drug. The donkey struck a trot, unwillingly, but he trotted nevertheless.

Warner had no exact directions to Fisher's place, so he wanted to arrive before everyone went to bed and the house got dark. He reckoned he would recognize it as Fisher's from the general layout Laura had given him. And he didn't figure there'd be very many two-story white frame houses out on the bald prairie. There was one rich man in Jack Fisher's county and he was it.

After about an hour's traveling, Warner struck a match and looked at his watch. It was five after eight. Soon, if he was on the right track, he should be able to see, even from a great distance, the lights of Fisher's house. Certainly there was very little in the way of high ground to impede his vision. All that really rough country now lay to the south. He had entered a region that had obviously been cleared for grazing. Now and again he saw an occasional steer or cow, but they were range cattle. From the looks of them, he could see why Fisher would be interested in acquiring some of Austin Vaughn's blooded stock. Of course he could simply have bought some of them to improve his herd, but Fisher apparently didn't think that way. Why buy what you could steal?

Some time later, perhaps half an hour, Warner spied a light to the west and a little to the south of his path. It was not exactly where he reckoned it ought to be, but then, he hadn't had a road map. He veered slightly and headed directly toward the beacon. As he rode, he caught glimpses of another light, more to the south. He stopped and studied the two. The light to the north appeared brighter, but it was smaller, while the light toward the southwest, though dimmer and less distinct, looked bigger. On a hunch that the northern light was the cabin of a line rider with only a single lantern in a small window, he made toward the hazy light to the south.

As Warner traveled, the light began to grow the closer he got. Within half an hour he could see the one big light and then several other lights surrounding it. He reckoned it was not too long after nine o'clock. He figured to hurry, not knowing what hours his adversary kept and wanting to be there in plenty of time to use the lights as a guide to who was where and how many there were.

He stopped a full half mile away, using a mesquite thicket for cover. There was no doubt it was Fisher's place. Warner could clearly see lights in the upstairs and downstairs windows. Laura had said there was a long bunkhouse facing the back of the house, some fifty yards separating the two buildings. He could see enough lights that were far enough apart for him to identify the bunkhouse. She'd said there was a smaller house set between the bunkhouse and the main house. Laura had said the buildings stood in a direct line, but Warner could see that the smaller house was more toward the north, off by itself. Laura had reckoned that was where the foreman lived, or else Fisher's top gunhand or ramrod, or whoever would be considered second-in-command of an operation like Fisher's. She'd said he might live there with his wife, though she hadn't seen any women around the place in her short visit there. She'd said, with a touch of malice, "You'd think a man with Fisher's power and money would have the house overrun with floozies and loose women, but there weren't any I could see. Maybe he doesn't like girls."

Warner didn't give a damn what Fisher liked so long as it wasn't Warner's horses or reputation. Laura had made the caustic observation to explain why Fisher was so vicious and amoral.

But Warner sat there studying the house and the outbuildings. He knew there were several barns and corrals, but they were of no interest to him. He could feel the wind, what little there was, in his face, and that had also been part of the reason for his approach from the south. The wind was always out of the north or northeast in that part of the country at that time of the year and he wanted to be downwind so that none of Fisher's horses or dogs, if he had any about the place, could wind them and sound an alarm. Warner knew the Andalusian wouldn't neigh at the smell of other horses. That was a peculiarity of the breed that he liked. He also knew the donkey wasn't going to smell and bray because he'd rubbed some brandy inside the donkey's nostrils and he wouldn't be smelling anything for quite some time.

Wilson's antelope rifle, because of its length, fit awkwardly in the saddle boot, but it hadn't fallen out. Warner reached behind his right leg and drew it out, then dismounted, dropping the reins to the ground. The Andalusian wasn't going anywhere, and the donkey was tied to the saddle horn, so he wasn't going anywhere either.

Warner stepped out of the cover of the mesquite trees and, bent over, began slowly moving down a little incline toward the lights of the ranch below. He wasn't too worried about being seen. The sky had become dappled with big masses of slow-moving clouds, and each time one of them blocked the moon, the night became too dim to see into its darkness. He was walking in weeds up to his knees, and hunched over, he would look as much like a calf or a steer as anything else. He threaded his way slowly. He'd left his hat on his saddle horn, and the breeze was light and cool on his head.

He remembered Wilson once telling a belligerent who was challenging him that he'd be wise to not buy any green fruit, the implication being that the man, if he kept on with his ways, might not be around long enough for it to ripen. As never before, the significance of that remark came home to Warner. He wasn't scared. He was too determined for that. But inside him was already a sense of sadness at what could happen to him during this awful risky plan he was going to attempt. It was simple and direct and could work, but there were a great many elements that could go wrong. And the worst part of it was that, once he began, there would be no pulling back, no breaking off and running for cover. He would be committed, and he would have just this one chance to take Fisher down. And Fisher would take him down in short order if he failed.

Warner kept on until he was some two hundred yards from the lighted buildings. They lay in a kind of valley between two gentle slopes in the prairie. When he thought he was close enough he lay down carefully on his belly, resting on his elbows, his rifle near to hand, his eyes just above the tops of the weeds.

The place seemed to be settling down for the night. Now and again a light would go off in the bunkhouse. He had counted down the line when the building was fully lighted up and had figured there were twelve windows. He reckoned the place to be at least fifty or sixty feet long. With bunks on both sides, that would hold a power of men.

Most of the lights were still burning on the ground floor of the two-story main house, and Warner could see men still wandering back and forth around the common ground, going into the big house or the barn or off into the darkness to relieve themselves one last time before bed. Just looking, he knew that there must be twenty-five to thirty men about the place, not counting Fisher and the cooks and servants. But, he told himself, he had a long-range rifle and a long-range horse, and he was counting on those advantages to even out the odds.

Warner lay and watched, trying not to think too much. It wasn't good to think about what was ahead. All it would do was make him more nervous and skittish, and he was already chock full of those commodities. Instead, he made his mind think of Laura and his ranch and the stock they were breeding and how well they had been doing until Carl Hamm showed up with his unwelcome message. He remembered back to that morning, how he'd been having his breakfast and fretting over a load of trivial details and aggravations. Well, he thought, that just showed to go you. When you thought you had troubles, a man could come along and show you what real troubles looked like. Warner would gladly have gone back to those minor aggravations and thrown in a thousand dollars and a good saddle to boot. A man never knew when he was well off.

He waited and he waited. Finally, one by one, the lights began to go off. The bunkhouse went dark, and then so did the foreman's house. Only a single lamp burned on the ground floor of the big house. It was, he thought, probably Jack Fisher sitting up, plotting more devilment.

He got out his watch and tried to see it by the light of the moon as it ducked out from behind a cloud. But there wasn't enough light, and he damn sure wasn't going to risk striking a match.

Warner had wondered if Fisher kept watchmen on duty through the night. He hadn't seen any, and because of the man's enormous conceit, he doubted that Fisher would feel that any such a precaution was necessary. He doubted that Fisher would expect anyone to even trespass on his land, much less contemplate a raid on his headquarters.

But still, he waited and watched. He heard a dog howl and another one answer, but they sounded far off, away from the main buildings. He didn't know what he was going to do if Fisher kept a pack of hounds around the place and they set up a baying at his approach. He'd just have to handle that problem as it came about.

Finally, as the moon began to descend, Warner calculated he'd waited long enough. The light that had been on downstairs at the big house had gradually grown dim and then gone out, as if it had run out of lamp oil. Well, Warner had a fresh supply for them. He was going to give them some light.

He got up cautiously and, still hunched over, slowly made his way back to the clump of mesquite. The Andalusian stamped his foot, but the donkey looked bored. Warner unhooked the two sack, which had been hanging off one of the kerosene cans and tied it to the saddle horn of the Andalusian. Then, deep in the mesquite grove, he turned his back to the ranch below him and flicked a match with his thumb and, in its brief flare, took a quick look at his watch. It was a quarter after three. As good a time as any.

Warner untied the donkey and, taking him on lead, started down the slope toward the buildings. He went slowly, walking hunched over, hiding as much of himself as he could behind the reluctant donkey. In his left hand he carried Wilson's antelope gun. He had taken two boxes of the .32 caliber cartridges out of his saddlebags, each box containing fifty bullets. He'd emptied the contents of one box into his shirt and pants pockets. The other box he'd stuck inside his shirt. He could feel its sharp corners against his belly.

Finally, at the edge of the weeds, he stopped. He reckoned the distance to the buildings to be about a hundred yards. That was going to be either the longest hundred yards he'd ever traveled or the shortest. The span would be measured by how well things went. Warner laid his rifle down at the edge of the weeds, memorizing its position in relation to that of the ranch buildings. When he came back, he judged he'd be in too big a hurry to spend much time looking for it.

He untied the lead line from the donkey's rope halter and let it fall to the ground, then tugged the two kerosene cans off the back of the donkey and set them down. There didn't seem to be any good way to carry them, so he knelt down and put the strap over his own neck and stood up. It made his sore back groan with pain, and he began to wish he'd taken a little sip of the laudanum before setting out, but it was too late now. He figured the cans couldn't weigh more than seventy pounds, but his sore back thought they were made of lead.

With his unwieldy burden he started first for the bunkhouse, judging that nest to contain the most dangerous hornets. Now was not a time to go slowly, now was a time to hurry.

He got to the bunkhouse, arriving at the southeast corner. He knelt down below the level of the windows and carefully unscrewed the cap of the can on his right side after placing the other can next to it. Then he felt something come up, and he jerked his head to the left, his right hand going toward the butt of his revolver. His heart almost stopped. It was the donkey. The beast had not been willing to be led, and now he was following along like a pet dog. When Warner had his nerves back under control he freed the open can from the tie at the end of the strap and then, holding it in both hands and walking bent over, began to move slowly along the side of the bunkhouse splashing out kerosene as he went. He tried to gauge the amount he was pouring out so that he would have enough to completely encircle the building but it was a hard thing to judge. He felt like the can was half empty by the time he'd finished with just the back side. The bunkhouse was much longer than it was wide, but he would still have to cut down on the amount he was pouring. He turned right at the corner and started on the western end. When he was near the corner, only some two or three feet away, he heard a noise. He couldn't identify it, but it sounded close. It wasn't the donkey, which was right behind him. He set the can down and straightened up, taking his revolver by the butt and half drawing it from the holster.

A man wearing only the bottoms of a pair of long johns suddenly came around the corner, yawning and looking down as he fumbled with the buttons of his underwear. He was almost to Warner when he looked up. His eyes widened and he opened his mouth to either speak or yell. The only sound, though, was the dull crack when Warner slammed the barrel of his revolver down on the man's bare head. He crumpled without a sound and flopped to the ground, his arms and legs sprawled out.

Without a pause Warner picked up the can and continued on around the building. There were two doors to the bunkhouse with a little porch in front of each. He gave them both a good dose of the kerosene.

It was hard, awkward work, and he was perspiring by the time he reached his starting point. So far all was quiet. He had heard a few more yowls from dogs, but they still sounded far off.

He had only the one can to go. He set the empty can down and picked up the full one and laboriously made his way across the open ground to the big house. This was the dangerous time. Someone else could have a full bladder. A man could come outside for a smoke, unable to sleep. The dogs that were howling might be moving closer. He felt an intense desire to hurry, but he forced himself to walk casually, as if he belonged there, as if he were on some errand for Fisher.

Warner's heart was beating wildly as he reached the back porch of the ranch house and doused it with kerosene. Then, unable to keep himself from hurrying, he walked rapidly down the south side of the house pouring out the kerosene liberally. He no longer felt the need to completely encircle the house, just get enough kerosene on it to get it started good. After that the wood would take care of itself.

He turned at the corner and then climbed up on the front porch, making sure to douse it good. He didn't want anyone coming out the front door. He wanted Fisher to have to try to get out the back way.

The kerosene played out halfway down the far side. It was enough. It would have to do. He knelt and struck a match and got the fuel burning. Kerosene burned slowly, but it would burn for a long time, using the dirt it had soaked into like a wick.

Once he had the fire started at the house he started back toward the bunkhouse, again forcing himself to walk when he wanted desperately to break into a run.

Somehow, after what seemed like an hour, he reached the corner of the bunkhouse where he'd started. He knelt and struck a match and lit the kerosene that was dripping out of the first can he'd emptied. In a moment the flame caught. He waited to make sure it was burning good and then started, as deliberately as he could, to find his way back to his rifle. The donkey had retreated a little ways back and was standing, watching, as Warner passed. He thought the donkey might not think the scene so peaceful in a very few minutes, so he grabbed the animal by his rope halter and led him along until he reached the edge of the weeds. His rifle was right where he had left it. He looked back, saw that the fire was starting to encircle the buildings and then carefully walked back up toward his horse. He figured the Andalusian and the mesquite thicket were about eight hundred yards from the ranch headquarters. He planned to take up his position at about six hundred yards.

At that distance he found a small clump of bushes that would hide his frame. He let go of the donkey, made little shooing motions at him, and then settled down behind the bushes on his belly, carefully running the long rifle through the foliage and finding an inch-thick branch to use as a firing rest. He could see the fire progressing. As near as he could tell, it was already most of the way around the big house, or as far as his kerosene had lasted, and nearly all the way around the bunkhouse. He could see white smoke starting to rise against the horizon, and he knew by that that the wood had caught and was starting to burn.

13

Warner was amazed at how long it took the occupants to realize that the buildings were on fire. The men in the bunkhouse were the first to become aware of the danger, but they did so only when Warner could see flames leaping up as high as the windows. The breeze had freshened and, even at a distance of six hundred yards he could hear their cries and yells of surprise and alarm. Then, finally, they started pouring out. Since they were coming out the doors on the other side of the building from him, he saw them only when they came running out onto the common ground. By now the main house was also well ablaze, and the common ground between the two structures was as well lit as by day. Warner saw several figures run out the back door of the big house. Finally one appeared that Warner instantly recognized as Jack Fisher. He had taken time to put on boots and hat and trousers, but his shirt was flapping open and he hadn't bothered with vest or coat or tie. He ran down the steps, buckling on his gun belt as he ran, and disappeared into the mass of men.

Most of the men were just milling around, disorganized, some of them half asleep, none of them fully aware of what was happening. They appeared to be about of the number Warner had expected. He began to fire, slowly, trying to pick his targets, his intent to reduce their number as much as he could. But he was careful to not direct his fire anywhere near Jack Fisher. He didn't want to kill Jack Fisher, not with a rifle bullet at long distance.

At first he was firing too high. It was easy to tell because he would sight in on a man and fire, and another man, ten yards closer to Warner, would suddenly grab at his back or stomach and stumble to his knees and fall over. He reckoned his miscalculation was due to the slope the terrain made down into the little valley.

By now both buildings were burning fiercely. Warner could see Fisher darting this way and that, shouting orders and conflicting instructions. No one seemed to notice the men who were falling or when someone would suddenly clap a hand to his shoulder or grab at his leg. He didn't think they could hear the reports of the rifle. But then, it just made a little crack, and the wind was in his favor, and the two fires must have been making such a roar that the men could barely hear each other.

Most of them were only half dressed, though all of them had on their boots. A man who spent his life on horseback had tender soles, and the first thing he reached for when he got out of bed was his socks and boots—even if the roof over his head was on fire. Most of them had on trousers and their gun belts, but there were few shirts except for undershirts.

Warner could faintly hear them yelling at each other. *"Water! Get water!"* *"Bucket brigade. Start a bucket brigade! Hurry!"* *"Save the big house first!"*

He kept firing as they tried to put themselves into some kind of order. He calculated that he had hit, either wounding or killing, some eight or ten men before they gradually became aware that they faced another danger besides the fires. Men began to bend over their downed comrades, seeing the blood and then looking up and around. Warner kept firing.

Now, though, he could see them beginning to talk among themselves and to frantically search the surrounding terrain. He thought it was about time he made his presence felt and known. He came out from behind the bush and walked fifty yards down the slope toward the fires and the bewildered men. At the top of his lungs he yelled, *"Jack Fisher! You swill-sucking, pig-fucking bastard.* You son of a bitch from hell! This is Warner Grayson, and *I am having my revenge.* You are a dead man, Fisher! Make your peace with the devil, because you will soon meet him!"

Then he turned and started walking slowly back toward his horse. He could hear a few scattered shots from behind him, but he wasn't worried. They didn't have a rifle that could reach him.

He took his time, reloading his rifle as he walked and checking the amount of ammunition he had left in his pockets. At his Andalusian he checked the cinch, made sure his grub sack was secure, and checked his saddlebags, making sure that the valise was secure with its vital contents of brandy and ammunition and laudanum. He was hurting badly from his exertions with the kerosene cans and then running up the slope and then lying still so long on the cold ground in one position. The laudanum was tempting, but he was afraid it might affect his judgment and his aim, so he settled for a swig of brandy. Just as he was about to mount he heard something behind him and he whirled around. It was the donkey, hurrying up the slope. Warner just shook his head and mounted the Andalusian. He rode out from behind the mesquite thicket and sat his horse in plain sight of those below.

Warner figured it was going to take more than a few minutes for all of them to mount and collect their weapons and set out in pursuit. He was sure they expected to run him to ground in short order, and he was going to do everything in his power to keep them thinking that as he slowly tolled them away from the ranch. A few individuals were still in sight, though not one of them was extra short and wearing a big white hat. Sitting in the saddle, he sighted offhand and fired nine deliberately placed shots at the men. He saw only one fall. That didn't matter; he just wanted to be sure they knew he was still there. There were sporadic bursts of return fire, but all of it fell short. He waited, watching. If he had read his man right, Fisher would be beside himself with anger at this astounding attack on his homeplace. This was what Fisher did to other people; they didn't do it to him. Especially one lone man, setting fire to his home, to his ranch, and then having the nerve to fire on him and his men while standing on his land.

Warner figured that Fisher would come after him like a swarm of angry wasps, not stopping to think, not waiting to consider any course of action other than immediate retaliation. He had probably even told his men to try to wound Warner, so he could kill him at his leisure. The man was so full of conceit and had such a history of lording it over others that there was no other way for him to react. Besides, Fisher had no precedent on which to base any other response. In the past no one would have dared to set foot on his land without permission, much less attack him. The sign at the crossroads said it all: This Is Jack Fisher's Road. You Take the Other.

Warner did not have long to wait. In less than five minutes a crowd of horsemen came boiling out of the barn. They circled around the burning bunkhouse and charged straight up the slight slope toward him. He sat his horse, firing calmly into their midst. He saw two men go down and two horses suddenly break out from the pack and start pitching and bucking around. He hated to shoot the horses, but it was impossible to shoot that accurately at that distance into a moving mass target.

He let them get to about four hundred yards of him because he wanted them to run as much life out of their horses as they could. That wouldn't seem important to them now, but they'd understand later what a price they'd paid.

When they were close enough so that he felt there was a danger of a wild rifle shot hitting either him or his horse, he whirled the Andalusian to his left, to the northwest, and started off at a slow lope, looked back to judge the progress of the chase party, and then kicked the Andalusian up into a gallop. As he rode, he studied the sky, trying the guess the time. The night was warmly dark, the stars starting to dim and fade. It usually got light at a little after six. He had to figure it was at least five o'clock, if not later. What he wanted to do now was keep a decent lead over the chase party, staying far enough ahead so that there was no danger from their frustrated, random rifle shots, but not so far as to discourage them. They were angry now, but that would wear off and someone with a drop of common sense might recognize that they were not doing much of a job of overtaking their quarry.

He was also alert to ride carefully and to watch the ground ahead. So far he was on smooth prairie, but it wasn't far to where the land would become choppy and broken and he would have to be concerned about the safety of his horse. It would not do for the Andalusian to go lame by throwing a shoe or suffering a stone bruise to the frog of his foot or even breaking a leg. Warner would be dog meat if that happened. He could match Fisher and his men in a running gun battle, especially with a superior weapon and a superior horse, but if he was forced to fight on foot, they would quickly overwhelm him.

For the first half hour he kept the rifle in the saddle boot and concentrated on maintaining a safe distance between himself and his pursuers. After the first all-out dash, they had seen they were not going to come up on him immediately, and they had slowed their horses to a bare gallop. In turn he had pulled the Andalusian down into his peculiar lope that was slightly above a trot but was as smooth as sitting in a stuffed chair. The horse could keep that gait up all day long. Warner calculated that they had come some four or five miles from Fisher's ranch and the run was all straight toward Del Rio. It had been too dark, and matters had been too hurried for him to take a count of the men in pursuit, but he calculated it to be somewhere around fifteen or sixteen. He guessed that he had either wounded or killed a round dozen back at the ranch as the gunmen milled around in the light of the fires. Looking back, he could just make out the big hat up front, leading the pack. Come along, Mr. Fisher, come along with me and let us have our showdown. Come along like a good boy. Come along like a goat on a rope, you and your hired killers.

But then the Andalusian suddenly stumbled and Warner's heart rose in his throat, jamming his breathing, until the Spanish horse caught his balance and continued on in his smooth gait as if nothing had happened.

He looked back and saw that his chasers were slowing more and more. They didn't know it, but they were riding plain, ordinary horses, compared to the Andalusian. Warner had to remind himself that Fisher, in his conceit, claimed to be a horse breeder and handler. Warner had not seen any signs of excellence in Fisher's animals.

He became afraid that the men would get discouraged too soon or that their animals would quit. He slowed the Andalusian to a walk, but the copper-colored horse's walk was almost as fast as the trot of an ordinary horse. He pulled him to a slow walk so that Fisher and his men would have a sense of gaining on him. He kept a constant watch over his shoulder, gauging their progress, gauging the condition of their horses. He calculated they'd come at least ten or twelve miles from the ranch, which wasn't an exceptional distance, but the pursuers had not husbanded their horses' strength carefully, spending their mounts endurance in some fruitless dashes and gallops when they had no chance of catching him.

Warner glanced toward the east and thought he could see a dim glow in that direction. He was anxious for the sun to rise and the light to come, because that would signal the beginning of the next phase of his plan. It should also bring them into rougher country, which would be to his benefit. It would bring them into that country, he reminded himself, if he could keep nursing this chase party along.

He glanced over his shoulder and saw that the gang of men was making another dash at him. He watched them narrow the distance. At about a quarter of a mile they let off a ragged volley. He had not thought they were so close until he heard an errant round whine over his head. That was too close. He could not afford to let them get too close. He immediately touched spurs to the Andalusian, who had been chafing under the slow pace. The Spanish horse shot ahead and was into a gallop before Warner could take him in hand. As rapidly as he could, he slowed the horse. The damn fool animal had almost taken them out of eyeshot of the chase party. He slowly came back down to a walk and looked back. The distance had opened up again, but his pursuers were cantering dutifully forward.

In the next hour the sun rose fully above the horizon, bringing a welcome warmth after the cool morning air. Warner had been so intent upon his objective that he hadn't noticed how much his body and face hurt or how thirsty it made a person to breathe through his mouth all the time. He reckoned he'd drunk half a canteen of water through the night.

Now he figured they'd come about eighteen miles, and ahead the country was breaking up into shallow ravines and knolls along with brushy patches of briers and stunted post oak and cedar and mesquite trees. He doubted if he was still on Fisher's land. There were fewer cattle around, and surely no one could own land this distant from his headquarters.

The chase party was clearly showing signs of fatigue and wear. Warner stopped his horse and studied them, squinting his eyes and moving his lips as he made a count. It was a difficult task, but as best he could figure there was sixteen men in the chase party besides Fisher. It was, he decided, about time to start doing something about the disproportion in their numbers. About half a mile ahead a small, graduated knoll appeared to rise thirty or forty feet above the level of the prairie. He touched the Andalusian and let him build up into a rapid gallop. Within a minute he pulled his horse to a stop on top of the knoll. He dismounted and picked up one of the Andalusian's hooves, as if worrying that he might have thrown a shoe or gone lame. He let the horse's foot back down to the ground and then took him on lead and walked him down the far side of the knoll. Just before his head descended out of sight he glanced back. He could see that Fisher had smelled blood and was urging his party forward.

Warner descended a few feet farther and then jerked Wilson's rifle out of the boot and scrambled back up the knoll, leaving his hat on the saddle horn. He lay as flat as he could with one eye peeping around a rock on the raised ground. They were coming on rapidly on their tired horses. He watched them, calculating, waiting until the last safe second. He judged that to be at around three hundred yards. Warner opened fire, shooting into the bunch, but being careful to not hit Jack Fisher. He fired all nine shots in the cylinder and then quickly reloaded and fired five more. The sudden fusillade threw the party into confusion. He saw two men go out of the saddle, saw another slump forward and catch himself, and saw one horse go down. But by then, they were too close, and he scrambled down the rise, quickly mounted the Andalusian, and put rapid distance between himself and Fisher's party. As he rode, he calculated that he must have thinned their ranks by four guns. That would bring them down to a dozen men besides Fisher. He wondered how long they would continue to chase him before they realized they couldn't get him in rifle range, much less catch him.

But then, he had an ally in the conceit and madness of Jack Fisher. From time to time Warner stopped to shout insults and taunts at the man. That usually worked, causing Fisher to hurry his men and horses on faster, but the taunts exacted a cost from Warner. His throat was still very sore from the hands of Quince, who had tried to squeeze the life out of him.

All the rest of that morning Warner led them on. He could see how tired their horses were getting. Once—with the exception of Fisher, who stayed in the saddle—the men got down and walked to give their horses a little rest. But that cost them two more men, because Warner quickly found a convenient post oak tree, dismounted, and, using a limb as a firing rest, opened fire. He could tell by the way one man suddenly sat down, clutching his stomach, that he was gutshot. But Fisher and the others just mounted up and rode on, leaving him to die a painful death. Warner was sure that he had severely wounded more than one of Fisher's men, but they never stopped to see to their care or to drop off a man to help the wounded.

Fisher's gang seemed baffled by the range of the rifle. Each time Warner fired on them from a safe distance of five or six hundred yards, they would futilely fire back, their bullets falling well short.

About noon Fisher and his men came to a little creek that Warner had already crossed. As he had expected, they dismounted to water themselves and their horses. He reckoned that, in their haste, they'd never thought to bring water or provisions. But he gave them no time at the creek. From behind another tree he fired down on them, killing or wounding three more men. The party was now down to six men and Fisher. They were leading three extra horses, the mounts of men who had been killed, and they tried to rotate these among themselves to save what horseflesh they had left. But it wasn't going to do them much good. The Andalusian was just starting to work up a lather. He could go forty miles in a day without food or water and think it was just another day's work. And Warner had crammed him full of grain and hay on the train and then made sure he got a little water as they rode along.

Now and again he saw the donkey off in the distance, moving parallel to their course. It just made Warner shake his head. The damn beast appeared to have the homing instinct of a dog.

By the middle of the afternoon they'd arrived on a broad, sweeping plain with very little cover. The chase had deteriorated to a walk. On one occasion the pursuers stopped, and Warner judged that the men were arguing with Fisher. He saw Fisher draw his revolver and fire it over their heads. After a moment they began to move sullenly forward, trudging after him. They were no longer willing, however, to come within range of his rifle, and no ploy or charade that Warner could think of would induce them to charge him on their dead-tired horses.

Now, he decided, was the time to reverse the roles. The broad, flat, featureless prairie gave him the ideal terrain, and he figured the bunch of them were so worn down that there would be very little fight left in them.

Without warning he suddenly turned the Andalusian left, to the south, and put him into a gallop, making a wide, sweeping circle around the chase party until he came to a stop about six hundred yards behind them. He was now blocking the path they would have to take to get back to Fisher's ranch. They stopped and sat their horses, acting confused.

He was not long in letting them know his intentions. He dismounted and, kneeling on one knee, raised the rifle to his shoulder and fired off six shots. He saw one man go out of the saddle and a riderless horse suddenly stagger sideways and fall. The gang instantly put their horses into a trot heading, as he wanted them to, west toward

Del Rio. He mounted up and, for a time, until the Andalusian could have a blow after his hard run, was content to follow along behind them.

Then, in midafternoon, they stopped, and all of them, even Fisher, turned their horses to face him. He figured they were going to try a charge. Well, that suited him fine. They were over a quarter of a mile away, and he knew he could shoot down the five who were left, not counting Fisher.

But he was wrong. One of the men was wearing a white shirt, and Warner watched while he took it off and rode forward waving it over his head. Warner judged it to be his undershirt, since it was more gray than white. He let the man come on for a hundred yards, sighting at him over the barrel of his rifle. He was keeping the one hand in the air, swinging the undershirt, and his other hand on the reins. But he still could have had a pistol in his rein hand. Warner let him get within fifty yards and then yelled for him to stop. He said, "Get both your hands up where I can see them. Take a rein in each hand if you have to. Try anything and I'll put a hole in you."

The man dipped his right hand down, the one holding the undershirt, and then came back up, a rein in each hand, holding them up high enough so Warner could see them. He had to urge his tired mount forward with his spurs.

Warner let him get within five yards and then stopped him again. He took the rifle down from his cheek but held it pointed straight at the man's chest. Warner said, "Speak your piece. Make it quick. I don't want your horses getting too much rest."

The man had a high, whiny voice, but his face was full of meaness. He said, "Lissen, feller, Mistuh Fishuh says he don't want no more trouble. He's willin' to call it quits. He accidentally shot 'at lady wuz with you. But you done burnt him out and kilt his hired hands. He figgers ya'll is quits. He be willin' to let bygones be bygones."

Warner laughed without mirth. "They must have sent you because you was the only one with underwear clean enough for me to tell it was white. It sure wasn't for your brains. I ain't got no bygones for Fisher. Except him. Here is *my* deal. I will swap you and the others your lives in exchange for Fisher. You go back and disarm him, take his guns away, and then strip him naked. Put his clothes and his boots in his saddlebags and run his horse off a couple of hundred yards toward Del Rio. Then the rest of you throw away your weapons, and I will let you ride away alive."

The man opened his mouth and then closed it and then opened it to say, "Us put hands on Mistuh Fishuh? Shit, feller. He'd kill us daid as hell."

"Grab his gun away from him. Do something.

You ain't got long. If you don't do what I tell you I'm going to pick the rest of you off one by one within the next hour, and then I'll have Fisher solo. This way you save your worthless lives and maybe keep me from having to shoot Fisher in the leg."

The man thought for a moment and then looked back toward the group waiting on exhausted horses. He said, "Hell, I dunno."

Warner said, "You got ten more seconds to make up your mind. You can have yours here and now if you want. Save you laying out there on the prairie with a bullet in your belly."

The man's eyes widened. He said, "You want him stripped nakkid?"

"As the day he was born." He repeated his instructions about Fisher's clothes and his horse. "I don't want the man to have a weapon on him or anywhere near. If he fires at me I'll run the rest of you down and kill every one of you. Savvy?"

The man looked at him for a moment and then nodded slowly. As he started to rein his animal around, the man said, "Say, what kind o' horse is that you got thar? Don't he never git tahred?"

"Never," Warner said. "Now get going. I'll give you five minutes to get the job done, and then I start shooting again. And one thing—don't kill Fisher. If you kill him, the deal is off and I'll finish with the rest of you."

The man blinked as if the thought had been in his mind. Then he nodded again.

Warner called after him, "When you're finished, ride home and don't look back."

He watched the brief scuffle as Fisher's gunmen disarmed him and then relieved him of his horse and his clothes. Warner looked on in some amusement as Fisher stamped his feet and jumped up and down, like a child throwing a tantrum, while his men rode away. He waited until they were out of sight over a hump in the prairie before gathering up Fisher's horse and leading him over to the naked man. He stared at Fisher's scrawny body for a second, wondering how such a puny man had brought such misery into so many people's lives. Fisher was babbling, but Warner didn't pay him any mind. He went through Fisher's saddlebags and threw him his clothes garment by garment and boot by boot as he made sure there were no weapons hidden in them. He said tersely, "Get dressed, Fisher. We got a long ride ahead."

He took down his lariat as Fisher finished dressing and mounted his tired horse. Warner made a loop and cast it just as Fisher settled into the saddle. It went over his shoulders and Warner jerked it tight around the man's middle. Fisher turned a startled face toward him. He said, "Now, look here, Grayson, I know you are mad as hell right now, but we can work somethin' out. You've put me considerable out of pocket, burnin' me out like you done, but I'm a wealthy man and I can make this whole mess worth yore while." All of the arrogance, all of the banty rooster, all of the cocksureness was gone from him. Even his hat was muddied and misshapen. Now he was just an undersized bully who'd lost all of his power and his bluster at the same time.

Warner said quietly, "Fisher, get one thing straight—there is nothing I want to discuss with you. At all. If you say one more word I will yank you out of the saddle and drag you. I have a great desire to kill you here and now, to belly-shoot you and put a bullet in every joint of your body. But I think it is going to hurt you worse to be drug back to Del Rio and forced to endure the humiliation and degradation of being made to answer for your crimes. I—"

Fisher started to say, "I know you feel bad about the lady, but I—"

He got no further. With a hard jerk, Warner tumbled him out of the saddle. He landed hard, but Warner gave him no time to get his breath. With a quick hand he took a turn of his lariat around the saddle horn and then wheeled the Andalusian around and set him off at a brisk trot, dragging Fisher behind him. He could hear Fisher screaming, but he paid him no mind. Warner rode for a hundred yards and then turned and dragged Fisher back to his horse. It was a long moment before Fisher could even sit up. His shirt was torn, and Warner could see scratches on his face and his arms. He said flatly, "Get mounted, Fisher, or I'll drag you to Del Rio."

He waited while Fisher staggered to his feet, groaning and touching the sore places on his body. Warner flipped the lariat to hurry him along. When he was finally remounted, Warner rode around to face him. He said, "I'm not going to warn you again. I consider you about the lowest form of human being I have ever seen, and I don't want to hear another word out of you. A moment ago you used the word 'lady.' You're a lucky man. You might have used her name. For that I would have drug you ten miles. Was I you Fisher, I wouldn't even think about anything in the feminine gender. I wouldn't even think at all. We've got twenty miles or so to go and if you do exactly as I tell you you may save yourself some pain. I intend to deliver you to the sheriff in Del Rio. I'm not going to feed you, and I'm not going to water you, and there ain't going to be no use in asking me to. My job is to get you from here to there, and that is all I am willing to do. The sight of you disgusts me. The sound of your voice would be more than I could bear. If you open your mouth you had better yawn or cough; otherwise I am going to give you a ride on the end of this rope. Now point yourself in the direction of Del Rio and start moving. We would make it without stopping, except I know your horse is nearly done in. Move!"

At about ten o'clock the next morning Warner turned in at the Vaughns' ranch. It was about a mile out of his way, but he thought they deserved an early look at Fisher. Besides, Warner wanted to get cleaned up, get a good meal if he could, and maybe rest for an hour. Ahead of him, Fisher was reeling in the saddle, and his horse was nearly as played out. He was bare from the waist up because, the night before, Warner had used Fisher's shirt, torn into strips, to tie him upright to a mesquite tree while he, Warner, had a meal and a few drinks and several hours' sleep.

Warner reckoned he'd borrow a horse from the Vaughns, if they had one to spare. He didn't think Fisher's horse could last another ten miles.

The Vaughns met him, standing on their porch, staring. They said a hired hand had seen them coming several miles off and had come to notify them. They hadn't known it was Warner until he came into view. And they hadn't believed their eyes until Fisher was sitting before them, slumped down, about to fall out of his saddle.

Warner said, "Ya'll got a place a man could have a wash and change his shirt and maybe get a bite to eat? I been eating out of cans for two days, and I am plumb sick of it."

They hustled him inside, and Preston watched Fisher while Austin got his wife busy in the kitchen and showed Warner where he could wash up. They didn't have a bathtub inside the house like Wilson did in his casino and whorehouse, but Warner made do with a bucket of heated water and a big towel. After that he shaved and brushed his teeth and then sat down to a steak Mrs. Vaughn had cooked for him along with fried potatoes and some pinto beans. When he was through, they all sat outside and looked at Jack Fisher, who had not been moved or given any relief. Warner had put on one of the clean shirts he'd brought. Mrs. Vaughn had brought them out some lemonade, and Warner was having a tall glass sweetened with some whiskey while the Vaughns sat in big porch chairs and studied Fisher like they were judging a head of livestock. Austin said, "He looks kind of drawed down. Shrunk out. Not that he had that far to go."

Warner said, "He ain't had no water or nothing to eat for at least twenty-four hours."

Preston said, "He looks like he's lost a little hide."

Warner smiled. That had happened that morning. He'd asked Fisher what Quince's first name was, but Fisher hadn't wanted to tell him. He'd wanted to tell him about one second later, but Warner had given him ten minutes on the end of the rope, seeking out every brier patch or clump of cactus he could find.

When Warner explained, in brief detail, how he had come to capture Fisher, the Vaughns just stared at him for a long moment. Then Preston said, "But it sounds so simple."

Austin said carefully, "I reckon it is simple if you are willing to take ten-to-one odds on getting out with your life. I couldn't have done it, and I don't think I know another soul who would have dared it."

Preston said, "Wasn't no barnum about that. It was sheer nerve."

Now Warner asked if they could loan him another horse to carry Fisher on into town. He said, "That poor beast he's riding is about to crater. I'll tell you, it was the Andalusian done the trick as much as me."

They looked at Fisher's horse before Preston left to get another animal. Austin said, "That animal don't look like no big advertisement for Mr. Fisher's claims to being the breeder of superior horseflesh. I can see why he would need some help from you."

Warner looked at Fisher. "He's going to need some help from somebody. And soon. I don't know that the man has a single friend. And I ain't never heard of a man's enemies coming to his aid."

• • •

It was almost one o'clock before Warner urged Fisher, on the borrowed horse, down Del Rio's main street. He'd asked the Vaughns if they wanted to come in and enjoy Fisher's finish, but they had said, gratefully, that they didn't want to be in the way, that they didn't want to distract from Warner's credit.

Heads turned as Warner drove his prisoner down the street. The horse and vehicle traffic parted in front of him. He could hear people on both sides of the street stopping to whisper among themselves. "Ain't that Jack Fisher? That looks like Jack Fisher. Who is that feller a-drivin' him at the end of that rope?"

Behind him a little crowd on foot and horseback fell in to follow. As he came up on Wilson Young's Palace Saloon & Casino he saw Wilson Young standing on the edge of the boardwalk looking at him with a little amused smile.

Warner said, "Much obliged for the loan of the rifle. It done the job."

Wilson walked along the boardwalk, keeping pace with him. "I'll swap you it for the button horse. Throw in five hundred dollars' worth of boot."

"Horse ain't mine. I'm going to give him to Charlie. Wasn't for Charlie finding and making that little horse, I might not could have outrun Fisher in that first race."

365

"You rich enough to give away a fifteen-hundred-dollar horse?"

"Last offer I heard was twelve hundred. Where is Laura?"

Wilson pointed up with his hat brim. "She's up yonder in the room ya'll been sleeping in. She's taking a nap."

"She all right?"

"She was. Been up and around a little. But she's going to be mad as hell when she finds out you lied to her. She's been fretting for you to get back for the last twenty-four hours. I told her not to worry."

"Wasn't me lied to her. You did the telling."

Wilson made a little motion with his hand, indicating Fisher. "Where'd you get that?"

"Oh, found him wandering around lost. I give him a hand finding his way."

"Looks like you gave him more than a hand."

"How about you go warn Laura? I got to deliver this baggage."

A block farther on, Warner turned both horses in to the hitching rail in front of the sheriff's office and called out, "Sheriff! Sheriff Shank! Sheriff Ryan Shank!"

In a moment the tall, spare frame of the sheriff filled the doorway of his office. He looked at Warner and then at Fisher without comment.

Warner said, "I brought you the man who shot Laura Pico and who put Willis Quince up to

366

killing me by strangulation. I will bring the lady, and we will both swear out charges later."

Then he put his left hand on Fisher's shoulder and shoved. Fisher went off the side of the horse. Warner heard the breath whoosh out of him as he hit the ground. He reached down and took the reins of the Vaughn's horse. He started to wheel away from the rail.

The sheriff said, "Mr. Grayson?"

Warner stopped. "Yes?"

"Your face looks like hell. You ought to see a doctor."

"I'm on my way there now," he said. He backed the Andalusian away from the rail and started both horses back down the street. As he neared the livery stable he saw the donkey trotting down the street toward him. Warner simply shook his head and turned in at the hotel. He didn't reckon he was ever going to get rid of the donkey. A boy came out to meet him in front of the stables. He eased down from the saddle and told the boy to grain and water both horses but to take special care of the Andalusian. Then he said, "And if a donkey comes wandering in here, well, take care of him too. I reckon he belongs to me."

Then he started for Wilson's place. Laura was going to give him all kinds of hell, but if he could live through it he figured the reward at the end would make it all worthwhile.

Center Point Large Print

600 Brooks Road / PO Box 1
Thorndike, ME 04986-0001 USA

(207) 568-3717

US & Canada:
1 800 929-9108
www.centerpointlargeprint.com